CHINESE ZHI GUAI

-GHOST STORIES FROM

THE WEI-JIN, NAN-BEI DYNASTIES

中英魏晉南北朝志怪選

Compiled by Yu Ya-Tzu
尤雅姿 編譯

臺灣 學士書局 印行

Preface

During my sabbatical year in the Institute of Chinese and Korean Studies in Tuebingen University, Germany, spring 2007, I received double scholarship from the National Science Council of Taiwan and the German Research Foundation for the research project of "An Exploration of the Research and Translation Results of the German Sinology Circle of Ancient Chinese Zhi Guai." Therefore I gladly welcomed a new phase in my career of academic research.

While searching for information in the Tuebingen University Library, I realized that the Sinology circle focuses more on "Fang Shi" and "Taoism" during the Wei Jin Nan Bei Dynasties, along with poetry in terms of literature. The only research translation project featuring Zhi Guai I could find was the work done by Professor Dr. Ylva Monschein of the Sinology Research Institute of Heidelberg University. I was enthralled by the fact that Dr. Ylva had translated around ten articles of Zhi Guai into German with her research project "Der Zauber der Fuchsfee: Entstehung und Wandel eines "Femme-fatale"-Motivs in der Chinesischen Literature (The

Conjuration of the Fox Spirits-The Development of the Theme of Seductive Women in Chinese Literature)". This book, borrowed by Herr Thomas Gaiser of the Chinese and Korean Studies Institute, was a great assistance in my research project.

In May, 2007, I gave lectures respectively in the Institute of Chinese and Korean Studies and in the "Conference of Humanities and Social Science of Taiwanese Scholars in France" with the topic of "The Sexual Adventure and Awakening in the Lacking World-the One-Night Affair among Humans and Spirits in Zhi Guai". The participants showed great curiosity about this topic, and at the same time, indicated that they had no idea that there were so many fantasy stories from ancient China. Furthermore, Professor Doctor Hans Ulrich Vogel, the director of the Institute of Chinese and Korean Studies, suggested me to translate the stories into English and introduce them to Western Sinologists. Upon arrival to Tuebingen, I had presented him with my doctoral dissertation-"The Study of Yan Zhi-Tui and his Family Instructions", and much to my surprise, he later showed me a book of "The Family Instructions Master Yen" in both Chinese and English he had bought on a trip to China. He believed that he could understand my study with this book. It was hard for me to believe that such work, which is not so popular, has a translated version in China. I thought to myself, "Perhaps I should really make a bilingual Zhi Guai to introduce to the West".

Back in Taiwan I received help by Professor Lin Fu-Shi's Project Spark (Liao-Yuan) of the Literary Institute of my college to proceed in this project of Zhi Guai translation. With a selection of one hundred Zhi Guai stories, I categorized them into sixteen interesting themes according to their features and contents. With the assistances from the bright and diligent Chen Tzu-Ting, Ho Tsai-Ju, Brandon William Wunder, and illustrations from Yeh Shao-Yung. This whole process from selecting to publishing lasted up to three years. I really appreciate their consistent help towards this project. Another special appreciation goes to Dr. Liu Yuan-Ju of the Institute of Chinese Literature and Philosophy of Academia Sinica, who generously supported my translation work and took efforts to lend me important reference books from Taipei. She is also a reason I am involved in Zhi Guai.

I hereby convey my gratitude to the sponsor of the National Science Council and DFG for granting me the opportunity to fly over ten thousand miles to Germany and start a new phase of my academic career. In addition, I would like to thank Institute of Chinese and Korean Studies for providing a great study environment for me. Staying in the beautiful town of Tuebingen was a truly precious experience of both studying abroad and wandering outdoors. I used to hike among the beautiful woods almost every day, enjoyed admiring the clouds and the sunset, and with nostalgia, watch the airplanes from Stuttgart precisely divide the sky into two while missing my family from afar. Beaches dominated the woods where I stood listening to the echoes of my footsteps, coming with the rustling sound of the snappy movements of chipmunks at times. Sometimes not until it was dark did I start to take my time walking back along the trails. "My existence in the deep woods remains unknown to humans; only the bright moon comes to shine on." During my visit, Frau Nina Berger, the secretary of the institute of Chinese and Korean Studies took care of me in every possible way-a friend that I give my deepest gratitude.

Yu Ya-Tzu Taichung,
December 28th, 2010.

自序

　　2007年春季，我於教授休假期間前往德國杜賓根大學漢韓研究所訪問三個月，我以研究計畫：〈德國漢學界對於中國魏晉南北朝志怪小說的翻譯與研究成果綜述〉獲得中華民國國科會與德國學術研究委員會的雙邊獎助，欣欣然展開學術生涯的另一階段旅程。

　　在杜賓根大學圖書館查閱資料時，我發現西方漢學界對魏晉南北朝研究較多的是方士與道教信仰，而在文學方面則是偏重於詩歌，有關志怪的翻譯與研究，我只找到海德堡大學漢學研究所Professor Dr.Ylva Monschein教授的「狐狸精的幻術──致命吸引力女性故事主題在中國文學中的發展」，伊芙教授以德文翻譯了十篇左右的志怪，令我喜出望外，漢韓研究所的職員蓋瑟先生 Herr Thomas Gaiser為我從海德堡大學將此書借來參閱，使我的研究計畫有了眉目。

　　我在2007年五月時，先在漢韓研究所，之後又前往巴黎的「旅法台灣學人人文與社會科學研討會」發表專題演講，講題為「匱乏世界中的情慾冒險與覺醒──六朝志怪中的人／妖一夜情」，不論是在杜賓根，或是在巴黎，與會的中外學者們對這個主題都感到十分有趣，同時也向我表示，他們以前並不知道中國古代有這麼多奇幻的鬼怪故事，而且故事內容還可以延伸出許多嚴肅的文化議題。漢韓研究所的所長傅漢斯教授Professor Doctor

Hans Ulrich Vogel.熱心地建議我，不妨將這些故事翻譯成英文，好介紹給西方漢學界。我初到杜賓根的時候，曾致贈我的博士論文——《顏之推及其家訓之研究》給漢斯教授，他看著書名，意味深長地微笑著；其後，漢斯教授前往中國，返德時買回了一本中英雙語的《顏氏家訓》，他開心地秀給我看，笑著說，這樣他就知道我在研究什麼了。當時，我真不敢相信，中國大陸連這麼冷門的書都做了翻譯的推廣工作！也許我真的該編譯一本中英雙語對照的魏晉南北朝志怪。

返回台灣之後，適逢林富士研究員接掌中興大學文學院，林院長為激活文學院的研究產能，熱血地策動了「燎原計畫」，他爽朗明快地支持我進行這項英譯工作，使我得到人力與物力上的一些資助。我精選了一百零八篇的志怪作品，依故事內容特性將它們分成十六個主題來介紹，每個主題都觸及了人類的生命處境與文化議題，因此，各篇之前均列有前言作一提示；前言之後，是志怪的文言原文，原文之後是英文翻譯。顧慮到東西文化風俗上的差異，有些專屬中國特有的名物制度或禮俗，也隨文提供簡單的註腳作一說明。

整個翻譯計畫從選文到出版，前後共進行了三年餘，負責文書處理的陳姿廷，擔任翻譯工作的何采儒、布蘭登，以及義務繪製插圖的葉紹雍等人；個個都是勤勉穎慧，認真負責的有為青年，我非常感謝他們對這項計畫的喜愛與協助；尤其是何采儒，她的英文能力和文學素養出色，能夠貼切細膩地傳譯我的文章和情思；布蘭登是本系的留學生，遠從美國來台灣學習中國文學與武術，他謙虛好學，每事問地與我推敲譯文的內容與修辭，並且建議我增列文化禮俗上的註腳，以利理解故事中的一些關鍵事物。另外我要特別感謝中央研究院文哲所劉苑如研究員，她慷慨磊落地支持我的英譯寸心，還不辭辛勞地從台北惠借重要參考書籍給我，而且，晚近我之所以「涉足」六朝志怪，也是因為1999年劉博士邀請我參加由李豐楙研究員主持的「空間、地域與文化研討會——中國文化空間的書寫與闡釋」，當初為了撰寫論文〈虛擬實境中的生命諦視——談魏晉文學中的臨界空間經驗〉才真正接觸了魏晉南北朝的志怪作品，由此而派生出另一條治學之路。

我也感謝國科會和德國學術委員會DFG的資助，以及杜賓根大學漢韓研究所的周到禮遇，使我有機會飛到萬里之遠的德國從事漢學研究，開展了學術生涯的新局面。客居於美麗的杜賓根小鎮，是我人生極為珍貴的「留學」與「流浪」經驗，我幾乎天天在美麗的樹林中健行，喜歡在黃昏時追落日，望晚霞，帶著鄉愁遙望那從斯圖加特飛來飛去的飛機，看它們在天空中準確地瓜分著航線，想念著家鄉也思索著我未來的旅程。森林遍植優雅的櫸木，落葉聲中細聽花栗鼠與自己的跫音迴響，彷彿踏進了「深林人不知，明月來相照」的詩境！從早春到初夏，我總是在星月爭輝的藍色夜空下，才悠閒地沿著附近人家的花草小徑散步回去。

漢韓研究所的秘書妮娜·柏格女士 Frau Nina Berger，在我訪問期間對我細心照顧，關懷備至，也是我想念在心的朋友。她在雨中騎著腳踏車來火車站接我，在初春的暖陽下偕友人與我悠遊內卡河畔的古城風景，邀我一起逛斯圖加特的動物園，驚喜地望著初生的小花豹蹣跚地學步；在杜賓根戲院一起看德語版的「蜘蛛人」，在她溫馨的廚房，我們一邊話著家常，一邊享用著她巧手烹飪的白蘆筍，餐桌上洋溢著清新的薄荷茶香味，如同她為人一般散發著美善氣息！最後要謝謝台灣學生書局以及編輯部陳蕙文女士，當英譯工作接近尾聲，我正為出版之事踟躕時，學生書局挺身襄助，勇於任事，使這本小書得以展開漢學傳播之旅。今書初成，特誌於此，以示不忘。海內存知己，天涯若比鄰；有朋來自遠方，不亦樂乎！

尤雅姿　序於台中開心小書齋　2010.12.28

2012.2.04 定稿

CHINESE ZHI GUAI

–GHOST STORIES FROM THE

WEI-JIN, NAN-BEI DYNASTIES

中英魏晉南北朝志怪選

Content table

主題一：陰陽生死戀

Theme 1 : Yin Yang Love Stories between Life and Death

The dead woman resting in the coffin under the grave is supposedly the most helpless and loneliest with her eternal sleep in the world of love and desire. She is taken to grave by her nubile age, whether she is willing to leave the world or not, having met the man of her life, able to bid farewell with her fiancée. Though readers grieve over the death of the woman and the unfinished love stories, no one can change the cruel fact of death.

Yet in ghost stories, writers fulfill the young and meandering female ghosts' desire to come back to life and make up for the defects in their love lives. When it falls dark, the sexual energy of both male and female and that of both the living and the dead stir up altogether. The restless atmosphere the man lost in the wild walking toward the dim light; or there is the lone and poor student crooning by the light, "The fair lady is the mate of a young man," and vaguely hears the knock on the door as if it is pounding in his heart. A beautiful woman ghost at age fifteen or sixteen, who comes without invitation, spends a night with the lonely man. Yet it may just be a fling and never lasts long. The derailed desire will at last vaporize and the woman ghost will have no choice but to bid farewell. Yet some among the women ghosts can come back to life and earn the opportunity to build a family and live on.

Men in the stories are all living humans without exception, and the female characters are beautiful and young ghosts mostly coming from wealthy families. Some of them are couples that have unforgettable love though fate has brought an end to it; some are total strangers to each other; some are appointed by the gods to revive. The ending also differs; some can revive and are able to give birth to children; some leave with regrets failing to fulfill their goals. In terms of the techniques of the narratives, the smooth dialogue between the male and female characters appropriately shows the emotion and personalities of the characters; the arrangement of the properties, including a pearl robe as a mortuary object, a piece of ripped cloth, a pair of rings as tokens of love, and a woman's shoe, specifically points out the sorrowful atmosphere of the love between ghost and human. Simple and unadorned as the love stories may seem, they have significant and profound influence on Chinese novels.

一、墳場一夜情　東晉·戴祚：《甄異傳》

　　沛郡人<u>秦樹</u>者，家在<u>曲阿</u><u>小辛村</u>。<u>義熙</u>中，嘗自京歸，未至二十<u>里</u>❶許，天暗失道。遙望火光，往投之。見一女子秉燭出，云：「女弱獨居，不得宿客。」<u>樹</u>曰：「欲進路，礙夜，不可前去，乞寄外住。」女然之。

　　<u>樹</u>既進，坐竟，以此女獨處一室，慮其夫至，不敢安眠。女曰：「何以過嫌？保無慮，不相誤也。」為<u>樹</u>設食，食物悉是陳久。<u>樹</u>曰：「承未出適，我亦未婚，欲結大義，能相顧否？」女笑曰：「自顧鄙薄，豈足伉儷？」遂與寢止。

　　向晨，<u>樹</u>去，仍俱起執別。女泣曰：「與君一覿，後面莫期。」以指環一雙贈之，結置衣帶，相送出門。<u>樹</u>低頭急去，數十步，顧其宿處，乃是冢墓。居數日，亡其指環，帶結如故。

One Night Stand in the Graveyard

Dong Jin Dynasty (317- 420CE) Dai Zuo（？-？）"Zhen Yi Zhuan"

　　There once was a man named Qin Shu（秦樹）from a small village in Pei County（沛郡）. One evening on returning home from the capital, just 10 kilometers left he became lost. The night had fallen dark. He saw a remote light ahead and went

---

❶　里 li : The character li is a traditional Chinese measuring unit of distance. Its length is close to half a kilometer.

forward to ask for accommodations. A girl answered the door with a lamp, saying, "As a young girl living alone, I shouldn't take any guests overnight." Shu（樹）said, "I was supposed to keep traveling but failed due to the obscurity in the night. Please allow me to stay outside for one night." The girl agreed.

When Shu sat down in the house, he had been worrying about the girl's husband blaming them for staying under the same roof and so Shu could not sleep. "Why do you mistrust me？ I guarantee you that there is no trouble at all," the girl told him. She prepared him some food that had been preserved for a long time. Shu said, "According to what you say I know you have not married yet, and neither have I. I have intentions to marry you, would you think this over?" The girl smiled, "I am afraid that I am too humble and petty to be your wife." Then she slept with him.

When the dawn arrived, Shu was about to leave. The two got up and held hands saying goodbye. The girl cried, "I might not be able to see your face again." She gave him a pair of rings, tying them up on his belt, and sent him off. Head down, Shu quickly walked away. After some steps, he looked back to last night's stop only to find it as a tomb. Some days later, the rings had gone but the knot on his belt had still remained.

二、鬼妻的珠袍　　魏・曹丕：《列異傳》

　　<u>漢談生</u>者，年四十，無婦，常感激讀《詩經》。夜半，有女子
年可十五、六，姿顏服飾，天下無雙，來就<u>生</u>，為夫婦。乃言：「我
與人不同，勿以火照我也。三年之後，方可照耳。」

　　與為夫婦。生一兒，已二歲，不能忍，夜伺其寢後，盜照視之。
其腰已上，生肉如人，腰已下，但有枯骨。婦覺，遂言曰：「君負
我。我垂生矣，何不能忍一歲而竟相照也？」<u>生</u>辭謝。涕泣不可復

止，云：「與君雖大義永離，然顧念我兒，若貧不能自偕活者，暫隨我去，方遺君物。」生隨之去，入華堂室宇，器物不凡。以一珠袍與之，曰：「可以自給。」裂取生衣裾，留之而去。

後生持袍詣市。睢陽王家買之，得錢千萬。王識之曰：「是我女袍，那得在市？此必發冢！」乃取拷之。生具以實對，王猶不信。乃視女冢，冢完如故。發視之，棺蓋下果得衣裾。呼其兒視，正類王女。王乃信之。即召談生，復賜遺衣，以為女婿。表其兒為郎中。

The Ghost Wife's Pearl Robe

Wei Dynasty (220-266CE) Cao Pi (187-226CE) "Lie Yi Zhuan"

During the Han Dynasty（漢朝）（202BCE-220CE），a student named Tan Sheng（談生）remained unmarried even at the age of 40 and often turned to "The Book of Songs"（詩經）for consolation. On one late night, a girl, 15 or 16 with stunning beauty, came to him and wanted to marry him. However she warned him, "I am no ordinary woman. For three years you must not shine lights on me."

They had a son after they married. Finally, when the boy had reached the age of two Sheng（生）could not contain his curiosity anymore. While his wife lay asleep, he held a lamp over her. Her illuminated body was like any other woman from the waist up, but from the waist down she was nothing but skeletons! Just then his wife woke up.

"You have wronged me." she cried. "I would have soon become mortal. Why couldn't you wait for one more year instead of holding that lamp over me?"

Sheng made abject apologies.

"Although we will never be a couple again, I still have concern for my son," she said in tears, "if one is so poor, they will not be able to support the family. Come with me now, I have something for you."

He followed her into a splendid hall, a rare building that was well furnished, and where she gave him a robe made of pearls.

"You can live on this," she told him.

She tore down a piece of cloth from his gown, and with this she left.

Later Sheng took the robe to the market to sell. One of Duke Sui Yang's（睢陽王） family members spent ten million dollars to buy the robe. As soon as the prince set eyes on it, he said:

"That robe belonged to my daughter. This fellow must be a grave robber."

Sheng was captured by the prince and tortured to tell the truth. However, the prince refused to believe his story. Yet upon inspecting the grave, they found it intact. And when they opened the tomb, they discovered the strip of Sheng's garment. What's more, they discovered that Sheng's son resembled the princess. At last, the duke was convinced and summoned Tan Shen. He returned the robe and made him his son-in-law, while the child was ennobled.

三、忘了穿鞋的鬼情人 東晉·陶潛：《搜神後記》卷四

晉時，武都太守李仲文在郡喪女，年十八，權假葬郡城北。有張世之代為郡。世之男字子長，年二十，侍從在廨中。夜夢一女，年可十七、八，顏色不常，自言前府君女，不幸早亡，會今當更生，心相愛樂，故來相就。如此五、六夕。忽然晝見，衣服熏香殊絕，遂為夫妻，寢息，衣皆有污，如處女焉。

後仲文遣婢視女墓，因過世之婦相問。入廨中，見此女一隻履在子長牀下，取之啼泣，呼言發冢！持履歸，以示仲文，仲文驚愕。遣問世之：「君兒何由得亡女履耶？」世之呼問兒，具道本末。李、張並謂可怪。發棺視之，女體已生肉，姿顏如故，右腳有履，左腳無也。

子長夢女曰：「我比得生，今為所發。自爾之後，遂死肉爛，不得生矣。夫婦情至，謂偕老，而無狀忘履，以致覺露，不復得生。萬恨之心，當復何言！」涕泣而別。

Ghost Lover Without Her Shoe

Dong Jin Dynasty (317-420CE) Tao Qian "Sou Shen Hou Ji"

During the Jin Dynasty(晉朝)(265-420CE), the daughter of the chief magistrate of Wu Du County（武都郡）, Li Zhong-Wen(李仲文), died. She died during her father's term and was buried in the northern part of the county due to the difficulties of traveling back home for funeral. She was only 18 years old by then. Afterwards Li（李）was succeeded by Zhang Shi-Zhi （張世之）, whose son, named Zi-Chang（子長）, 20, accompanied his father in the official house. One night while sleeping, a young and beautiful girl, about 17 or 18, approached Zi-Chang with adoration in his dream. She revealed herself as the daughter of the ex-magistrate and that she died young but was granted with a chance for resurrection. After five or six nights of this encounter, the girl suddenly appeared in the daylight with clothes emitting a wonderful fragrance. The two became a couple and slept together. As if virgin blood, the girl's clothes were stained with blood.

Afterwards Li sent his maid to check the lady's tomb and visit Zhang's（張）wife. As soon as the maid entered the house, she saw a shoe of her lady under Zi-Chang's bed. She took the shoe out and cried to it, screaming "The lady's tomb was raided!" When the maid came back with the shoe and presented it to Li, he was stunned and went forward to question Zhang, "Why does your son possess my dead daughter's shoe?" Zhang asked his son and Zi-Chang relayed the whole story to them. Yet both Li and Zhang found it strange. They opened the coffin of the lady and found that the body had grown new flesh and its complexion and appearance were just the same as when alive. Just one thing though, she was without one shoe on the left foot.

Zi-Chang then dreamed of the girl telling him, "I was about to revive but now the coffin had been opened. Now my body will rot and never again come to life. Our love was deep and as a couple I thought we could be together forever. To my surprise, it was my mistake of forgetting to put on my shoe that exposed and failed our chance to be together. I regretted it deeply but there was nothing I can do about it." She cried and bade farewell to him.

四、陰間救美　南朝　宋·劉敬叔：《異苑》卷八

臨海樂安章沈，年二十餘死，經數日，將欲而蘇。云：被錄到天曹，天曹主者是其外兄，斷理得免。初到時，有少年女子同被錄

送，立住門外。女子見沈事散，知有力助，因泣涕，脫金釧一隻及臂上雜寶，託沈與主者，求見救濟。沈即為請之，并進釧物。良久出，語沈已論，秋英亦同遣去。秋英即此女之名也。

於是俱去，腳痛疲頓，殊不堪行。會日亦暮，止道側小窟，狀如客舍，而不見主人。沈共宿嬿接，更相問次，女曰：「我姓徐，家在吳縣烏門，臨瀆為居，門前倒棗樹即是也。」明晨各去，遂並活。

沈先為護府軍吏，依假出都，經吳，乃到烏門，依此尋索，得徐氏舍。與主人敘闊，問：「秋英何在？」主人云：「女初不出入，君何知其名？」沈因說昔日魂相見之由，秋英先說之，所言因得，主人乃悟。惟羞不及寢嬿之事，而其鄰人或知，以語徐氏。徐氏試令侍婢數人遞出示沈，沈曰：「非也。」乃令秋英見之，則如舊識。徐氏謂為天意，遂以妻沈，生子名曰：天賜。

Romance From Hell

Nan Chao Song Dynasty (420-479CE) Liu Jing-Shu (？-468CE) "Yi Yuan"

There once was a man named Zhang Chen（章沉）of Lin Hai（臨海）who died at his 20s. When he died his body was kept outside in the open for several days but came to life when he was about to be encoffined. He announced to everyone he was captivated by the ghost officials and taken to the court, but it happened that the chief of the court was his cousin, so he was set free after the trial. A young girl had also been taken to the court like him, and when she stood outside waiting for her trial, she knew that Chen (沉) had support from someone influential so that he could get away from the court. She took off her golden bracelet and other jewelry and asked Chen, in tears, to give them to the chief to save her life. Chen quickly did what she asked, and later on the chief walked out and told Chen that the judgment was done and that Qiu-Ying (秋英) was free just as Chen. Qiu-Ying is the name of the girl.

Then the two left the court together, but they could no longer walk due to the pain of their feet and fatigue. As the night fell, they stopped at a small cavern on the road side and rested there. Though the cavern looked like an inn, but they couldn't find a host. Then Chen and Qiu-Ying slept together. He further inquired more information about the girl. "My family name is Xu (徐), and my hometown is in Wu Men (烏門) in Wu County (吳縣). Nearby my house is a stream and there is a crooked jujube tree in front of my house." In the next morning, the two revitalized, and left on their own.

In the past Chen was an officer of military affairs. He took the opportunity and left the capital city during his break and went to Wu Men. He traced the house of Xu by the clues the girl gave him. He greeted the host and asked Qiu-Ying 's whereabouts. The host said, "My daughter has never set foot outside the house before. How could you know her name?" To the host, Chen then relayed the story of how they once became ghosts and met. Since Qiu-Ying had told him the story before, the host thus came to a realization. Yet, Chen was too embarrassed to mention their sexual relationship. However, one neighbor happened to know it and told Xu. In order to test Chen, Xu had some maids come out respectively and asked Chen to identify which one was Qiu-Ying. Chen gave all negative responses. So Xu had Qiu-Ying come out to meet him, and when they met they felt they had known each other for a long time. Xu believed that it was god's will and betrothed his daughter to Chen. The two gave birth to a son whose name was "Tian-Si"（天賜）, meaning "God's giving."

五、髮妻　　東晉‧陶潛：《搜神後記》卷四

　　晉時，東平馮孝將為廣州太守。兒名馬子，年二十餘，獨臥廨中。夜夢見一女子，年十八、九，言：「我是前太守北海徐玄方女，不幸蚤亡，亡來今已四年。為鬼所枉殺，案生錄當八十餘，聽我更生，要當有依馬子，乃得生活，又應為君妻。能從所委，見救活不？」馬子答曰：「可爾。」乃與馬子剋期當出。

　　至期日，牀前地頭髮正與地平，令人掃去，則愈分明，始悟是所夢見者。遂屏除左右人，便漸漸額出，次頭面出，又次肩項，形體頓出。馬子便令坐對榻上，陳說語言，奇妙非常。遂與馬子寢息。每誡云：「我尚虛爾，君當自節。」即問何時得出，答曰：「出當得本命生日，尚未至。」遂住廨中。言語聲音，人皆聞之。

女計生日至，乃具教馬子出己養之方法，語畢辭去。馬子從其言，至日，以丹雄雞一隻，黍飯一盤，清酒一升，醊其喪前，去廨十餘步。祭訖，掘棺出，開視女身，體貌全如故。徐徐抱出，著氈帳中，唯心下微煖，口有氣息。令婢四人守養護之，常以青羊乳汁瀝其兩眼，漸漸能開。口能咽粥，既而能語。二百日中，持杖起行。一期之後，顏色肌膚氣力，悉復如常。

乃遣報徐氏，上下盡來。選吉日下禮，聘為夫婦。生二兒一女：長男字元慶，永嘉初為秘書郎中；小男字敬度，作太傅掾；女適濟南劉子彥，徵士延世之孫云。

What The Hair？！

Dong Jin Dynasty (317-420CE) Tao Qian (365-427CE) "Sou Shen Hou Ji"

During the Jin Dynasty（晉朝）(265-420CE)，Feng Xiao-Jiang（馮孝將）of Dong Ping（東平）served the post of chief magistrate of Guang Zhou（廣州）. His son, Ma-Zi（馬子），who was in his 20's, slept alone in the official house. One night he dreamed of a girl, about 18 or 19 years old, telling him, "I am the daughter of the ex-chief magistrate, Xu Xuan-Fang（徐玄方）. Unfortunate as I was, I died young. I have been dead for 4 years already. I was supposed to live until my 80s, but the ghost made a mistake and took my life. After the judgment, I was granted with a chance to revive and must rely on you, than I can become your wife. Can you do me this favor to save my life?" Ma-Zi agreed. Then the two made an arrangement on the time to bring her out of the earth.

When the time arrived, hairs emerged on the floor in front of the bed , Ma-Zi sent someone to sweep the hair away but was unsuccessful. However, the hair grew more and more. He then remembered the previous dream, so he ordered others to leave him alone. Gradually the forehead of the girl emerged from the floor and then her face, her neck, her shoulder, and the entire body came out. Ma-Zi put her on the bench at the opposite side and what the girl said was extraordinary. Ma-Zi and the girl then slept together, and often the girl warned Ma-Zi , "My body is still very weak, so you must contain yourself." When Ma-Zi asked her when she could show herself to others, she answered, "It must be the same day as I was born, which has not yet arrived." The girl continued to live in the official house, and people were familiar with her voice and of the noise of her movements.

When the girl figured out her birthday was coming, she carefully taught Ma-Zi how to dig her body out from the grave and how to take care of it afterwards. After she was done, she then left. Ma-Zi followed her instructions. On her birthday, he had a big red rooster, a bowl of sticky rice, and one liter of wine as offering on her tomb, which was a mere 10-steps away from the official house.

After he finished the ritual, he dug out the coffin and opened it to check the girl's body. It was intact and alive. Slowly he took her out of the coffin and put her in a tent made of carpet. Yet only her heart was warm and she was breathing very little. He ordered four maids to attend to her and often used the milk of black sheep to moisturize her eyes. Gradually her eyes could open up and she could swallow down some porridge and talk. After 200 days, she could walk with the help of canes. A year later, her complexion, muscle, skins, and spirits became normal.

Ma-Zi sent someone to tell Xu(徐)about the news, and the whole family of Xu came along. They picked a favorable day and presented betrothal gifts and held a wedding ceremony for the two. The couple later on gave birth to two sons and one daughter; the older son, Yuan-Qing（元慶）, served as magistrate official; the other one, Jing-Du（敬度）, magistrate official of the Prince's teacher; and the daughter was married to Liu Zi-Yan（劉子彥）, grandson of the scholar Liu Yan-Shi（劉延世）.

六、幽魂公主的眼淚　東晉·干寶：《搜神記》卷十六

　　吳王夫差小女，名曰紫玉，年十八，才貌俱美。童子韓重，年十九，有道術。女悅之，私交信問，許為之妻。重學於齊、魯之間，臨去，屬其父母，使求婚。王怒，不與女。玉結氣死，葬閶門之外。

　　三年重歸，詰其父母。父母曰：「王大怒，玉結氣死，已葬矣。」重哭泣哀慟，具牲幣，往弔於墓前。玉魂從墓出，見重，流涕謂曰：「昔爾行之後，令二親從王相求，度必克從大願，不圖別後遭命；奈何！」玉乃左顧宛頸而歌曰：「南山有鳥，北山張羅。鳥既高飛，羅將奈何！意欲從君，讒言孔多。悲結生疾，沒命黃墟。命之不造，冤如之何！」「羽族之長，名為鳳凰。一日失雄，三年感傷。雖有眾鳥，不為匹雙。故見鄙姿，逢君輝光。身遠心近，何當暫忘！」歌畢，歔欷流涕。要重還冢，重曰：「死生異路，懼有尤愆，不敢承命。」玉曰：「死生異路，吾亦知之，然今一別，永無後期，子將畏我為鬼而禍子乎？欲誠所奉，寧不相信！」重感其言，送之還冢。玉與之飲讌，留三日三夜，盡夫婦之禮。臨出，取徑寸明珠以送重，曰：「既毀其名，又絕其願，復何言哉！時節自愛。若至吾家，致敬大王。」

　　重既出，遂詣王，自說其事。王大怒曰：「吾女既死，而重造訛言，以玷穢亡靈。此不過發冢取物，託以鬼神！」趣收重，重走脫，至玉墓所訴之玉曰：「無憂，今歸白王。」王粧梳，忽見玉，驚愕悲喜，問曰：「爾緣何生？」玉跪而言曰：「昔諸生韓重來求玉，大王不許，玉名毀義絕，自致身亡。重從遠還，聞玉已死，故齎牲

幣詣冢弔唁。感其篤終，輒與相見，因以珠遺之。不為發冢，願勿
推治。」夫人聞之，出而抱之，玉如烟然。

Tears of the Ghost Princess

Dong Jin Dynasty (317-420CE) Gan Bao (？-336CE) "Sou Shen Ji"

Fu Chai（夫差）（？-473BCE），the King of Wu（吳），had
a gifted and beautiful daughter of eighteen named Zi-Yu（紫
玉）. She fell in love with a learned youth of nineteen, Han
Zhong（韓重）. They exchanged secret pledges and she
promised to marry him. When Han was heading to the area
between Qi（齊）and Lu（魯）for studying, he asked his parents
to propose the marriage; but the king refused in great anger.
The princess ended up dying of a broken heart and was buried
outside the Chang Gate（閶門）.

Three years later, Zhon（重）returned and asked his
parents about the proposal.

"The king flew into a rage and the princess died of a
broken heart," they told him. "She already has been buried."

At that Han wept in extreme sorrow. He prepared
sacrifices at her grave and mourned for her. Miraculously, the
princess then appeared from her grave and said with tears:

"When you left you asked your parents to approach my

father, and I thought our wish would surely come true. But alas! Fate was against us."

With a sidelong glance, she hung her head and sang:

The crow was on the southern mountain,

Nets upon the north were spread;

High away the crow has fled.

Nets were laid, but laid in vain,

Intentions were to follow you

Many hurtful rumors barred the way;

Falling ill of grief I died,

Under yellow earth I lay;

Misfortune with no other way,

Feeling wronged and depressed!

The head of birds

Are named Feng, Huang ❷（鳳凰）

When Huang lost her mate,

For three whole years she wept.

Though there are still opportunities

Widowed Huang remained forlorn.

So despite my looks of fright,

Here I meet with you glowing bright;

---

❷　鳳凰 Feng Huang: A Chinese legendary bird. The male is called Feng and the female is called Huang.

Our bodies are separated but our hearts are near,

For not even a moment will I forget you dear!

After the song she sobbed bitterly, unable to control her grief, and begged Zhong to accompany her into the grave.

"The dead and living must go different ways," said Zhong. "I fear that would hardly be fitting. I better not."

"I know that the dead and living go different ways," she replied. "But once we part we shall never meet again. Are you afraid that now I am a ghost I will harm you? I am completely sincere——why don't you trust me?"

Touched by her words, Zhong sent her back. In the grave they feasted for three days and three nights, and completed the rites of marriage. When he was leaving she gave him a pearl that was one-inch in diameter.

"My reputation was ruined and I never attained my wish to marry you," she sighed, "What more is there to say? Take good care of yourself, and if you pass the palace, please pay my respects to the king."

When Zhong left the grave he went to the king and told him what had happened. Fu Chai flew into a rage.

"My daughter is dead!" he exclaimed. "This fellow is lying to dishonor the dead. He is simply a grave robber who has stolen this pearl and made up this story of a ghost as an excuse. Arrest him at once!"

But Zhong escaped and retreated to the grave where he complained to the princess.

"Don't worry," she said. "I shall explain to the king myself."

Then she appeared to her father as he was dressing. Joy, sorrow and amazement overcame him.

"What brings you back to life?" he demanded.

"When the young student Han Zhong asked to marry me, you refused him," she replied, kneeling. "Having lost my good name and broken faith, I died. Recently he came back from far away, and hearing that I was dead he prepared sacrifices to mourn at my grave. I was so touched by his loyalty that I appeared to him and gave him that pearl. He is no grave robber. Please don't punish him."

When the queen heard this she came out to embrace her child. But the princess vanished like a puff of smoke.

七、倩女幽魂來送絹　南朝 宋·祖沖之：《述異記》

清河崔基，寓居青州。朱氏女姿容絕倫，崔傾懷招攬，約女為妾。後三更中，忽聞扣門外，崔披衣出迎，女雨淚嗚咽，云：「適得暴疾喪亡，忻愛永奪。」悲不自勝。女於懷中抽兩疋絹，與崔曰：
「近自織此絹，欲為君作褌衫，未得裁縫，今以贈離。」崔以錦八
尺答之。女取錦，曰：「從此絕矣！」言畢，豁然而滅。

　　至旦，告其家。女父曰：「女昨夜忽心痛，夜亡。」崔曰：「君
家絹帛無零失耶？」答云：「此女舊餘兩疋絹在箱中。女亡之始，
婦出絹，欲裁為送終衣，轉晒失之。」崔因此具說事狀。

The Enchanting Silk

Nan Chao Song Dynasty (420-479CE) Zu Chong-Zhi "ShuYi Ji"

Cui Ji（崔基）of Qing He（清河）lived in Qing State（青
州）. There was an extremely beautiful woman in the Zhu（朱）
family that he pursued, whom then agreed to become his
concubine ❸. Later, some time in the midnight, Cui（崔）heard
a knocking on the door and threw on his clothes to answer it.
Outside the door was the woman he pursued, crying endlessly
saying, "I just died of a sudden illness. The love of my life is
lost forever." In grave grief, she took out two bolts of silk
fabrics, gave them to Cui and said, "I made these recently. I
wanted to make you a set of clothes but never finished. I give

---

❸ During the Wei Jin Dynasties, a prominent family can only marry within
the same class. Since Cui is from a prominent family and Zhu is not,
therefore Zhu can only become Cui's concubine.

you this as a farewell gift." Cui gave her eight feet of brocade as a reciprocal gift. The woman took the brocade, saying, "Farewell." She then disappeared.

At dawn, Cui went to the woman's family and told them what happened. Her father said, "My daughter suddenly felt cardiac pain last evening and died during the night." Cui asked, "Has the silk fabrics in your house become less?" His father replied, "My daughter made two bolts of silk fabrics and put them in a box. When my daughter had just passed away, my wife took out the silk fabrics, wanting to make her some clothes to be buried in. However, the fabrics disappeared within the blink of an eye." Then Cui explained to them about the gift of silk fabrics.

主題二、精怪色誘篇

Theme 2 : Seduction of Demons and Sprites

This theme centers on the transfiguration or masquerade of human's sexual desire. Lurking in the stories are the sexual desire, dreams, and fantasies of humans (especially men) who are both storytellers and listeners at the same time. The theme also involves the problems about the control and indulgence of "self-consciousness," "social norms," and "primitive desire." Storytellers deliberately spreading these stories not only want to "record of the strange and mythical events", but also have the intention to warn, to tease, and to announce this alternative appetite for sex, which is worthwhile to chew over.

In these stories, the narrator excitedly yet with great caution recounts the strange stories for example: a fisher meets a woman who is a total stranger to him by the misty swamp. Their flirting back and forth during this encounter is both provoking and interesting; a traveler, bored and cannot resist the temptation of a woman falling into his arms, triumphantly believes it is his lucky day, yet after all the flirtation, the woman unexpectedly turns out to be an alligator under the moonlight; after one night, a woman gets out of bed, and as she moves quietly, the man finds out that under her skirt isn't a pair of woman's feet, but that of a turtle's a tail to go with it. Utterly discomfited, the men seek to vindication, who believed they are victims of their sexual deception. However, the adept and experienced demons and sprites can mostly remain calm and depart in a short moment, leaving the men to face upon their bad luck but can do nothing about it. It happens with the women in the stories too. A lonely and bitter wife has some affair with any other man, and when it comes to light, the woman and the demons often are doomed. Who's fooling who? Is it mere self-deception? Or are they actually deluded? Or is it their sexual desire that arouses the fantasy?

Within the construction of abnormal fantasies, there exists the reciprocal action of contradiction. In other words, it approves a standardized situation, yet on the other hand, it allows the existence of many kinds of variations; it protects the social order that is required in the human world, and meanwhile it gives the world a certain kind of freedom to reverse the order. Human's sexual desire are thus allowed to temporarily transgress the bound of social norms, and it gradually becomes possible that animals, insects, aquatic life, reptiles, and birds alike can transform into human figure, for they are the metaphor of desire, or the symbol of "vice." However, when secretly the men and women are having an ignominious affair, their flaws are very quickly shown to others. The order of the reality world rejects at once any disgraceful sexual affairs. After all, people and animals are not the same, and they have to run their own course of life. Stories of this theme are thus set to affirm the norms of human's sexuality and reproduction, and, by "demonizing" the objects of human's sexual desire, to show that the infamous sexual affairs are the faults of the demons' deceptions, and thus their offspring is not allowed to enter the world of humans, but to be eliminated or banished.

From the analytical view of psychology, when humans cannot satisfy their desire, they tend to act differently, so as to relieve pressure by acting unusual. Thus, the absurd sexual affairs often exist in certain circumstances where the subjective life needs to diverge from the objective society. Nevertheless, human society does not permit any taboo sexual affairs. Though we cannot keep away that remnant of disorder in the society, it is necessary to review and repent the errors to take precautions. Consequently stories of this theme can also reflect upon the legitimacy and normalization of sexuality and standard of reproduction.

一、烏龜來搭訕　晉·孔約：《志怪》

會稽吏謝宗赴假吳中，獨在舡。忽有女子，姿性妖婉，來入舡。問宗：「有佳絲否？欲市之。」宗因與戲，女漸相容。留在舡宿，歡宴繼曉。因求宗寄載，宗便許之 。

自爾舡人恆夕但聞言笑，兼芬馥氣。至一年，往來同宿。密伺之，不見有人。方知是邪魅，遂共掩之。良久，得一物，大如枕；須臾又得二物，並小如拳。以火視之，乃是三龜。

宗悲思，數日方悟。自說此女子一歲生二男，大者名道愍；小者名道興。既為龜，送之於江。

Falling in Love with a Turtle

Jin Dynasty (265-420CE) Kong Yue（？-？）"Zhi Guai"

One day Xie Zong（謝宗），an official of Kui Ji（會稽），went on a vacation to Wu（吳）area. When he was cruising alone, a lustful woman entered the boat and asked him,"Do you have some fine silk? I would like to buy some." Zong（宗）then flirted with her and she also accepted it. They spent the whole night having fun together on the boat. After that, she asked Zong to stay with him in his boat, and Zong agreed.

Other boatmen always heard them chatting with laughs at night and also smelled some kind of fragrance. The woman lived with Zong for almost one year, and even though the other boatmen spied on Zong, they didn't see any trace of the woman. Because of this, the boatmen then realized that it must be some kind of evil spirit that bewitched Zong. They launched a sneak attack and finally caught an object that looked like a pillow and two other smaller ones with their size like a fist. They used a flame's light to inspect those objects and found out that they were turtles.

Zong was very depressed about the truth. Later on, he came to realize what had happened to him. He said that the woman gave him two sons in one year, named Dao-Min（道愍）and Dao-Xing（道興）. They sent them back to the river.

二、臂彎裡的大鱷魚 _{東晉·干寶：《搜神記》卷十九}

　　鄱陽人張福，船行還野水邊。夜有一女子，容色甚美，自乘小船，來投福，云：「日暮畏虎，不敢夜行。」福曰：「汝何姓？作此輕行。無笠，雨駛，可入船就避雨。」因共相調，遂入就福船寢。以所乘小舟，繫福船邊。

　　三更許，雨晴月照，福視婦人，乃是一大鼉，枕臂而臥！福驚起，欲執之，遽走入水。向小舟是一枯槎段，長丈餘。

Nightmare on the River

Dong Jin Dynasty (317-420CE) Gan Bao (？-336CE) "Sou Shen Ji"

One night when Zhang Fu（張福）of Bo Yang（鄱陽）parked his boat in a remote place on the riverside, a beautiful woman came to him by a raft. The woman said, "The night is dark and I am afraid of tigers, I don't dare to travel alone." Fu（福）then replied, "What's your name? How can you travel so light? Without an awning, how can you row in this rain? You may come aboard my boat to escape the rain!" They started to chatter and flirt with each other. Fu tied her raft to his boat and they slept in his boat together.

In the midnight, moonlight shined into the boat after the rain stopped. Fu looked at the woman sleeping in his arms but found that she had transformed into an alligator. With terror, he jumped out of bed and tried to catch the monster but the alligator escaped into the river. The raft was actually a three-meter-long piece of drift wood.

三、水獺女郎　東晉·戴祚：《甄異傳》

河南<u>楊醜奴</u>，常詣<u>章安</u>湖拔蒲。將暝，見一女子，衣裳不甚鮮潔而貌美。乘船載荨，前就<u>醜奴</u>：「家湖側，逼暮不得返。」便停舟寄住。

借食器以食，盤中有乾魚、生菜。食畢，因戲笑。醜奴歌嘲之，女答曰：「家在西湖側，日暮陽光頹，託蔭遇良主，不覺寬中懷。」俄滅火共寢。覺其臊氣，又手指甚短，乃疑是魅。此物知人意，遽出戶，變為獺，徑走入水。

Treat of the Otter

Dong Jin Dynasty (317- 420CE) Dai Zuo（？-？）Zhen Yi Zuan"

Yang Chou-Nu（楊醜奴）of He Nan（河南）often went picking cattail leaves at Zhang An Lake（章安湖）. One day as the night approached, he saw a beautiful woman in dirty clothes riding on a boat loaded with water-shield plants. She was riding towards him and told him, "My house is by the lake, but it is too dark to return to." Then she berthed the boat and stayed in the house of Chou-Nu（醜奴）.

She borrowed some tableware to use to offer dried fish and vegetables. After they finished eating, the two flirted with each other. Chou-Nu sang songs to joke around with her, and the girl responded singing, "My home is in the west of the lake. The sun is setting and darkness is creeping in. Fortunately, a good man I met. Naturally, I cherish this relief." Soon the fire was put out and the two slept together. However Chou-Nu discovered that there was an offensive smell of raw fish on her and that her fingers were rather short, so he suspected that it must be some monster. The thing knew what was on Chou-Nu's mind, so it quickly slipped away and transformed into an otter, going straight to the water.

四、露出龜腳　南朝‧佚名：《續異記》

　　山陰朱法公者，嘗出行，憩於臺城東橘樹下。忽有女子，年可十六、七，形甚端麗。薄晚，遣婢與法公相聞，方夕欲詣宿。至人定後，乃來，自稱姓檀，住在城側。因共眠寢，至曉而去，明日復來。如此數夜。每曉去，婢輒來迎。復有男子，可六、七歲，端麗可愛，女云是其弟。

　　後曉去，女衣裙開，見龜尾及龜腳。法公方悟是魅，欲執之。向夕復來，即然火照覓，尋失所在。

Before Giving the Show Away

Nan Chao Dynasty (317-420CE) Anonymous"Xu Yi Ji"

Once while Zhu Fa-Gong（朱法公）of Shan Yin（山陰）was traveling, he rested under the orange tree at the east side of Tai Castle（臺城）. Suddenly a beautiful girl, about 16 or 17, came and sent her maid to greet Fa-Gong（法公）. The maid told him that the girl would be coming over for the night. She came at midnight while everyone else was asleep. She said her family name was Tan（檀）, living near the city. She then slept with Fa-Gong together and left at dawn. The next day she came back, and this went on for several nights. The girl always left at dawn and her maid would meet and greet her. Still there was one adorable boy, about 6 or 7 years of age, who the girl claimed was her little brother.

One morning as she left, her skirt opened wide and her turtle-like tail and feet were exposed. It was then that Fa-Gong realized she was a monster and wanted to catch her. That evening, Fa-Gong lit a torch as soon as the girl showed up, but lost sight of her immediately.

五、母豬賽貂蟬　東晉・干寶：《搜神記》卷十八

晉有一士人，姓王，家在吳郡。還至曲阿，日暮，引船上當大埭。見埭上有一女子，年十七、八，便呼之留宿。至曉，解金鈴繫其臂。使人隨至家，都無女人，因逼豬欄中，見母豬臂有金鈴。

Woman or Sow?

Dong Jin Dynasty (317-420CE) Gan Bao (？-336CE) "Sou Shen Ji"

There was a scholar named Wang（王）lived in Wu County （吳郡）in Jin Dynasty（晉朝）(265-420CE). When he was returning to Qu E（曲阿）, the night had fallen. He docked his boat up at the Dang Da Pier（當大埭）, and there he saw a girl, about 17 or 18, and asked her to stay for the night.

In the morning, he took off a golden bracelet and tied it up on the girl's arm. Then he sent someone to follow the girl to her house. But there wasn't a woman in the house, so the man approached the pigpen and saw a sow with the golden bracelet on its leg.

六、獺糞變成口香糖 南朝 宋·劉義慶：《幽明錄》卷六

宋永興縣吏鐘道得重病初差，情欲倍常。先樂白鶴墟中女子，至是猶存想焉。忽見此女振衣而來，即與燕好。

是後數至。道曰：「我甚欲雞舌香。」女曰：「何難？」遂掬香滿手以授道。道邀女同含咀之。女曰：「我氣素芳，不假此。」女子出戶，狗忽見，隨咋殺之，乃是老獺。口香即獺糞，頓覺臭穢。

Refreshment of Excrement

Nan Chao Song Dynasty (420-479CE) Liu Yi-Qing (403-444CE) "You Ming Lu"

Zhong Dao（鐘道）, an official of Yong Xin County（永興縣）in Song Dynasty（宋代）（420- 479CE）, was sickened with a serious illness. As he was recovering from it, his sexual desire was stronger than before. He used to have affections for a woman living in White Crane Village（白鶴墟）and missed her a lot during these days. Suddenly he saw the girl patting off the dust on her clothes and coming towards him, and she made love with him. The girl came to Dao's house often after this.

One day, Dao（道）said to her, "How much do I want to hold clove fruit in my mouth!" "That's not a problem at all," the girl answered, and held the clove fruit up in both hands to Dao. Dao invited the girl to taste it with him, but the girl said, "I always have good breath so I don't need that." Yet when the girl went out, the dog found her to be strange. The dog snapped and killed her. It then appeared that it was an old otter and the clove fruit was the excrement of the otter. Dao felt his mouth stinking and filthy.

七、披麻帶孝的白狗 東晉·干寶：《搜神記》卷十八

北平田琰，居母喪，恆處廬。向一期，夜忽入婦室。密怪之，曰：「君在毀滅之地，豈可如此！」琰不聽而合。

後琰暫入，不與婦語，婦怪無言，並以前事責之。琰知鬼魅。臨暮竟未眠，衰服掛廬。須臾，見一白狗，攬銜衰服，因變為人，著而入。琰隨後逐之，見犬將升婦牀，便打殺之。婦羞愧而死。

The Dog in Mourning Clothes

Dong Jin Dynasty (317-420CE) Gan Bao (？-336CE) "Sou Shen Ji"

Tian Yan（田琰）from Bei Ping（北平）was in mourning for his mother ❶ . He left his house and lived in a small hut near the grave of his mother ❷. After one year, during the night one day, Yan（琰）entered his wife's bedroom suddenly and his wife silently criticized him saying," You shouldn't come to me during the mourning period for your mother." Yan did not listen to his wife and slept with her.

After that, Yan came home temporarily, but didn't speak with his wife. His wife was upset with his silence and complained him for sleeping with her. Hearing her words, Yan

---

❶ 守孝: In Chinese traditional culture, after one's parents pass away, for three years they cannot work or get married and must stay in a small hut near the tomb and maintain a sad state of mind in condolence for their parents.

❷ 廬: After a parent passes away, the eldest son must live in an earthen hut constructed next to the tomb in order to look after it for a period of three years.

knew that a monster had come and slept with his wife. Then Yan prepared to catch the monster, staying wide awake the whole night.

Just as usual, he hung his mourning clothes ❸ in the hut. Shortly after,he saw a white dog arrive. The white dog grabbed his mourning clothes and put them on, transformed into a man and then walked towards his house. Yan followed after and when the dog was about to climb into to his wife's bed, he beat it to death. Yan's wife was ashamed and committed suicide.

八、狐精與逃兵　東晉·干寶:《搜神記》卷十八

後漢建安中,沛國郡陳羨為西海都尉。其部曲王靈孝無故逃去,羨欲殺之。居無何,孝復逃走。羨久不見,囚其婦,婦以實對,羨曰:「是必魅將去,當求之。」因將步騎數十,領獵犬,周旋於城外求索,果見孝於空塚中。聞人犬聲,怪遂避去。

羨使人扶孝以歸,其形頗像狐矣,略不復與人相應,但啼呼「阿紫」,阿紫,狐字也。後十餘日,乃稍稍了悟。云:「狐始來時,

---

❸ 孝服: After one passes away, their relatives must wear a thick white clothing, similar to a potato sack. According to the relation between relatives, this clothing should be worn between three months to three years.

於屋曲角雞棲間，作好婦形，自稱『阿紫』，招我。如此非一，忽
然便隨去，即為妻，暮輒與共還其家。遇狗不覺。」云樂無比也。

　　道士云：「此山魅也。」《名山記》曰：「狐者，先古之淫婦
也，其名曰『阿紫』，化而為狐。故其怪多自稱『阿紫』。」

The Escapist

Dong Jin Dynasty (317-420CE) Gan Bao (？-336CE) "Sou Shen Ji"

　　In Jian-An（建安）period(196-220CE), post Han Dynasty
（後漢）（25－220CE），there was a commander named Chen
Xian（陳羨）of Pei County（沛郡）. One of his subordinates ❹
, named Wang Ling-Xiao（王靈孝），defected from the troops
with no reason. Xian（羨）intended to execute him but Xiao
（孝）came back at last. However, soon after Xiao escaped
again. For a long time Xian couldn't find Xiao, so in return
Xian then imprisoned Xiao's wife, trying to find out Xiao's
location. But his wife said that she truly didn't know of his
whereabouts. Xian concluded," Xiao must have been taken by
some kind of monster, we should rescue him." Therefore, he
led dozens of cavalry troops and some hounds in search for
Xiao around the suburbs and as suspected, found him in an

---

❹　部曲：A soldier belonging to a particular Commander or General's
　　jurisdiction.

empty tomb. After hearing the sound of dogs and humans approaching, the monster escaped.

As a result, Xian ordered his subordinates to carry Xiao back. However, Xiao had come to look like a fox and almost lost his mind as well as his ability to communicate. He just kept crying out a name "A- Zi" (阿紫) . After some time, he regained consciousness. "In the beginning when the fox spirit came, she hid in the corner of the hen house. She had the figure of a beautiful woman, she called herself A- Zi and drew me near. After several times, I went with her and she became my wife. In the evening we returned to this tomb, our home. Even dogs couldn't detect her." Xiao said they had wonderful life.

Taoist alleged that this must have been a demon. *Records of Ming Shan* (名山記) says "Fox spirits are a kind of whore in ancient times called "A- Zi". Because of this, many other demons also called themselves "A- Zi" .

九、狸精變作心上人　　南朝 宋·祖沖之：《述異記》

陳留董逸少時，鄰女梁瑩年稚色豔，逸愛慕傾魂，貽椒獻寶，瑩亦納而未獲果。後逸郡人鄭充在逸所宿，二更中，門前有叩掌聲，充臥望之，亦識瑩，語逸：「梁瑩今來！」逸驚躍出迎，把臂入舍，遂與瑩寢。

瑩仍求去，逸攬持不置，申款達旦，逸欲留之，云：「為汝蒸豚作食，食竟去。」逸起，閉戶絕帳，瑩因變形為狸，從梁上走去。

One Night Stand with a Fox

Nan Chao Song Dynasty (420-479CE) Zu Chong-Zhi (429-500CE)
"Shu Yi Ji"

In Chen Liu（陳留）area, there was a young man called Dong Yi（董逸）. He was so fascinated by a pretty girl named Liang Ying（梁瑩）that he kept sending fragrant flowers and precious gifts to show his feeling. Even though Ying（瑩）accepted all of them, she didn't respond to Yi's（逸）affection. Once when Yi's neighbor, Zheng Chong（鄭充）, stayed at Yi's place for one night, Chong （充）was woken up by the sound of clapping ❺ at midnight and found out Ying came. Yi welcomed her with surprise, and then they went into Yi's room with their arms hooked together.

After they slept together, Ying asked to leave. But Yi held her tightly and kept conveying his love the whole night. The

---

❺　扣掌聲：During the Chinese Medieval time period, clapping was used as a way to call to others.

next morning, Yi wanted Ying to stay and told her, "I will cook pork for you, when finished eating you can leave." He got up and locked the door to prevent Ying from escaping. However, Ying transformed into a fox and ran away by climbing up the beams.

十、迷上蚱蜢精　　南朝·佚名：《續異記》

徐邈，晉孝武帝時，為中書侍郎。在省直，左右人恆覺邈獨在帳內，以與人共語。有舊門生，一夕伺之，無所見。天時微有光，始開窗戶，瞥睹一物從屏風裡飛出，直入鐵鑊中。仍逐視之，無餘物，唯見鑊中聚菖蒲根，下有大青蚱蜢，雖疑此為魅，而古來未聞，但摘除其兩翼。

至夜，遂入邈夢云：「為君門生所困，往來道絕，相去雖近，有若山河。」邈得夢，甚悽慘。門生知其意，乃微發其端。邈初時疑，不即道。語之曰：「我始來直者，便見一青衣女子從前度，猶作兩髻，姿色甚美。聊試挑謔，即來就己。且愛之，仍溺情。亦不知其從何而至此。」兼告夢。門生因具以狀白，亦不復追殺蚱蜢。

Infatuated by the Grasshopper

Nan Chao Dynasty (317-420CE) Anonymous"Xu Yi Ji"

During the Jin Xiao-Wu(晉孝武）(362-396CE) empire era, there was an official named Xu Miao（徐邈）. When he was on duty, his colleagues heard him chatting with someone in his own tent. One night, one of his ex- subordinates secretly investigated on Miao（邈）. He didn't discover anything until the day was dawning. As Miao opened the window he saw a creature fly out from the screen to a wok. He chased after it to get a closer look but found out nothing but a big grasshopper among sword grasses. Even though he had never heard that a grasshopper could be an evil spirit, he still had his suspicions, so he removed its wings.

That night the grasshopper entered Miao's dream. It said "I am trapped by your ex-subordinate. Though we are near each other, the path to find you is blocked. He enlarged the distance between us." Miao was very upset since then. His ex-subordinate noticed and asked him why. Miao hesitated at first but eventually told him "I met a pretty girl with her hair worn in two buns, dressed in a green gown. I attempted flirting with her and she accepted. She came to me and we fell in love. I really don't know where she came from." He also talked about the dream. His ex-subordinate therefore confessed what he had done and ceased trying to kill the grasshopper.

十一、人魚怪胎　　無名氏：《稽神異苑》

《三吳記》曰：「餘姚百姓王素有一女，姿色殊絕。有少年，自稱江郎，求婚。經年，女生一物，狀若絹囊。母以刀割之，悉是魚子。乃伺江郎就寢細視，所著衣衫皆鱗甲之狀，乃以石碪之。曉見牀下一大魚，長六、七尺。素持刀斷之，命家人煮食。其女後適於人。」

The Crossbreed

Anonymous "Ji Shen Yi Yuan"

It was recorded in"San Wu Ji" (三吳記), that in Yu Yao County (餘姚縣) lived a man named Wang Su (王素) who had a beautiful girl. One day a young man, who introduced himself as Jiang (江) (means river), proposed marriage with his daughter and was accepted.

One year later, the girl gave birth to an object similar to a silk-bag. With great suspicion, the girl's mother cut open the bag-like thing and found that it was full of fish spawn. She felt so weird that she examined Jiang when he fell asleep and found that his clothes were covered with scales. She then put a big stone on him. Next morning, a giant fish was found beneath the bed and it soon was killed and boiled by the girl's father. The girl then remarried.

十二、狸精越界來成親 南朝 宋‧劉義慶：《幽明錄》卷三

晉太元中，瓦官佛圖前淳于矜，年少潔白。送客至石頭城南，逢一女子，美姿容。矜悅之，因訪問。二情既和，將入城北角，共盡歡好，便各分別。期更克集，便欲結為伉儷。女曰：「得婿如君，死何恨。我兄弟多，父母并在，當問我父母。」矜便令女婢問其父母，父母亦懸許之。女因敕婢取銀百斤，絹百匹，助矜成婚。經久，養兩兒。

當作秘書監，明日，騶卒來召，車馬導從，前後部鼓吹。經少日，有獵者過，覓<u>矜</u>，將數十狗徑突入，咋婦及兒，并成狸。絹帛金銀并是草及死人骨及蛇魅等。

The Mysterious Wife

Nan Chao Song Dynasty (420-479CE) Liu Yi-Qing (403-444CE) "You Ming Lu"

In the Tai Yuan（太元）(376-396CE) period of Jin Dynasty（晉朝）(265-420CE）, there was a handsome young man called Chun-Yu Jin（淳于矜）. He once met a beautiful woman after sending a guest to Stone Castle's（石頭城）southern side. Jin（矜）was attracted to her and approached wanting to chat with her. They both felt good about each other and then had a one-night stand in the northern corner of the castle. Jin proposed the next time they met that they should get married. The woman said, "Why should I feel regretful to have such a great husband like you? However, we ought to ask my parents for their permission first." Jin sent the woman's maid to ask her parents about marriage and got their word. The woman ordered her maid to provide Jin（矜）with abundant silver and silk to help with their marriage. As time went by, they gave birth to two sons.

When Jin was sent to work in the Royal Library (秘書省),
the government sent cavaliers leading in the front and
following from behind, along with musical bands to take him
to the palace. Before long, surprisingly a hunter with many
dogs entered Jin's house wanting to visit him. However, the
hunter didn't find Jin; instead, his dogs attacked and killed
his wife and sons.

Their bodies transformed into foxes, and those treasures the
woman brought to Jin all became human bones, weeds and
wild berries.

十三、蛇郎君的洞房花燭夜

東晉‧陶潛:《搜神後記》卷十

晉太元中,有士人
嫁女於近村者,至時,
夫家遣人來迎,女家好
遣發,又令女乳母送
之。既至,重門累閣,
擬於王侯。廊柱下有燈
火,一婢子嚴粧直守。
後房帷帳甚美。

至夜,女抱乳母涕

泣，而口不得言。乳母密於帳中以手潛摸之，得一蛇，如數圍柱，纏其女，從足至頭！乳母驚走出外，柱下守燈婢子，悉是小蛇，燈火乃是蛇眼。

The Wedding Night of the Snake Man

Dong Jin Dynasty (317-420CE) Tao Qian (365-427CE) "Sou Shen Hou Ji"

During the Jin Dynasty(晉朝)(265-420CE), the daughter of a scholar was about to marry someone from a nearby village. On their wedding day, a party of people came to escort the bride to the groom's house. The bride's family sent the bride out discreetly followed by her wet nurse. The groom's house was a large mansion with lofty towers like the house of the nobility. There were also lights on the pillars of the corridors. Under each light a maid, dressed accordingly, stood to keep vigil. The curtain in the bedroom was extraordinarily beautiful.

On that night, the woman held the nurse and cried but could not let out a word. The nurse secretly searched in the curtains and found a snake as large as a pillar several inches thick. The snake strangled the woman tightly from head to toe. The nurse was so scared that she ran out. Afterwards she found the maids standing under the lights to actually be small snakes and the lights to be of snake eyes.

十四、三小猴　東晉・陶潛：《搜神後記》卷九

　　晉太元中，丁零王翟昭後宮養一獼猴，在妓女房前。前後妓女同時懷妊，各產子三頭，出便跳躍。昭方知是猴所為，乃殺猴及子。妓女同時號哭。昭問之，云：「初見一年少，著黃練單衣，白紗帢，甚可愛，笑語如人。」

Monkey Magic

Dong Jin Dynasty (317-420CE) Tao Qian (365-427CE) "Sou Shen Hou Ji"

　　During the Jin Dynasty(晉朝)(265-420CE)lived the King of Ding Ling(丁靈王). His name was Zhai Zhao(翟昭)and he raised a macaque in front of the House of Maids in his seraglio. Some of the maids got pregnant successively and gave birth to three creatures which were able to jump around at birth. The king then knew that it was done by the macaque so he killed the macaque and its offspring. The maids all cried loudly and the king asked how these creatures came from them. They answered, "First we saw a young man wearing a gown made of yellow silk and a white yarn cap. He was very adorable. He talked and laughed just like humans."

十五、冒牌雞老公　　南朝　宋·劉義慶：《幽明錄》卷六

臨淮朱綜遭母難，恆外處住，內有病，因前見。婦曰：「喪禮之重，不煩數還。」綜曰：「自荼毒以來，何時至內？」婦曰：「君來多矣。」綜知是魅，敕婦婢：「候來，便即戶執之！」及來，登往赴視。此物不得去，遽變老白雄雞。推問，是家雞。殺之，遂絕。

Intrigued by the Old White Rooster

Nan Chao Song Dynasty (420-479CE) Liu Yi-Qing (403-444CE) "You Ming Lu"

There was a man called Zhu Zong（朱綜）who lived in the Lin Huai（臨淮）area. His mother just passed away. He maintained to live outside for funeral purposes ❻, but later found out that his wife fell ill, and returned home to see her. His wife said to him, "Mother's funeral is the top priority for you now, so you shouldn't come to see me so often." Zong（綜）

---

❻ After a parent passes away, the eldest son must live in an earthen hut constructed next to the tomb in order to look after it for a period of three years.

whereupon asked her, "Did I come back home and see you after mother's death?" She answered him saying that he did return home very often.

Zong thus concluded that there must be some kind of evil spirit who bewitched his wife. To take action, he ordered his wife's maidservant, "Spy, and when it gets to the door, grab it!" Upon hearing that the spirit had been caught, Zong quickly returned home to check on it. The evil spirit couldn't get away, so it suddenly transformed into an old white rooster. After investigating, they found out that it was their household rooster. They killed the old white rooster and the evil spirit had vanished.

主題三、冤魂索命錄

Theme 3: Revenge of Ghosts

During the Chinese medieval times, when the "world" was in turmoil and chaos because of the war, it is, cruelly, often seen that the majorities and the powerful bully the minorities and the weak. In the political arena, different authorities wrestle with one another, and the losing one, though vows to revenge, is put to death as a warning to others. In the society, there are such stories like a woman being raped and robbed, deserted by an exhausted well, waiting for the time to redress the injustice; a sex scandal in the local government comes to light and the informer is silenced for his reporting on the scandal; the widowed man on a boat back home is pushed by others and drowned to death, and his ghost then carries his grievance afar to his mother's dream in hope of revenge. The victims in other stories with incidents of wrongful imprisonment, vicious arson, and murders cannot do anything but whimper in the night. How many cases can be justified in the real world? In the world filled with the din of human voices, who will hear the sorrows and grievances of the ghosts in tears? Who, then, are willing to step forward boldly to file an appeal for those who die spitefully? Who seek justice for them and bridge the wide gap between the world of legitimacy and the world of reality?

By examining and collecting materials from history, the extraordinary anecdotes in the country, writers of the abnormal fantasy have been the ones to establish the text of punitive justice, weaving the events together and conforming to the common understanding of "just punishment." The stories are aimed to redeem the society by punishing the culprits and doing justice to the victims, who can eventually exit the world peacefully.

Additionally, the techniques of narration have made the stories of this theme even more appealing to readers. Whether it is the scenario of people being murdered or that of revenge, writers are able to give a very vivid description so as to draw readers to heave a deep sigh for the victims and, at the same time, satisfy the primitive desire to take revenge upon the culprits. The ghosts in the stories come in various forms; one moves his head away and puts a sacrificial object into his neck; some only appear within traces of water; some appear indistinctly and show their faces in the mirror; some can penetrate into the culprits' chest and frighten them to pass out; some are grieved and look black, without pupils in their eyes, and wait gloomily in the swamp for the enemies; some will produce an apparition to lure the enemies, and when they approach the water, the ghosts thrust their deadly hands towards the enemies' and grasped their nostrils making blood run out of them. These stories also reflect the judicial process in ancient China.

一、誰用斧頭劈死了主人 北齊・顏之推：《冤魂志》

宋世永康人呂慶祖家甚溫富。嘗使一奴名教子守視墅舍。以元嘉中便往案行，忽為人所殺。族弟無期先大舉慶祖餞，咸謂為害。

無期齎羊、酒、脯至柩所而咒曰：「君荼酷如此，乃云是我！魂而有靈，使知其人！」既還，至三更，見慶祖來云：「近教子畦疇不理，許當痛治奴，奴送以斧斫我背，將帽塞口，因得嚙奴三指，悉皆破碎，便取刀刺我頸，曳著後門。初見殺時，諸從行人亦在其中，奴今欲叛，我已釘其頭著壁。」言畢而滅。

無期早旦以告父母。潛視奴所在，壁果有一把髮，以竹釘之。又看其指，並見破傷。錄奴詰驗，具伏。又云：「汝既反逆，何以不叛？」奴云：「頭如被繫，欲逃不得。」諸同見者，事事相符，即焚教子並其二息。

Who Axed the Master?

Bei Qi Dynasty (550-577CE) Yan Zhi-Tui (531-595CE) " Yuan Hun Zhi"

In the Song Dynasty（宋代）（420-479CE）, there was a wealthy man named Lü Cing-Zu（呂慶祖）of Yong Kang（永康）. He once sent one servant, named Jiao-Zi（教子）, to look after his villas and fields. On his inspection tour of his fields, Lü（呂）was killed. His cousin, Wu-Qi（無期）, had held a farewell feast for Lü and everyone was oddly convinced that Wu-Qi killed Lü.

Wu-Qi brought lambs, wine, and meat jerky as sacrifice to Lü's coffin and said, "You were murdered cruelly, and people said I did it. If your spirit is aware of it, let me know who the murderer is!" After he went back, and in the midnight, Lü came to him and said, "Recently Jiao-Zi did not take care of the farm, which had been deserted, so I scolded him saying I will punish him severely. He then fiercely hacked my back with an axe, and stuffed my mouth with his bandana, I took this opportunity to bite through three fingers of his. Then he stabbed my neck with a knife, dragging me to the back door. While I was being murdered, my fellow companions were there. As the servant wanted to flee away, I had already nailed his head on the wall." After Lü told his cousin he vanished.

Wu-Qi told this to his parents at daybreak. He secretly went to check on the place the servant lived where he found a bundle of hair nailed on the wall, and the injured fingers on the servant's hand. Wu-Qi then caught him and inquired, and the servant confessed everything. "Now that you rebelled against Lü, why don't you run away? " asked Wu-Qi. " My head was nailed and I couldn't get away even if I want to," the servant answered. Wu-Qi further inquired those witnesses, whose statements corroborated the facts. Then Lü's family burned Jiao-Zi and his two sons to death ❶.

二、性醜聞秘辛　　北齊・顏之推：《冤魂志》

晉富陽縣令王範，有妾桃英，殊有姿色，遂與閣下丁豐、史華期二人姦通。範嘗出行不還。帳內都督孫元弼聞丁豐戶內有環珮聲，覘視，見桃英與同被而臥。元弼叩戶，面叱之，桃英即起，攬裙理鬢，躡履還內。元弼又見華期帶珮桃英麝香。二人懼元弼告之，乃共謗元弼與桃英有私。範不辨察，遂殺元弼。

有陳超者，當時在座，勸成元弼罪。後範代還，超亦出都看範。

---

❶ In ancient China, when one commits a crime serious enough, the criminal and their offspring were executed together.

行至赤亭山下，值雷雨日暮。忽然有人扶超腋，徑曳將去，入荒澤中。電光照見一鬼，面甚青黑，眼無瞳子，曰：「吾孫元弼也。訴怨皇天，早見申理。連時候汝，乃今相遇！」超叩頭流血，鬼曰：「王範既為事主，當先殺之。賈景伯、孫文度在太山玄堂下，共定死生名錄。桃英魂魄亦收在女青亭者，是第三地獄名，在黃泉下，專治女鬼。」投至天明，失鬼所在。

超至揚都詣範，未敢說之。便見鬼從外來，逕入範帳。至夜，範始眠，忽然大魘，連呼不醒。家人牽青牛臨範，上并加桃人左索。向明小蘇。十許日而死，妾亦暴亡。

超亦逃走長干寺，易姓名為何規。後五年，三月三日臨水，酒酣，超云：「今當不復畏此鬼也！」低頭，便見鬼影已在水中，以手撋超鼻，血大出，可一升許。數日而殂。

Slaughter after the Illicit Scandal

Bei Qi Dynasty (550-577CE) Yan Zhi-Tui (531-595CE)" Yuan Hun Zhi"

Tao-Ying（桃英）, the beautiful and beloved concubine of the chief magistrate of Fu Yang County（富陽縣）, Wang Fan（王範）, had an affair with officers Ding Feng（丁豐）and Shi Hua-Qi（史華期）. While Wang（王）was away on an inspection tour, a military officer named Sun Yuan-Bi（孫元弼）heard a sound of jade pendants coming from the room of Ding Feng.

He went forward to check on it, only to find Ding Feng sleeping with Tao-Ying on the bed. Sun (孫) knocked at the door and lashed at them. Tao-Ying then got up, put on her skirt, fixed her hair, and walked back to the inner room with her shoes halfway on. Afterwards, Sun also found Shi (史) was wearing Tao Ying's perfume sachet. Afraid that Sun would report them to the chief magistrate, Ding(丁)and Shi together accused Sun and Tao-Ying of adultery. Without further evidence, Wang killed Sun.

There was a man named Chen Chao (陳超) in the jury, who decreed Sun's (孫) death sentence. Later when Wang had served his term, Chen (陳) especially went to visit him. Just as Chen walked to the foot of Chi Ting Mountain (赤亭山), a storm came with darkness falling upon the sky. Suddenly someone grabbed Chen's arm and dragged him away into a barren swamp. Then a bolt of lightning lit up the figure, it was a dark-faced ghost without pupils in its eyes. The ghost said, "I am Sun Yuan-Bi and I have appealed to the heaven about the injustice. I am vindicated now. Having been waiting here for you for so long, I finally meet you now." Chen kowtowed ❷

---

❷　叩頭 Kowtow: The highest form of respect in Chinese etiquette used to show one's obedience or used to apologize or plea for forgiveness from a severe mistake. It is the act of kneeling down and placing one's hands and

incessantly until bleeding. "Since Wang is the arch-criminal, I should kill him first. Jia Jing-Bo（賈景伯）and Sun Wen-Du（孫文度）are collating the files of death in hell. Tao-Ying's （桃英） spirit has been taken into custody in Nü Qing Station（女青亭）, the name of the third hell under the nether world designed for the remedy and punishment of female ghosts." Said the ghost, and he was gone after dawn.

When Chen arrived at the Yang Du（揚都）, he went to visit Wang. He didn't dare mention what happened in the barren swamp. Soon the ghost came from outside and entered Wang's tent. In the night, as Wang fell into sleep, he had a nightmare and did not wake up even when others were calling him. His family members took to Wang's bedside a black ox carrying a puppet made of peach tree and rope made of reed ❸. As the sun was about to rise, Wang was slightly awake for some time. He died after more than 10 days and his concubine, Tao Ying, died suddenly too.

Chen fled for his life, hiding in Chang Gan Temple （長干寺）, and changed his name to He Gui（何規）. After five years,

---

forehead on the ground. When used an apology, one must knock his/her forehead on the ground.

❸ These three objects can dispel ghosts and evil sprits.

on the 3rd of March ❹ he came to the water side, drunk, saying, "I should not have to worry about the ghost now." Just when he lowered his head, he saw the shadow of the ghost on the surface of the water. The ghost clutched Chen's nose, and about one liter of blood poured out from it. Chen died several days later.

三、刑場上含恨奏琵琶　　北齊‧顏之推：《冤魂志》

宋元嘉中，李龍等夜行劫掠。於時丹陽陶繼之為秣陵縣令，微密尋捕，遂擒龍等。取龍引一人，是太樂伎，忘其姓名。劫發之夜，此伎推同伴往就人宿，共奏音聲。陶不詳審，為作款列，隨例申上。及所宿主人士貴賓客並明相證，陶知枉濫。但以文書已行，不欲自為通塞，遂并諸劫干人，於郡門斬之。

此伎聲伎精能，又殊辨慧。將死之日，親隣知識看者甚眾。伎曰：「我雖賤隸，少懷慕善，未嘗為非，實不作劫！陶令已當具知，枉見殺害……若死無鬼則已，有鬼必自陳訴！」因彈琵琶數曲而就死。眾知其枉，莫不殞泣。

月餘日，陶遂夜夢伎來至案前云：「昔枉見殺，實所不忿。訴之得理，今故取君！」便入陶口，仍落腹中。陶即驚窹，俄而倒絕，

---

❹　三月三日：The 3rd of March is a festival where people gather around the riverside to clean their face or hands in order to dispel bad luck.

狀若風顛，良久方醒。有時而發，輒天矯，頭反著背。四日而亡。
亡後家便貧頓，一兒早死，餘有一孫，窮寒路次。

Bitter Songs of the Pipa on Execution Grounds

Bei Qi Dynasty (550-577CE) Yan Zhi-Tui (531-595CE) " Yuan Hun Zhi"

During Emperor Wen's（文帝）time(424-453CE) in the Song Dynasty（宋代）(420-479CE), a criminal gang led by Li Long（李龍）plundered and robbed in the night. The then chief magistrate of Mo Ling County（秣陵縣），Tao Ji-Zhi（陶繼之），tracked them down secretly and caught Li Long and his fellow companions. When they arrested Li Long, they coaxed him into revealing other criminals, one of which was a musician in the imperial palace whose name could not be recalled. The musician defended, saying that on the day of plundering, he and his companion were staying at someone's house for the night, performing music for the host. Tao Ji-Zhi did not inquire further but reported the musician as a criminal in his verdict for the higher authorities. It was not until the host of the house and the audience of the musician that night came out to prove the musician's innocence that Tao（陶）realized he had done the musician an injustice. Yet the verdict had been sent out and he did not want to admit his mistake, so the musician was executed in the Gate of the County along with other gangsters.

The musician was brilliant at his skills and talented. When he was to be executed, friends, relatives, and neighbors came to see him. The musician said, "Even though I am just a petty musician, I have been doing good deeds since I was young. I have never done any evil and I did not rob nor plunder. The chief magistrate should have known the case well, but still he has done this injustice and decreed my death sentence. When I die, if possible, I will plea for vindication to the ghosts." Then he played the pipa（琵琶）❺ and was executed after a couple of songs. Tears dropped on everyone's face, knowing he was treated unjustly.

After more than a month, Tao dreamed of the musician, who came toward his desk and said, "I was killed by injustice and my mind can not settle. My appeal has been put on a trial. Now I come here to take away your life!" Then he jumped into Tao's mouth and fell into his stomach. Immediately, Tao woke up with a start, but fainted down as if he had a stroke. It was a long time before he woke up. This happened occasionally

---

❺　琵琶 pipa : A kind of stringed musical instrument made of wood similar to the lute.

and when it did, his body would bend over in the opposite side, with his head bending to his back. He died after four days. After his death, the family suffered from poverty. One of his sons died young, leaving only a grandson starving and freezing on the street.

四、遇害女鬼的悲憤控訴

東晉·干寶:《搜神記》卷十六

漢九江何敞,為交州刺史,行部到蒼梧郡高要縣,暮宿鵠奔亭。夜猶未半,有一女從樓下出,呼曰「明使君,妾冤人也!」須臾,至敞所臥牀下跪曰:「妾姓蘇名娥,字始珠,本居廣信縣,修里人。早失父母,又無兄弟,嫁與同縣施氏。薄命夫死,有雜繒帛百二十疋,及婢一人,名致富。妾孤窮羸弱,不能自振,欲之旁縣賣繒,從同縣男子王伯賃車牛一乘,直錢萬二千,載妾并繒,令致富執轡,乃以前年四月十日,到此亭外。於時日已向暮,行人斷絕,不敢復進,因即留止。致富暴得腹痛,妾之亭長舍,乞漿取火。亭長龔壽,操戈持戟,來至車旁,問妾曰:『夫人從何所來?車上所載何物?丈夫安在?何故獨行?』妾應曰:『何勞問之。』壽因持妾臂曰:『少年愛有色,冀可樂也……』妾懼怖不從,壽即持刀刺脅下,一創立死。又刺致富,亦死。壽掘樓下,合埋,妾在下,婢在上,取財物去。殺牛燒車,車釭及牛骨,貯亭東空井中。妾既冤死,痛感皇天,無所告訴,故來自歸於明使君。」敞曰:「今欲發出汝屍，以何為驗？」女曰：「妾上下著白衣、青絲履，猶未朽也。
願訪鄉里，以骸骨歸死夫。」掘之果然。

　　敞乃馳還，遣吏捕捉，拷問具服。下廣信縣驗問，與娥語合。
壽父母兄弟，悉捕繫獄。敞表壽：「常律殺人，不至族誅。然壽為
惡首，隱密數年，王法自所不免。今鬼神訴者，千載無一。請皆斬
之，以明鬼神，以助陰誅。」上報聽之。

Accusation From the Victimized Ghost

Dong Jin Dynasty(317-420CE) Gan Bao (？-336CE) "Sou Shen Ji"

　　During the Han Dynasty（漢朝）（202BCE-220CE），He
Chang （何敞）of Jiu Jiang（九江），the Governor of Jiao State
（交州），went on an inspection tour in Cang Wu County（蒼
梧郡）and stayed in Hu Ben station（鵠奔亭）❻. At midnight,
a woman came from the bottom of the building and shouted,
"To the wise magistrate, I am a victim of injustice!" Soon, she
knelt down on He's bedside and said, "My name is Su E(蘇娥),
Shi-Zhu（始珠），originally from Xio Li（修里）of Guang Xin
County(廣信縣). My parents were gone and I had no brothers.
My husband died young, leaving one hundred and twenty

---

❻　亭 station：A guard station with a two-story building, established in a
　　suburban area. The first floor is used to provide shelter for travelers
　　overnight, and the second floor is used as the office for local officers.

bolts of different kinds of silk and a maid named Zhi-Fu(致富).
I was lonely, poor, weak, and could not live independently. So
I rented a bull cart from a man named Wang Bo（王伯） to sell
silk in the neighboring counties. The rent for the bull cart was
twelve thousand dollars. I had Zhi-Fu ride the cart with me,
reaching this station on April 10th, two years ago. It was dark
with no men to be seen, so we stopped not daring to go further.
Suddenly Zhi-Fu felt funny in her stomach, so I went to the
officer of this station to look for water and firewood. The
officer, Gong Shou （龔壽）, took the halberd ❼ with him and
came by the cart, asking, 'Where did you come from, madam?
What is on the cart? Where is your husband? Why are you
traveling alone?' I answered, 'Don't bother to ask!' Shou （壽）
then grabbed my arm and said, 'Young men are attracted to
beautiful women, I hope we can have some fun...' I was scared
and rejected him. Shou then stabbed me in my chest with the
knife and killed me. He killed Zhi-Fu too, and buried us in a
hole he dug at the bottom of the building. I was buried under
the maid. Our belongings were taken away and the bull was
killed too. My cart was burnt and the remains were buried in
the dried well on the east side. Injustice brought my death,

---

❼　戈戟 Halberd：A Chinese traditional weapon found as early as the Bronze
　　Age. It is the combination of a spear along with a dagger on one end.

and heaven pitied me, but I had no one to appeal to. So I came here to talk to you, the wise magistrate." Chang (敞) said, "Now I plan to dig out your body, but how can you prove your story?" The woman said, "I wore white clothes and my shoes were black. The body is not rotten yet. I hope my body can be sent home and buried together with my husband." After the digging, her body was found just as she said.

Chang then traveled quickly back to the city and sent officers to catch Shou. After being interrogated by torture, Shou pleaded guilty. Then Chang went to Guang Xin County to look for evidence, and found it matched with Su E's words. Shou's parents and brothers were all taken into jail. Chang wrote in the verdict, "In a normal case of murder, laws would not go so far as to kill the relatives; but Shou is guilty of a heinous crime and has been hiding for many years, which is not to be tolerated at all. His crime made her ghost appeal to me, which is rarely seen in history. I ask to execute them all to show that the ghost truly exists and to help do justice in hell." The authorities approved this decree.

五、鏡子裡有鬼　東晉·干寶：《搜神記》卷一

孫策欲渡江襲許，與于吉俱行。時大旱，所在燋屬。策催諸將

士，使速引船。或身自早出督切，見將吏多在<u>吉</u>許。<u>策</u>因此激怒，
言：「我為不如<u>吉</u>耶？而先趨附之！」便使收<u>吉</u>。至，呵問之曰：「天
旱不雨，道路艱澀，不時得過，故自早出。而卿不同憂戚，安坐船
中，作鬼物態，敗吾部伍！今當相除！」

令人縛置地上，暴之，使請雨。若能感天，日中雨者，當原赦；
不爾，行誅。俄而雲氣上蒸，膚寸而合。比至日中，大雨總至，溪
澗盈溢。將士喜悅，以為<u>吉</u>必見原，並往慶慰。<u>策</u>遂殺之。將士哀
惜，藏其屍。天夜，忽更興雲覆之。明旦往視，不知所在。

<u>策</u>既殺<u>吉</u>，每獨坐，彷彿見<u>吉</u>在左右。意深惡之，頗有失常。
後治瘡方差，而引鏡自照；見<u>吉</u>在鏡中，顧而弗見；如是再三，撲
鏡大叫，瘡皆崩裂，須臾而死。

Ghost Mirror

Dong Jin Dynasty(317-420CE) Gan Bao（？-336CE）"Sou Shen Ji"

Sun Ce（孫策）（175－200CE）lead his troops to cross the
river for a sneak attack on Xu County（許縣），with the Taoist
priest, Yu Ji(于吉)（？－200CE）. There was a severe drought,
with extreme heat everywhere. Ce（策）urged his soldiers to
steer the ships as fast as possible. Sometimes when he came
out to urge the soldiers personally, he found most of the
soldiers gathered around Ji（吉）. He became irritated from
this and said to himself, "Am I no better than Ji? They all

have gone to his side!" Then he had Ji caught. When he had Ji, Ce questioned him in a loud voice, "The drought is slowing us down, and we may not be able to make it in time, we need to set out as soon as possible. But you cannot either share my burden, nor can you stay in your part of the ship without causing trouble with your tricks. The discipline in the military has been ruined. I must eliminate you today!"

He gave orders to have Ji tied and put on the ground under the heated sunshine. If Ji were able to make rainfall by praying, he would be forgiven, if not, then he would be executed. Soon, steam rose and gathered gradually. At noon, the rain poured down and the river was refilled with water. Glad as the soldiers were, they thought Ji would be forgiven and went to congratulate him. Yet Ce still killed him. Soldiers felt deeply sorry for him and hid his corpse. That night, steam rose again and covered the body. The next day when they checked on the body, it was gone.

After Ce killed Ji, he felt he had seen Ji around him every time he sat alone. Thus, he became rather suspicious and behaved strangely. Later, when he was checking on his recovering wound on his face, he saw in the mirror the figure of Ji, but did not find Ji when he looked back. It happened again and again. Then, screaming out loudly, Ce threw himself on the mirror and his wound split open. It was not long before he died.

六、噎在喉嚨裡的眼珠　　北齊·　顏之推：《冤魂志》

　　梁太山羊道生，為梁郡邵陵王中兵參軍。其兄海珍任漢州刺史。道生乞假省之。臨還，兄於近路頓待道生。道生見縛一人於樹，就視，乃故舊部曲也。見道生，洟泣哀訴，云漢州欲賜殺，求之救濟。道生問何罪，答云：「失意叛逃。」道生曰：「此最可忿！」即下馬以珮刀剜其眼睛吞之。部曲呼天號地。須臾，海珍來，又勸兄決斬。

至座良久，方覺眼在喉內，噎不肯下。索酒嚥之，頻傾數盃，終不能去。轉覺脹塞。遂不成宴而別。在路數日死。當時見者，莫不以為天道有驗矣。

Eyeballs in the Throat

Bei Qi Dynasty (550-577CE) Yan Zhi-Tui (531-595CE) "Yuan Hun Zhi"

Yang Dao-Sheng（羊道生）of Tai Shan（太山）served as an officer in Duke Shao Ling's（邵陵王）regional government. His brother, Hai-Zhen（海珍）, served as the Governor of Han State（漢州）. One day Dao-Sheng（道生）took a few days off to visit his brother. On his way back, his brother held a feast in his honor on the road side. Dao-Sheng saw someone tied on the tree and went forward to find a former subordinate[8] of his. Once the man saw Dao-Sheng, he sobbed and informed Dao-Sheng about the Governor of Han's（漢）order to execute him, and hoped that Dao-Sheng could save his life. Dao-Sheng inquired what crime he committed. "I betrayed and fled away due to frustration," he answered. Dao-Sheng said, "This is

---

❼ 部曲：A soldier belonging to a particular Commander or General's jurisdiction.

most unforgivable!" He then dismounted from the horse, took his knife, dug out his eyeballs and swallowed them. The soldier cried out loud. Soon, Hai-Zhen came by and Dao Sheng suggested the man to be executed.

After Dao-Sheng was seated for a while, he found the eyeballs got stuck in his throat. He asked for wine, wanting to swallow them down, and poured in a great deal of wine, but in vain. He then found his stomach bloated, so he left halfway through the feast. Several days later, Dao-Sheng was found dead on the road. The witnesses all believed justice served him well.

主題四、異次元時空往返

Theme 4: Extraordinary Travels

Travelling to fairyland and hell is the chief topic of this section's theme. The title of this theme, "Extraordinary Travels" comes from the characters and settings in the stories shuttling back and forth in daily and extraordinary time and space, with the speed of travelling and management of space different from the mortal world. The visitors passing through fairyland often go there physically, while the visitors to hell go with their souls leaving their bodies for a short period of time; all visitors are mainly male, especially upon visiting a fairyland where men, who need to support themselves financially, can go deer hunting, fishing, or bark-stripping for constructing paper materials.

From an individual's consciousness, it is common for humans to experience feelings of being tired, depressed and lost, so we may often yearn for a world without sorrows. Consequently, there is "Peach Blossoms"（桃花源）and

"Shangri-la" in the East, while there is "Utopia" in the West. The word "Utopia" originates from two word roots of Greek; one is "eutopos," which means "happy" and "lucky"; and the other, "outopos" means "no place." Accordingly, utopia originally means a paradise that does not exist, just as the Peach Blossoms (桃花源) is not to be found again. This implies that paradise only exists in the minds of humans. Fantasy can reach such a place, yet the physical body has to remain in the world and go through the bitterness and joys of life. It is the significance of the plot of departure and return in the stories of this theme.

Apart from fairyland, the travel to hell is also another principle material in the theme. The task of the visitors to hell is to witness and spread the word about the judicial process there, propagating the ideas of hope and fear as the purpose of preaching religion. Thus the stories have their concept and meaning of redemption. The criminals in hell are punished by their own crime, the journey to "Hell" can be seen as an adventure, where the criminal experiences punishment for greed, rage, infatuation, and sins committed. After they fall into hell, they repent on their crime, reform themselves, and come back to life to exhort the living humans to do right in life. Thus, the stories about hell have cured the minds of criminals. The fairyland, on the other hand, is the dream that common men yearn for in their daily lives: there is no need to work to support themselves, no torture of aging, illness, and death; there are only beautiful women around and everything they wished for is in "Fairyland", which is why stories about fairyland often center on life with wine, food, music, and carefree sex. However, this journey has an end, which is to go back to the human world, signifying that people still take to heart the world they live in, though there are sufferings and tortuous circumstances. In the dilemma where people need to choose between "becoming a fairy" or "returning to the world," there is a possible concern that when people become fairies, it is not easy to live an endless and idle life. Furthermore, since the bustling world has already offered various kinds of entertainment such as food, wine, songs, dances, and sex, why bother going to the mountains looking for a fairyland?

Other than the religious travels to the extraordinary spaces, traveling to outer space also appears in the stories of abnormal fantasy. Characters in such stories take the "space ship" and travel to the Milky Way, meeting a Female Weaver （織女）and the Cowherd（牛郎）; there are also stories about Mars visiting and playing with children on earth. Such material for stories, representing the curiosity and imagination about the universe in ancient China, is rarely seen in Chinese classic novels.

From an aspect of anthropology, these fairylands that men encounter are probably where Chinese ethnic groups resided. Because of differences in wedding customs, clothing, housing construction and interior decoration, along with topographical isolation elements all create a mysterious feeling for outsiders causing them to believe they have entered a fairy-like land.

一、獵人的追尋與歸去 東晉・陶潛：《搜神後記》卷一

會稽剡縣民袁相、根碩二人獵，經深山重嶺甚多，見一羣山羊六、七頭，逐之。經一石橋，甚狹而峻。羊去，根等亦隨，渡向絕崖。崖正赤壁立，名曰赤城。上有水流下，廣狹如匹布。剡人謂之瀑布。羊徑有山穴如門，豁然而過。既入，內甚平敞，草木皆香。有一小屋，二女子住其中，年皆十五、六，容色甚美，著青衣。一名瑩珠，一名□□。見二人至，欣然云：「早望汝來。」遂為室家。忽二女出行，云復有得壻者，往慶之。曳履於絕巖上行，琅琅然。

二人思歸，潛去歸路。二女追還，已知，乃謂曰：「自可去。」乃以一腕囊與根等，語曰：「慎勿開也。」於是乃歸。後出行，家人開視其囊。囊如蓮花，一重去，一重復，至五蓋，中有小青鳥，飛去。根還知此，悵然而已。後根於田中耕，家依常餉之，見在田中不動，就視，但有殼如蟬脫也。

The Pursuit of the Hunters

Dong Jin Dynasty (317-420CE) Tao Qian (365-427CE) "Sou Shen Hou Ji"

One day, Yuan Xiang（袁相）and Gen Shuo（根碩）of Shan County（剡縣）went hunting together. They went across the mountains and saw a herd of goats, about six or seven of them. So they chased and followed them across a narrow and lofty stone bridge to the red cliff named Red City（赤城）. Water from a waterfall the villagers called Pu-Bu（瀑布）, having the width of a bolt of cloth, fell down from the cliff rapidly. On the herd's path was a cave that was broad like a gate and very spacious inside, flourished with trees and flowers. There was a small house where two beautiful girls in blue lived, both around the age of 15 or 16. As soon as the girls saw the two come, they gladly said, "We have been waiting for you for so long." Then they became couples. Later the girls went out, saying they were going to congratulate someone who also had just received her husband. They walked nimbly on the cliff with their shoes making loud, clear sounds.

After a period of time, Yuan（袁）and Gen（根）wanted to go back home and secretly began to creep back. When the girls found out, they chased them back and told them, "If you really want to leave, than you may go." They gave the men a small bag and told them, "Do not ever open it." Then the men went home.

After returning, Gen went out to the fields, and his family opened to check inside the bag. Yet the bag, like a lotus flower, had many layers. It was not until they opened the fifth layer that they found there was a small blue bird, which flew out when the layer was opened. After Gen got back and knew about this, he wasn't happy at all. Later he went to work in the fields, and when his family members routinely brought food for him, this time they found Gen still, motionless in the field like a cicada which had left its shell.

二、山林迷踪三百年 南朝 宋·劉義慶：《幽明錄》卷一

漢明帝永平五年，剡縣劉晨、阮肇共入天台山取穀皮，迷不得返，經十三日，糧食乏盡，饑餒殆死。遙望山上有一桃樹，大有子實，而絕巖邃澗，永無登路。攀緣藤葛，乃得至上。各噉數枚，而饑止體充。復下山，持杯取水，欲盥漱，見蕪菁葉從山腹流出，甚新鮮，復一杯流出，有胡麻糝，相謂曰：「此知去人徑不遠。」便共沒水，逆流二、三里，得度山。

出一大溪，溪邊有二女子，姿質妙絕，見二人持杯出，便笑曰：「劉、阮二郎捉向所失流杯來。」晨、肇既不識之，緣二女便呼其姓，似如有舊，乃相見而悅。問：「來何晚耶？」，因邀還家。其家

筒瓦屋，南壁及東壁各有一大牀，皆施絳羅帳，帳角懸鈴，金銀交錯。牀頭各有十侍婢，敕云：「劉、阮二郎，經涉山岨，向雖得瓊實，猶尚虛弊，可速作食。」食胡麻飯、山羊脯、牛肉、甚甘美。食畢，行酒。有一羣女來，各持五、三桃子，笑而言：「賀汝壻來。」酒酣作樂，劉、阮忻怖交并。至暮，令各就一帳宿，女往就之，言聲清婉，令人忘憂。

十日後，欲求還去，女云：「君已來是，宿福所牽，何復欲還邪？」遂停半年。氣候草木是春時，百鳥啼鳴，更懷悲思，求歸甚苦。女曰：「罪牽君，當可如何！」遂呼前來女子，有三、四十人，集會奏樂，共送劉、阮，指示還路。

既出，親舊零落，邑屋改異，無復相識。問訊得七世孫，傳聞上世入山，迷不得歸。至晉太元八年，忽復去，不知何所。

Three Hundred Years Lost in the Mountains

Nan Chao Song Dynasty (420-479CE) Liu Yi-Qing (403-444CE) "You Ming Lu"

During the Han Dynasty（漢朝）（202BCE-220CE），Liu Chen（劉晨）and Ruan Zhao（阮肇）went into Tian Tai Mountain（天台山）to gather some tree bark. They became lost in the mountain and couldn't find their way back. After 13 days, they ran out of food and were dying. Far away they saw a fruited peach tree, but there were cliffs and a rushing river between them and the tree. They could find no way to go up there, so they climbed up some vines slowly making their way. After reaching the tree, the two had some peaches to satisfy their hunger and restore energy. Then they climbed down to the stream and drank some water with the cups they carried. They saw fresh turnip leaves flow out from the mountain followed by a cup with rice balls in it. The two said in one voice, "There must be households nearby." So they went into the water and swam upstream for two or three kilometers. Finally, after passing through the center of the mountain they came out of the stream.

There were two beautiful girls by the riverside. When, Liu (劉) and Ruan (阮) came ashore the women saw them holding the cup, then smiled and said, "Mr. Liu and Mr. Ruan come with our cup which just flowed away." Though the two did not know them before, they felt warm when the girls called their names as if they had already known each other. The girls asked them why they were late and invited them to go home with them.

The girl's house was made of cylindrical terra cotta, and beside the walls on the east and the south were two large beds. The beds were covered by crimson gauze canopy with bells decorated with gold and silver hung on the corners. There were ten maids near each bed waiting to serve them. The girls ordered the maids saying, "Mr. Liu and Mr. Ruan have traveled over mountains and rivers, their bodies are weak. Though they have eaten the precious peach, go and prepare food for them." There was rice with sesame, goat meat, and beef, which all tasted delicious. They drank wine after they finished eating. A group of girls came and each carried some peaches in their hands, smiling, "Congratulations on the arrival of your husbands." Then they had great fun after they were drunk, while Liu and Ruan felt gleeful yet scared. In the night, they went to sleep on the decorated beds. The girls then came over, with tender and melodious words to accompany them through a wonderful night.

After ten days, Liu and Ruan asked to go back. The girls said, "You are able to come here because of an accumulated blessing in the past. Why do you want to go back?" Then they stayed for half a year. In the spring the birds were singing in the air, which made Liu and Ruan feel nostalgic. They put on great effort in asking to return home. The girls said, "Your karma led you this way, what else can we do?" Then they had about 30 to 40 girls gather together playing music. They sent off Liu and Ruan and showed them the way home.

After they had left they found their relatives and friends had all died. The houses in the village were changed beyond recognition. They inquired about their offspring, and found the grandchildren of their seventh generation. The grandchildren said the rumor was that their ancestors left for the mountain in the previous dynasty and never returned after getting lost. In the eighth year of the Tai Yuan（太元）（383CE）era, the two then suddenly left without anyone knowing where they had gone.

三、搭太空船一遊銀河　西晉·張華：《博物志》卷十

　　舊說云：天河與海通，近世有人居海渚者，年年八月有浮槎來，甚大，往反不失期。人有奇志，立飛閣於槎上，多齎糧，乘槎而去。十餘日中，猶觀星月日辰，自後茫茫忽忽，亦不覺晝夜。

　　去十餘日，奄至一處，有城郭狀，屋舍甚嚴，遙望宮中多織婦。見一丈夫牽牛，渚次飲之。牽牛人乃驚問曰：「何由至此？」此人具說來意，并問此是何處，答曰：「君還至蜀都，訪嚴君平則知之。」竟不上岸，因還如期。後至蜀，問君平，曰：「某年月日有客星犯牽牛宿。」計年月，正是此人到天河之時。

Travel to Milky Way
Xi Jin Dynasty (265-316CE) Zhang Hua (232-300CE) "Bo Wu Zhi"

Legend has it that the ocean was once connected with the

Milky Way. A man living nearby the sea, every year in August saw a humungous raft drift over. The raft always came on time. Therefore the man came up with an intriguing idea——he started to build an air corridor and prepare food supplies, and then he boarded the raft. During the first ten days on the raft, he could still see the sun, moon and stars. Yet afterwards, everything became so blurry that he could not tell whether it was day or night.

After some ten days of this, the raft suddenly reached a place where the buildings were like castles and the houses were all well arranged. From a distance, he saw many weaving maids in the palace. He also saw a man taking his cow to drink water at the riverside. The man with the cow asked him with astonishment, "How did you get here?" He then told the man everything in detail, and inquired where he was. The man with the cow answered, "When you get back and find Yan Jun-Ping (嚴君平) in Shu City (蜀都), you then should know." He went to Shu (蜀) and asked Jun-Ping (君平) about it. Jun-Ping answered, "There was a time when an irregular star disturbed Altair (牽牛星)." After calculation, they found out that it was the exact time when the man had reached the Milky Way.

四、火星遊地球　東晉·干寶：《搜神記》卷八

　　吳以草創之國，信不堅固，邊屯守將，皆質其妻子，名曰：「保質」。童子少年，以類相與娛遊者，日有十數。

　　孫休永安三年三月，有一異兒，長四尺餘，年可六、七歲，衣青衣，忽來從群兒戲。諸兒莫之識也，皆問曰：「爾誰家小兒，今日忽來？」答曰：「見爾群戲樂，故來耳。」詳而視之，眼有光芒，爚爚外射。諸兒畏之，重問其故。兒乃答曰：「爾恐我乎？我非人也，乃熒惑星也。將有以告爾：三公歸於司馬！」

諸兒大驚，或走告大人，大人馳往觀之。兒曰：「舍爾去乎！」聳身而躍，即以化矣。仰而視之，若曳一匹練以登天。大人來者，猶及見焉。飄飄漸高，有頃而沒。

時吳政峻急，莫敢宣也。後四年而蜀亡。六年而魏廢，二十一年而吳平。是歸於司馬也。

Apocalypse of Mars

Dong Jin Dynasty(317-420CE) Gan Bao (？-336CE) "Sou Shen Ji"

During the Age of the Three Kingdoms（三國）, due to the new political establishment, the kingdom Wu（吳）（222-280CE）was in a political turbulence. Because of this the chief generals who were stationed at the borders had to leave their wives and children held as hostages by the government. The young children and teenagers usually gathered and played together everyday in about ten different groups.

In March of the 3rd year of Sun Xiu's（孫休）（260 CE）reign, a peculiar child dressed in blue, about six or seven, and about four feet tall, suddenly came to play with the children. None of the children knew this child and they all asked him, "Which family are you from? How come you suddenly join us today?" He answered, "You all seemed happy playing together, so I came." With careful examination of him, they found his eyes were glowing, as if fire blazing out. The children were scared of his eyes and asked him more. The child answered, "Are you afraid of me? I am no human being. I am Mars ❶ (熒惑星). I have to inform you that the Si-Ma (司馬) family will reign over the world."

The children were so terrified that some of them ran back to tell the adults, who then came over to see the child. Mars then said, "I will leave you now." He stood up straight, jumped, and his body transformed. Everyone looked up and saw him flying into the sky as if dragging two strips of silk. Some adults that came later were just in time to see him fly into the sky.He flew higher and higher and soon disappeared into the sky.

The regime was at a critical time where it could not disclose the news about the event. After four years, the kingdom of Shu(蜀)(221-263CE) diminished. Six years later, the kingdom of Wei (魏) (220-265CE) was wiped out and Wu (吳)(222-280CE)followed after twenty-one years. Since then the Si-Ma family came into power.

---

❶ 熒惑 Ying Huo : In ancient Chinese Astronomy, Mars is called Ying Huo.

五、泰山府君有請　東晉‧干寶：《搜神記》卷四

　　胡母班，字季友，泰山人也。曾至泰山之側，忽於樹間逢一絳衣驛，呼班云：「泰山府君召。」班驚楞，逡巡未答。復有一驛出呼之。遂隨行。數十步，驛請班暫暝。少頃，便見宮室，威儀甚嚴。班乃入閣拜謁，主為設食，語班曰：「欲見君無他，欲附書與女婿耳。」班問：「女郎何在？」曰：「女為河伯婦。」班曰：「輒當奉書，不知緣何得達？」答曰：「今適河中流，便扣舟呼青衣，當自有取書者。」班乃辭出。昔驛復令閉目，有頃，忽如故道。

　　遂西行。如神言而呼「青衣」，須臾，果有一女僕出，取書而沒。少頃復出，云：「河伯欲暫見君。」婢亦請暝目。遂拜謁河伯。河伯乃大設酒食，詞旨殷勤。臨去，謂班曰：「感君遠為致書，無物相奉。」於是命左右：「取吾青絲屨來！」以貽班。班出，暝然忽得還舟。

　　遂於長安經年而還。至泰山側，不敢潛過，遂扣樹，自稱姓名：「從長安還，欲啟消息。」須臾，昔驛出引班，如向法而進，因致書焉。府君請曰：「當別再報。」班語訖，如廁，忽見其父著械徒作，此輩數百人。班進拜，流涕問：「大人何因及此？」父云：「吾死，不幸見遣三年，今已二年矣，困苦不可處。知汝今為明府所識，可為吾陳之，乞免此役，便欲得社公耳。」班乃依教，叩頭陳乞。府君曰：「生死異路，不可相近，身無所惜。」班苦請，方許之。於是辭出還家。

　　歲餘，兒子死亡略盡。班惶懼，復詣泰山，扣樹求見，昔驛遂迎之而見。班乃自說：「昔辭曠拙，及還家，兒死亡至盡。今恐禍

故未已，輒來啟白，幸蒙哀救。」府君拊掌大笑，曰：「昔語君『死
生異路，不可相近』故也。」即敕外召<u>班</u>父。須臾，至庭中，問之：
「昔求還里社，當為門戶作福，而孫息死亡至盡，何也？」答云：
「久別鄉里，自忻得還，又遇酒食充足，實念諸孫，召之。」於是
代之。父涕泣而出。<u>班</u>遂還。後有兒皆無恙。

The Request from Tai Mountain

Dong Jin Dynasty (317-420CE) Gan Bao（？-336CE) "Sou Shen Ji"

Hu-Mu Ban（胡母班）, otherwise known as Ji-You（季友）, of Tai Shan County（泰山郡）, went to the nearby area of Tai Mountain（泰山）❷. There in the woods he met a knight in red who said, "The master of Tai Mountain summons you." Shocked, he hesitated and moved back. Then another knight came forth and Ban（班）went followed with him. After some distance, the knight asked him to close his eyes. Shortly, Ban opened his eyes and saw a palace and guards. Ban then entered a hall to pay a visit with the master. The master had food prepared for him, and said, "Sorry to bother you, the reason I ask you to come is to help me give a letter to my

---

❷　泰山 Tai Mountain : Ancient Chinese believed that when one dies they then would live below Tai Mountain under the rule of the dead. The chief of this region is Master Tai Mountain.

son-in-law." Ban asked, "Where is your daughter?" "My daughter is the wife of the river god," the master answered. Ban said, "I will present this letter to him but I don't know how to get there." "Leave now and go to the center of the river, knock on the boat loudly, shout for Qing-Yi（青衣）, and someone will come and take the letter," the master replied. Then Ban left. The knight he previously met asked him again to close his eyes, and suddenly he came to the same road as before.

Then he went westward. He followed the instructions and shouted for Qing-Yi . Soon a maid came out and took away the letter. After a moment, she came out again and said, "The river god would like to meet you." The maid asked him to close his eyes. Then he met with the river god, who had also prepared a feast for him and treated him well. As Ban was about to leave, the god said, "Thank you for coming all the way here with the letter. I don't have anything valuable to offer you." He ordered the people around him and said. "Take my shoes of black silk." And he gave it to Ban. After Ban left, as if dreaming he suddenly returned back to the boat.

After one year in Chang An（長安）, he went back to Tai Mountain . When he went by the area, he did not dare pass quietly, so he knocked on the trees and shouted his name, "I come from Chang An and would like to report some information." Soon, the knight came out to lead Ban in the same way as before. Ban then presented the letter to the master who then said, "You are welcome to return anytime to report information." After that, Ban went to use the lavatory and saw his father in cuffs, and hundreds of people just like his father. Ban met his father and asked him in tears, "Why are you like this?" His father answered, "After my death, I was punished for committing crimes, and was given a three-year sentence. It has been two years now and the condition has been really hard to bear. I know now you are acquainted with the master, can you report my condition to the master and ask him to eliminate my penal servitude? In addition, I'd like to be the Earth God." Ban then followed his father's instruction and asked for the master's mercy. The master said, "The living and the dead are in two different worlds, and you should not have gotten involved with this dichotomy, however I won't hesitate to assist you." Ban pleaded with great effort, and then the master agreed. He then left and went back home.

After more than one year, the sons of Ban died one after another. Ban was scared and went to Tai Mountain again, knocking on the tree asking to meet the master again. The knight came out to lead him. Ban said himself, "I used to talk nonsense clumsily. When I got home, my sons soon died. I am afraid the catastrophe is not over, so I have immediately come to report this and ask for your mercy." The master clapped his hands, laughing, "I once told you, the living and the dead are in two different worlds and that you should not have gotten involved with this dichotomy. This is the reason why." He then ordered to meet Ban's father. Soon, when his father came to the court, the master asked him, "You requested to return to your home country to be an earth god, you should have guarded your family and brought them good fortune! How come your grandsons are all dead? Why is that?" "I'd left my home country for a long time, and was happy to be able to go back. And it was because the food was plenty and I really missed my grandsons, I had them all come here." Ban's father replied. The master then replaced the position of Ban's father. Ban's father was taken away in tears. Ban then came back, and his sons were all safe, and there was no misfortune after that.

主題五：半獸人檔案

Theme5: Profiles of Orcs

Stories in this theme involve legends of people's belief in totemic animals, metaphors of the degeneration of human nature, and certain descriptions of the abnormal behaviors of people with mental disorder. In the Si Chuan（四川）region, monkeys can be seen as objects of totemic belief in abnormal fantasy stories. In this region there is a tribe with monkeys as their totemic animal which has a tradition of marriage by capture. Other than monkeys, there are stories about tribes with tigers as totemic animals. People can transform into a tiger and then return to human figure. These legends show the cultural trace of regarding tigers as the totemic animals. Sharing mythical blood relationships with tigers, people of the tribe have similar soles on their feet as tigers. In some stories of tigers, people are able to transform into tigers and eat humans. This may be the distorted tales of the cannibals, but it can also be the behavior resulting from mental disorder.

Besides being the combination of magic animals and humans, the "Orcs" in this theme also serve the purpose to satirize the people who violate the social norms or have no conscience. These people are actually "Not Human at all", for they have only put on the appearances as being one. Thus they are categorized as the combination of animals and humans, or even closer to animals. In other words, they are the projections of the words "Brute," "Beasts," describing people that are less than humans.

On the whole, even though stories of this theme center on the combination of animals and humans, they have no intention to demean the animals of totemic legends; stories of metaphors on human nature then point out betrayals, plunders, injuring others, seduction and raping, imprisonment, threatening and other vicious behaviors. The boundary between humans and animals is rather distinct.

一、猿人搶妻　西晉·張華：《博物志》卷三

蜀中西南高山上，有物如獼猴，長七尺，能人行，健走，名曰猴玃，一名馬化，或曰猳玃。伺行道婦女有好者，輒盜之以去，人不得知。行者或每遇其旁，皆以長繩相引，然故不免。

此得男子氣自死，故取女也，取去為室家。其年少者，終身不得還。十年之後，形皆類之，意亦迷惑，不復思歸。有子者，輒俱送還其家，產子皆如人。有不食養者，其母輒死，故無敢不養也。及長，與人無異，皆以楊為姓。故今蜀中西界多謂楊率皆猳玃、馬化之子孫，時時相有玃爪者也。

Ape Marriage through Capture

Xi Jin Dynasty (266-316CE) Zhang Hua (232-300CE) "Bo Wu Zhi"

Up on the hill in southwest Si Chuan（四川）lived a kind of creature, which looked like an ape. These creatures stood seven feet tall and were able to walk and run very fast. They were called "Ho Jue," （猴玃）"Ma Hua," （馬化）or "Jia Jue." （猳玃）They lurked beside the road and captured healthy, good-looking women who passed by. No one knew where these women were taken. People would hold long ropes together when they passed through the mountains where the apes would appear. Despite efforts, the apes were still able to capture women.

The creatures would get killed if they encountered men, so they always captured women, who were then married to the creatures and could not return home for the rest of their lives. After ten years the women appeared just like the apes and were bewildered so that they would not want to go home anymore. After given birth, the women, along with their infants, were sent back to their original home. The children, who looked just like humans had to be raised by their mother's family. If a family didn't raise the child, the child's mother would die, so nobody dared to abandon them. When those children grew up, they were no different than other human beings. Their last names were all Yang（楊）. So now there are many people in west Si Chuan who believe people with the last name "Yang" are mostly the offspring of Jia Jue or Ma Hua and often find them having monkey-like claws.

二、騙神不是人　南朝 宋·祖沖之:《述異記》

宋元嘉中,南康平固人黃苗,為州吏。受假違期,方上行,經宮亭湖。入廟下願,希免罰坐,又欲還家,若所願並遂,當上猪、酒。苗至州,皆得如志,乃還。資裝既薄,遂不過廟。

行至都界,與同侶並船泊宿。中夜,船忽從水自下,其疾如風介。夜四更,苗至宮亭,始醒悟。見船上有三人,並烏衣,持繩收縛苗,夜上廟階下。見神年可四十,黃面,披錦袍。梁下懸一珠,大如彈丸,光耀照屋。一人戶外白:「平固黃苗,上願猪、酒,避回家,教錄,今到。」命謫三年,取三十人。

遣吏送苗窮山林中,鑲腰繫樹,日以生肉食之。苗忽忽憂思,但覺寒熱,生瘡,舉體生斑毛。經一旬,毛蔽身,爪牙生,性欲搏噬。吏解鑲放之,隨其行止。三年,凡得二十九人,次應取新淦一女,而此女士族,初不出外。後值與娣妹從後門出,詣親家,女在最後,因取之。為此女難得,涉五年,人數乃充。

吏送至廟,神教放遣。乃以鹽飯飲之,體毛脫落,鬢髮悉出,爪牙墮,生新者。經十五日,還如人形,意慮復常,送出大路。縣令呼苗具疏事,覆前後所取人,遍問其家,並符合焉。髀為戟所傷,創瘢猶在。苗還家八年,得時疾死。

Inhuman

Nan Chao Song Dynasty (420-479CE) Zu Chong-Zhi (429-500CE)
"Shu Yi Ji"

During the Song Dynasty（宋代）(420-479CE), Huang Miao（黃苗）of Ping Gu（平固）was a field official in the county government. Having overstayed his leave, on his way back to the city he passed by Gong Ting Lake（宮亭湖）and went into a temple to pray not to be punished for his over stay. In addition, he also wished he could return home. He promised when he got back he would offer pork and wine as sacrifice in order to repay god's kindness if the wishes came true. When he got to the city, everything went well as he had wished, so he went back where he served. Since he did not bring much stuff with him, he skipped the temple and did not offer the sacrifice as promised.

While arriving at the city's border, he and his companions brought their boats together in parallel on the lake for the night. At midnight, Miao's（苗）boat suddenly drifted quickly down a current in the water, as if there was wind pushing it. At about two or three in the night, Miao woke and realized that he had arrived at Gong Ting Lake. He saw three men dressed in black standing on the boat with rope in their hands to tie Miao up. That night he was taken to the stairs of the temple and saw a god, at about 40 years old, with a yellow face and dressed in a brocade robe. Under a roof beam hung a huge pearl, brightening up the whole building. A man outside the door reported, "Huang Miao of Ping Gu is under arrest now for promising to offer sacrifice of pork and wine but failing to do so and evaded it by going home." The god decreed his three-year sentence, and he was charged with the task to bring thirty people to justice.

The officer escorted Miao to the mountains, tied him up to a tree with chains around his waist, and fed him raw meat. Being out of his senses, he only felt heat and cold, and his body grew boils and fur with stripes. After ten days, his body was covered in hair and he had grown claws and fangs, becoming fierce and yearning for biting. The officer untied him and let him move around. Within three years, he had caught twenty-nine people. At last, he had to catch a woman from a family of gentry who rarely went out in the Xin Gan (新淦) area. Eventually, when the woman went out from the back door with her sisters to visit their relatives, because she was the last one in the group, Miao was able to capture her. Since it was rather difficult to catch the woman, it ended up taking him five years until he caught thirty people.

The officer escorted Miao to Gong Ting Temple (宮亭廟), and the god ordered to set him free. He was fed salt and rice, and then his fur fell off while his hair and mustache grew back; his claws and fangs fell off, and he grew back new finger nails and teeth. After fifteen days, he returned to human, and his mentality became normal. He was then sent off on his road home. The magistrate of the county asked Miao to report this event in detail, and then verified those Miao caught during this period and inquired their families about the related events. Everything corresponded with Miao's words. During the sequence of events, Miao was injured by a halberd ❶, and the wound remained. Eight years after Miao went back home, he died of an epidemic disease.

三、化虎吃人　　南朝 宋·東陽無疑：《齊諧記》

太元元年，江夏郡安陸縣薛道恂，年二十二，少來了了。忽得時行病，差後發狂，百藥救治不損，乃服散狂走，猶多劇。忽失蹤跡，遂變作虎，食人不可復數。有一女子，樹下採桑，虎往取之食。食竟，乃藏其釵釧著山石間。後還作人，皆知取之。

經一年，還家為人。遂出都仕官，為殿中令史。夜共人語，忽道天地變怪之事。道恂自云：「吾昔常得病發狂，遂化作虎，噉人

---

❶　戟 Halberd：A Chinese traditional weapon found as early as the Bronze Age. It is the combination of a spear along with a dagger on one end.

一年。」中兼便敘其處所並人姓名。其同坐人，或有食其父子兄弟
者，於是號泣。捉以付官，遂餓死<u>建康</u>獄中。

Cannibal

Nan Chao Song Dynasty (420-479CE) Dong-Yang Wu-Yi (？-？) "Qi Xie Ji"

During the East Jin Dynasty（東晉）(317-420CE)，there was a man called Xue Dao-Xun（薛道恂），22, from Jiang Xia County（江夏郡）. Since childhood he was very intelligent. Suddenly Dao-Xun（道恂）was infected with an epidemic disease. When he recovered from the illness, he became mentally insane, unable to be cured by medicine. Then he took a particular kind of medicine where one must walk in order for the medicine to disperse throughout the body. Even upon running extremely hard, the medicine still had no effect and he remained seriously ill. Then one day he suddenly disappeared without a trace and transformed into a tiger, eating many people. He preyed on a girl picking mulberry leaves, and after eating her, hid her hairpin and bracelet between some rocks. When the tiger returned to human figure, he knew that he had to retain these objects.

After one year, Dao-Xun returned to his home in human

figure. He served as an office clerk in the capital city. One night he chatted with others about bizarre events in the world. Dao-Xun claimed, "I used to fall ill and become mad, transforming into a tiger, eating people for one year." He further described where he ate the people along with their names. Of those who were present, some of them whose father, sons, or brothers were killed by Dao-Xun, burst into tears when they heard Dao-Xun's words. They caught Dao-Xun and brought him to court. Later Dao-Xun died of hunger in the Jian Kang（建康）Jail.

四、古墓狸女　南朝 宋·東陽無疑：《齊諧記》

　　國步山有廟，又一亭❷。呂思與少婦投宿，失婦。思遂覓，見一大城，廳事一人紗帽憑几。左右競來擊之，思以刀斫，計當殺百餘人，餘者便乃大走，向人盡成死狸。看向廳事，乃是古始大冢。冢上穿，下甚明，見一群女子在冢裡，見其婦如失性人。因抱出冢口，又入抱取於先女子，有數十，中有通身已生毛者，亦有毛腳、面成狸者。

---

❷　亭 station：A guard station with a two-story building, established in a suburban area. The first floor is used to provide shelter for travelers overnight, and the second floor is used as the office for local officers.

須臾，天曉，將婦還亭。亭吏問之，具如此答。前後有失兒女者，零丁有數十。吏便斂此零丁，至冢口迎此群女，隨家遠近而報之，各迎取於此。後一、二年，廟無復靈。

Fox Women

Nan Chao Song Dynasty (420-479CE) Dong-Yang Wu-Yi（?-?）"Qi Xie Ji"

Lü Si（呂思）and his wife stayed in a station near a temple in Guo Bu Mountain（國步山）. Si's（思）wife went missing, so Si left to search for her. He saw a big castle where a man wearing a gauze hat leaning on a table in the office. The guards of this man came forth and attacked Si. Si fought back using his sword and killed more than one hundred guards, while the rest of them ran away. Those who had been killed had all transformed into dead foxes. He then found that this was a huge tomb where the upper side had a deteriorated opening thus brightening the inside of the tomb. Si saw a crowd of women and found his wife among them. She had lost her mind. Si carried his wife outside the tomb, and then re-entered to carry the other women out. There were dozens of women, some of whom grew hair all over the body, and some were about to transform into foxes with hair growing on their feet or face.

Soon dawn came. Si took his wife back to the station and the officer asked about what had happened. Si told him everything. At that time, there were dozens of notices of missing people; many families had lost their daughters. The officer then collected these notices, went to pick up the women from the tomb, and according to the location of their homes, one by one informed the families to take back their daughters. After one or two years, the temple was not efficacious anymore.

五、誤入陷阱的虎人　　東晉·干寶：《搜神記》卷十二

　　江漢之域，有貙人。其先，稟君之苗裔也。能化為虎。長沙所屬蠻縣東高居民，曾作檻捕虎。檻發！明日，眾人共往格之，見一亭長，赤幘大冠，在檻中坐。因問：「君何以入此中？」亭長大怒，曰：「昨忽被縣召，夜避雨，遂誤入此中。急出我！」曰：「君見召，不當有文書耶？」即出懷中召文書。於是即出之。尋視，乃化為虎，上山走。

或云：「貙虎化為人，好著紫葛衣，其足無踵。虎有五指者，皆是貙。」

Tiger Man

Dong Jin Dynasty (317-420CE) Gan Bao（？-336CE) "Sou Shen Ji"

In the region where the Yangtze River（揚子江；長江）and the Han River（漢江）meet lived the "Chu"（貙）❸ tribe, whose ancestors were the offspring of Lin Jun（廩君）, and could all transform into tigers. In the past, habitants in Dong Gao County（東高縣）used trap cage to catch tigers. After the trap had been tripped, the next day the people would go and kill the tiger. However they found there was a district officer wearing a red bandana under a large cap sitting inside the cage. The people asked, "How did you get in the cage?" The officer answered angrily, "Yesterday, all of the sudden, I had been called upon by the magistrate to go pay him a visit. In order to escape the rainy night, I had mistakenly entered this cage. Quickly, set me free!" The people then asked, "Aren't you supposed to have some kind of document since you had been summoned upon?" The officer then took out the document

---

❸ 貙 Chu：A kind of fierce animal belonging to a tiger category. Legend says that Chu has five claws on its paw different from tiger's four.

from his robe. The people quickly let him out of the cage and followed after him. They found him transform into a tiger and run into the mountains.

Some people say, "When Chu transforms into a human, it likes to wear purple clothes made of linen. It has no heels on its feet. If a tiger has five claws on its paw, then it is Chu ."

六、變身求去的母親　東晉・干寶：《搜神記》卷十四

魏黃初中，清河宋士宗母，夏天於浴室裡浴，遣家中大小悉出，獨在室中良久。家人不解其意，於壁穿中窺之，不見人體，見盆水中有一大鱉。遂開戶，大小悉入，了不與人相承。嘗先著銀釵，猶在頭上。相與守之啼泣，無可奈何。意欲求去，永不可留。

視之積日，轉懈，自捉出戶外，其去甚駛，逐之不及，遂便入水。後數日，忽還。巡行宅舍，如平生，了無所言而去。

時人謂士宗應行喪治服❸。士宗以母形雖變，而生理尚存，竟不治喪。此與江夏黃母相似。

---

❸ 行喪治服: In Chinese traditional culture, after one's parents pass away, for three years they cannot work or get married and must wear a thick white clothing made of a material similar to a potato sack. During this time period, one must also maintain a sad state of mind in condolence for their parents.

Turtle Transformation

Dong Jin Dynasty (317-420CE) Gan Bao (？-336CE) "Sou Shen Ji"

  Sometime during the Wei Kingdom（魏國）（220-265CE）, one summer day the mother of Song Shi-Zong（宋士宗）from Qing He（清河）took a shower in the bathroom. She asked all her family members to leave the house, while staying inside alone for a long time. Her family did not understand what her purpose for this was, so they peeped through a hole in the wall, only to see nothing but a soft-shell turtle in the bathtub and no sign of their mother. They opened the door and went inside. Having transforming into a turtle, the mother was not able to communicate with them. The silver hairpin she wore was on the head of the turtle. The family cried and waited by the turtle's side, feeling helpless. The turtle intended to leave, not wanting to stay.

  After watching for several days, they relaxed their attention on the turtle, who then took the opportunity to quickly run out of the door. They chased after her, failing to catch up and the turtle slipped into the water. After several days, the turtle suddenly returned, going about the house as usual, than left without a word.

  People then thought that Shi-Zong（士宗）should hold a

funeral. However, Shi-Zong thought even though his mother's figure had changed, she was still alive. In the end, a funeral was not held for her. The whole event was very similar to that of Huang（黃）of Jiang Xia（江夏）, whose mother also transformed into a soft-shell turtle.

七、少女化成蠶繭　東晉・干寶・《搜神記》卷十四

　　舊說太古之時，有大人遠征，家無餘人，唯有一女。牡馬一匹，女親養之。窮居幽處，思念其父，乃戲馬曰：「爾能為我迎得父還，吾將嫁汝。」馬既承此言，乃絕韁而去，徑至父所。父見馬驚喜，因取而乘之。馬望所自來，悲鳴不已。父曰：「此馬無事如此，我家得無有故乎？」亟乘以歸。為畜生有非常之情，故厚加芻養。馬不肯食。每見女出入，輒喜怒奮擊。如此非一。父怪之，密以問女。女具以告父，必為是故。父曰：「勿言！恐辱家門。且莫出入。」於是伏弩射殺之，暴皮于庭。

　　父行，女與鄰女於皮所戲，以足蹙之曰：「汝是畜生，而欲取人為婦耶？招此屠剝，如何自苦？」言未及竟，馬皮蹙然而起，卷女以行。鄰女忙怕，不敢救之。走告其父。父還，求索，已出失之。

　　後經數日，得於大樹枝間，女及馬皮，盡化為蠶，而績於樹上。其蠒綸理厚大，異於常蠶。鄰婦取而養之，其收數倍。因名其樹曰「桑」。桑者，喪也。由斯百姓競種之，今世所養是也。言桑蠶者，是古蠶之餘類也。

The Girl in the Cocoon

Dong Jin Dynasty (317-420CE) Gan Bao (? -336CE) "Sou Shen Ji"

Once upon a time, the leader of a tribe went far away to fight, leaving his daughter and a male horse at home. His daughter took care of the horse by herself. When she missed her father, she told the horse, jokingly, "If you can bring my father back home, I will marry you." The horse understood what she had said, so it broke free from its reins and ran away. Without any rest, it traveled all the way to where her father was. The father was surprised and happy to see the horse, and rode on its back. Gazing at the direction it came from, the horse cried sadly and incessantly. The father said, "This horse came here out of nowhere, there must be something wrong back home." Then he immediately rode the horse back. Because of the horse's loyalty they increased his feed. But the horse was not willing to eat and would become moody and kick around excitedly every time the daughter came around. Curious, the father secretly asked his daughter what was going on. She then described what had happened and her father concluded, "This must be the reason. Don't speak of this with anyone. It is a disgrace to our family. Don't come in here!" Then he ambushed the horse with a bow and arrow, and skinned off its skin, spreading it in their yard.

When the father went out, the daughter went playing with a female neighbor in the place where the horse skin had been spread. Kicking the skins, the daughter said, "You are a mere animal. How could you ask for a human to be your wife? As a result, you have received death and have been skinned. How can you escape this bitterness." Before she was finished speaking, the skins stood up and wrapped around the girl, taking her away. Her female neighbor was scared and nervous, and did not dare to save her. She went to tell her father, yet when her father came back to look for her, there was no sign of his daughter.

After several days, the girl and the skins of the horse were found hanging from a big tree. They had become silkworms and were attached to the tree with silk. The fibers of the cocoon were especially thick, unlike any others. They then called the tree "Sang" (桑) (mulberry). The word for death (喪) is pronounced the same as "Sang". Afterwards people contended with each other to plant mulberry trees, the same mulberry trees found nowadays. Mulberry silkworms are one species of silkworms derived from ancient times.

主題六：家有仙妻

Theme6: Fairy Love

In this theme, due to uncertain reasons fairies fall into the world becoming the wives of men, then go returning to heaven when their mission has been fulfilled. The reasons are mostly because the heavens want to help the people, so the fairies fall into the world as missionaries of gods, taking on the mission to help men. The missions are often to improve the financial conditions of the family. Besides being the missionaries, some fairies are forced to become a wife after their treasured objects have been obtained by some man. Whatever the reason is, the stories of fairies symbolize men's expectations of family happiness and their projection of an ideal wife.

A fairy wife devotes herself fully to helping the man in a way similar to a religious feeling. She is kind, thoughtful, good at cooking and sewing, and even has super powers. Quietly helping a lonely and poor man, she lights up the hope in his weary life. For Xie Duan（謝端）, who loses his parents when young, the Lady of the Milky Way comes in to his life, giving him the warmth of a family; with the loving care from the Lady, he is able to enjoy a warm dinner atmosphere. As for Dong Yong（董永）, who sells himself to bury his dead father, he had also been relieved by the Weaving Maid from his slave duty. Thus the theme reflects the economic structure of a traditional farming family where men go out to work and women weave at home, along with the principle of achieving prosperity through hard work. Apart from the previous factor that "heaven helps those who help themselves," the falling of a fairy wife also indicates that men crave for some kind of possessions from their spouses.

In addition, stories in this theme slightly touch base on the men's attitude about having children. Though fairy wives are the men's ideal wife, there has never been a child given birth by a fairy, except for the three daughters of Gu Huo Bird （姑獲鳥）. Thus we see the fairy wives do not conceive. Is it possible for humans and fairies to bear children, or do they have no need or ability to do so? The answer remains unknown. The only explanation is in *Sou Shen Ji*（搜神記） where the fairy Cheng-Gong Zhi-Qiong（成公知瓊）makes an agreement with her human husband Xian Chao（弦超）before marriage, saying that she won't bear children for him or interfere his marriage. The stories are also concerned about men's desire for a love affair outside of marriage. Since humans have duties and burdens in life and are not able to enjoy a carefree marriage, they relay their wishes to the gods. While there are no wearies in heaven, there is also no love and relationships. The fairies thus come to earth, marrying the humans, and then their lives intersect and blossom. Due to their limited life span, humans give birth to children to continue their lineage in the future; since fairies live forever, they do not persist on bearing and rearing children.

The stories reflect men's hope for an ideal spouse. They are lustful fantasies in which men desire for precious women, implying men's dissatisfaction of the quality of life in marriage and the fantasies that stem from it. In whole, there is a correspondent relationship between "desire to have" and "lack of being" in men's psychological structure. The male writers who fabricate the stories and the male reader who relay them may be able to satisfy their fancies with these stories.

一、織女下凡為人妻　東晉·干寶：《搜神記》卷一

　　漢董永，千乘人。少偏孤，與父居。肆力田畝，鹿車❶載自隨。父亡，無以葬，乃自賣為奴，以供喪事。主人知其賢，與錢一萬，遣之。

　　永行三年喪畢，欲還主人，供其奴職。道逢一婦人，曰：「願為子妻。」遂與之俱。主人謂永曰：「以錢與君矣。」永曰：「蒙君之惠，父喪收藏。永雖小人，必欲服勤致力，以報厚德。」主曰：「婦人何能？」永曰：「能織。」主曰：「必爾者，但令君婦為我織縑百疋。」於是永妻為主人家織，十日而畢。

　　女出門，謂永曰：「我，天之織女也。緣君至孝，天帝令我助君償債耳。」語畢，凌空而去，不知所在。

The Descent of the Weaving Maid

Dong Jin Dynasty (317-420CE) Gan Bao（？-336CE) "Sou Shen Ji"

　　During the Han Dynasty（漢朝）(202B.C.E-220CE), there was a man named Dong Yong（董永）of Qian Sheng（千乘）. Yong（永）lost his mother when he was a child, and lived with his father. He worked hard in the fields and always took his father along carrying him in a cart. After his father died, he sold himself as a slave to pay for the funeral fees. Knowing

---

❶　鹿車：A cart with a wheel and hand rail which can bare goods or people.

that he was a kindhearted person, the master let him go after giving him ten thousand dollars.

After Yong had finished serving his three year mourning term ❷, he prepared to go back to his master as a slave. On his way back, he met a woman who said, "I am willing to be your wife." Then the two walked together to the master's house. The master said, "I gave you that money. There is no need to repay me." Yong said, "I am much indebted to you. Without your help, the funeral for my father could not be completed. Although I am a lowly person, but I am willing to help you with laborious work to repay your kindness." The master asked, "What is your wife capable of doing?" Yong said, "She could weave." The master said, "If it must be so, you just have to ask your wife to weave one hundred bolts of silk." Then Yong's wife weaved for the master and finished the task within ten days.

The woman walked out of the master's house and said, "I am the weaving maid of the heaven. Because of your kindness, the god of heaven sent me here to help you repay your debt."

---

❷ 行三年喪：In Chinese traditional culture, after one's parents pass away, for three years they cannot work or get married and must stay in a small hut near the tomb and maintain a sad state of mind in condolence for their parents.

As soon as she was finished speaking she rose into the air and disappeared without a trace.

二、田螺姑娘來煮飯　　東晉‧陶潛：《搜神後記》卷五

　　晉安帝時，侯官人謝端，少喪父母，無有親屬，為鄰人所養。至年十七、八，恭謹自守，不履非法。始出居，未有妻，鄰人共愍念之，規為娶婦，未得。端夜臥早起，躬耕力作，不舍晝夜。後於邑下得一大螺，如三升壺。以為異物，取以歸，貯甕中。畜之十數日。

　　端每早至野還，見其戶中有飯飲湯火，如有人為者。端謂鄰人為之惠也。數日如此，便往謝鄰人。鄰人曰：「吾初不為是，何見謝也？」端又以鄰人不喻其意。然數爾如此，後更實問，鄰人笑曰：「卿已自取婦，密著室中炊爨，而言吾為之炊耶？」端默然心疑，不知其故。

　　後以雞鳴出去，平早潛歸，於籬外竊窺其家中，見一少女，從甕中出，至竈下燃火。端便入門，徑至甕所視螺，但見殼。乃到竈下問之曰：「新婦從何所來，而相為炊？」女大惶惑，欲還甕中，不能得去，答曰：「我天漢中白水素女也。天帝哀卿少孤，恭慎自守，故使我權為守舍炊烹。十年之中，使卿居富，得婦，自當還去。而卿無故竊相窺掩，吾形已見，不宜復留，當相委去。雖然，爾後自當少差。勤於田作，漁采治生。留此殼去，以貯米穀，常可不乏。」端請留，終不肯。時天忽風雨，翕然而去。

端為立神座，時節祭祀。居常饒足，不致大富耳。於是鄉人以女妻之，後仕至令長云。今道中素女祠是也。

Coming Out of the Shell

Dong Jin Dynasty(317-420CE) Tao Qian (365-427CE) "Sou Shen Hou Ji"

During the Jin Dynasty（晉朝）(397-419CE)，there was a man named Xie Duan（謝端）of Hou Guan county（侯官縣）who lost his parents when he was young. Having no other relatives, he was raised by his neighbors. Around the age of 17 or 18, he had become modest and courteous and had never done anything bad. At first, when he moved out he had no wife. His neighbors pitied him and wanted to find him a wife, but in vain. Duan（端）went to bed late in the night and got up early in the morning. He worked diligently in the field day and night without taking breaks. Later he found a field snail as big as a teapot. He thought it was something extraordinary so took it back home and saved it in the vat, keeping it for more than ten days.

Every morning Duan went to work in the field. When he got back, there was food and drinks already prepared along with hot water and firewood, as if someone had taken care of everything. He thought it was from his neighbor. The situation kept on for several days, so he went to thank his neighbor. The neighbor said, "I had never done such a thing. Why are you thanking me?" Duan thought the neighbor did not understand what he meant, and this situation continued to happen. So later he went to ask about it again. The neighbor laughed, "You already have married a wife who you keep secretly at home to cook. Why would you say that I cooked for you?" Duan remained silent, wondering but not knowing what was going on.

Later, he went out as the rooster crowed and returned at dawn on purpose. He hid outside the fences and peeped into his house. He saw a girl come out of the vat and light a fire in the kitchen stove. Duan then came in and went directly to check on the field snail, only to find the shell of it. He then went into the kitchen and asked the girl, "May I ask where you came from and why you cook for me?" The girl panicked, wanting to return to the vat, yet failing to do so. She then answered, "I am the fairy from the Milky Way. The god of heaven pitied you for being a good person even after you had lost your parents at childhood. So he sent me to cook and care after your house, and within ten years, make you rich and find you a wife. Afterwards I then could go back. Now that you spied on me, my true identity has been exposed, I can no longer stay here. Although I will have to leave you, your circumstances will naturally get better. Work hard in the field, fish and gather to maintain your life. I leave this shell here for you to store grain, you will no longer be short of them." Duan asked her to stay; yet after all she was not willing. Suddenly it started to rain and the wind rose, and she disappeared within a short moment.

Duan set up an alter for her and offered sacrifices to her during festivals and the new years. Although Duan was not wealthy, he had no problems in his life. Someone in his county married his daughter to Duan . Later he became an official of the county. Today the Su-Nü Temple（素女祠）can still be found on roadsides.

三、鳥人的羽毛衣　東晉·郭璞:《玄中記》

　　姑獲鳥夜飛晝藏,蓋鬼神類。衣毛為飛鳥,脫毛為女人。一名天帝少女,一名夜行游女,一名鉤星,一名隱飛。鳥無子,喜取人子養之以為子。今時小兒之衣不欲夜露者,為此物愛以血點其衣為誌,即取小兒也。故世人名為鬼鳥,荊州為多。

　　昔豫章男子,見田中有六、七女人,不知是鳥,匍匐往,先得其所解毛衣,取藏之,即往就諸鳥。諸鳥各去就毛衣,衣之飛去。一鳥獨不得去,男子取以為婦,生三女。其母後使女問父,知衣在積稻下,得之,衣而飛去。後以衣迎三女,三女兒得衣亦飛去。

The Plumage Clothes

Dong Jin Dynasty (317-420CE) Guo Pu (276-324CE) "Xuan Zhong Ji"

The Gu Huo（姑獲）bird flew in the night and hid during the day, it must have been some kind of supernatural being. With plumage Gu Huo was a bird, and when the bird cast off its plumage, it became a woman. Some called her "Young Daughter of God"（天帝少女）, "Nocturnal Girl"（夜行遊女）, "Hook Star"（鉤星）, or "Concealed Flyer"（隱飛）. Gu Huo had no offspring and liked to take away other's children and raise them as if her own. Children's clothes nowadays should not be put outside in the night because Gu Huo liked to mark the child's clothes with blood, and later take the child away. Because of this, people also called her "Ghost Bird"（鬼鳥）, prevailing over the Jing State（荊州）area.

Once upon a time, a man in Yu Zhang（豫章）saw six or seven women in the field. Not knowing they were birds, he crept on the ground towards them, took away the plumage clothes they had taken off, and hid them. After that, he suddenly charged towards the group. All of them quickly ran back to put on their plumage clothes and fly away. However, one of them was unable to escape. The man made her as his wife and they gave birth to three daughters. Subsequently, the mother sent her daughters to question their father where the plumage clothes were hidden. When she knew that the plumage clothes were hidden under the granary, she retrieved them and flew away. Later she brought plumage clothes to give to her girls, whom also flew away.

主題七、活見鬼

Theme7: Ghost Encounters

The "ghosts" in this theme are mostly spirits of the dead. Some, however, derive from other objects in the world, doing evil deeds in the form of human beings. Various situations of ghost encounters appear in these stories. Some ghosts may appear for they cannot let go of their families after death, and some are just simply troublemakers providing night travelers with a fright. Among the spooked travelers, some are only being played around with; while others are confronted with the dangers of death. Some ghosts are starved craving for food, and in return, are cheated or sold out by clever humans. In Chinese folktales, ghosts do not only play the role of some scary apparition, but also show sincere concern for the relationship between humans and ghosts. There is a tale of a ghost discussing music with the great musician Ji Kang (嵇康), passing on the famous Guang Ling Tune(廣陵散). Death of loved ones is also a factor of human beings encountering ghosts, the ghosts appear in order to contact, in some way and inform others of their own death. These situations of experiencing ghost encounters are only temporary and the ghosts disappear afterwards, never to be seen or heard again.

一、鬼來搭便車　東晉·干寶：《搜神記》卷十六

　　吳赤烏三年，句章民楊度至餘姚。夜行，有一年少，持琵琶，求寄載。度受之。鼓琵琶數十曲，曲畢，乃吐舌擘目，以怖度而去。

　　復行二十里❶許，又見一老父。自云姓王名戒。因復載之。謂曰：「鬼工鼓琵琶，甚哀。」戒曰：「我亦能鼓。」即是向鬼。復擘眼吐舌，度怖幾死。

The Hitchhiker

Dong Jin Dynasty (317-420CE) Gan Bao (？-336CE) "Sou Shen Ji"

During the age of the Wu Kingdom（吳國）（229-280CE），Yang Du（楊度）of Gou Zang（句章）came across a young man in the night on his way to Yu Yao County（餘姚縣）. The young

---

❶　里 li：The character li is a traditional Chinese measuring unit of distance. Its length is close to half a kilometer.

man held a pipa ❷ in his hand and asked for a ride. Du（度）accepted his request. The young man then played many songs with the pipa. Afterwards, with his tongue and eyes popping out, he scared Du and left.

Du then continued on for 10 kilometers and saw an old man who called himself Wang Jie（王戎）. Wang Jie then also rode along with Du. Du told him, "Ghosts are good at playing pipa, and the music they play is rather sorrowful." Jie said, "I am also able to play the pipa." It just so happened that Jie was the previous ghost. He then again stuck out his tongue, popped out his eyes and almost scared Du to death.

二、捨不得　南朝 宋·劉義慶：《幽明錄》卷六

近世有人得一小給使，頻求還家，未遂。後日久，此吏在南窗下眠。此人見門中有一婦人，年五、六十，肥大，行步艱難。吏眠失覆，婦人至牀邊取被以覆之，回復出門去。吏轉側衣落，婦人復如初。

此人心怪，明問吏以何事求歸，吏云：「母病。」次問狀貌及年，皆如所見，唯云形瘦不同。又問：「母何患？」答云：「病腫耳。」

---

❷ 琵琶 pipa: A kind of stringed musical instrument made of wood similar to the lute.

而即遣吏假。使出，便得家信，云母喪。追計所見之肥，乃是其腫
狀也。

Reluctant to Let Go

Nan Chao Song Dynasty (420-479CE) Liu Yi-Qing (403-444CE)
"You Ming Lu"

A boy was hired to run errands for a family. Many times
he had asked for time off to go back home, failing to gain
approval. After some time, while the boy was sleeping under
the south-side window, the host of the family saw a woman,
around 50 or 60 years old, plump and walking with difficulties.
While the boy was sleeping his quilt had fallen off, so the
woman picked up the fallen quilt and covered him, and left.
When the boy turned in his sleep his clothes fell off and the
woman, just like before, put the clothes back on the boy.

The host felt strange and the following day asked the boy
why he had to take days off to go home. The boy answered, "My
mother is sick." Then the host inquired how his mother looked
and her age. The description the boy gave corresponded with
the features of the woman he saw, the only difference was
that the boy said his mother was thin. The host then asked
him about his mother's illness. The boy said, "The illness

makes her body grow plump." The host then agreed to let him take time off and go home. Later the boy received the letter from his home saying that his mother had passed away. The host inferred that the plump woman he saw was the boy's sick mother.

三、聰明人出賣糊塗鬼 東晉·干寶:《搜神記》卷十六

南陽宋定伯,年少時,夜行逢鬼。問之,鬼言:「我是鬼。」鬼問:「汝復誰?」定伯誑之,曰:「我亦鬼。」鬼問:「欲至何所?」

答曰：「欲至宛市。」鬼言：「我亦欲至宛市。」遂行數里。鬼言：「步行太遲，可共遞相擔，何如？」定伯曰：「大善。」

鬼便先擔定伯數里。鬼言：「卿太重，將非鬼也？」定伯言：「我新鬼，故身重耳。」定伯因復擔鬼，鬼略無重。如是再三。定伯復言：「我新鬼，不知有何所畏忌？」鬼答言：「惟不喜人唾。」於是共行，道遇水，定伯令鬼先渡，聽之，了然無聲音。定伯自渡，漕漼作聲。鬼復言：「何以有聲？」定伯曰：「新死，不習渡水故耳。勿怪吾也。」

行欲至宛市，定伯便擔鬼著肩上，急執之，鬼大呼，聲咋咋然，索下，不復聽之。徑至宛市中，下著地，化為一羊，便賣之。恐其變化，唾之。得錢千五百乃去。當時石崇有言：「定伯賣鬼，得錢千五。」

Sold-Out

Dong Jin Dynasty (317-420CE) Gan Bao（？-336CE) "Sou Shen Ji"

When Song Ding-Bo（宋定伯）of Nan Yang（南陽）was young, he met a ghost one night while he was traveling.

"Who are you?" he asked.

"A ghost, who are you?" "A ghost, too." lied Ding-Bo（定伯）.

"Where are you going?"

"To the city."

"So am I."

They went on together for a few kilometers.

"Walking is time-consuming. Why not take turns carrying each other?" The ghost suggested.

"Good idea," agreed Ding-Bo .

The ghost first then carried him for some distance.

"How heavy you are!" said the ghost. "Are you really a ghost?"

"I am a new one," answered Ding-Bo . "That is why I am heavier than usual."

Then it was his turn to carry the ghost, who weighed nothing at all. They continued on like this, taking turns carrying one another.

"As a new ghost," said Ding-Bo presently, "I don't know what we are most afraid of."

"Being spat at by men-that's all."

They went on together until they came to a stream. Ding-Bo let the ghost cross first, which it did without a sound. But Ding-Bo made quite a splash.

"Why do you make such a noise?" inquired the ghost.

"I just died recently. I am not used to crossing streams. You must excuse me."

As they approached the city, Ding-Bo threw the ghost over his shoulder and held it tight. The ghost gave a screech and begged to be put down, but Ding-Bo would not listen and moved forward to the market. When he set the ghost down it had turned into a goat. He promptly sold it, and spat at it to prevent it from changing back to its original form again. Then he left with one thousand and five hundred coins.

So the saying spread:

"Ding-Bo made money by selling a ghost."

四、饑餓能使鬼推磨 南朝 宋·劉義慶：《幽明錄》卷六

新死鬼，形疲神頓，忽見生時友人，死及二十年，肥健。相問訊，曰：「卿那爾？」曰：「吾飢餓，殆不自任！卿知諸方便，故當以法見教。」友鬼云：「此甚易耳！但為人作怪，人必大怖，當與卿食。」

新鬼往入大墟東頭，有一家奉佛精進，屋西廂有磨，鬼就推此磨，如人推法。此家主人語子弟曰：「佛憐我家貧，令鬼推磨！」乃輦麥與之。至夕，磨數斛，疲頓乃去。遂罵友鬼：「卿那誑我？！」又曰：「但復去，自當得也。」復從墟西頭入一家，家奉道，門旁有碓，此鬼便上碓，如人舂狀。此人言：「昨日鬼助某甲，今復來助吾，可輦穀與之！」又給婢簸篩。至夕，力疲甚，不與鬼食。鬼暮歸，大怒曰：「吾自與卿為婚姻，非他比，如何見欺？二日助人，不得一甌飲食！」友鬼曰：「卿自不偶耳！此二家奉佛事道，情自難動，今去，可覓百姓家作怪，則無不得。」

鬼復去，得一家，門首有竹竿。從門入，見有一羣女子，窗前共食；至庭中，有一白狗，便抱令空中行。其家見之大驚，言：「自來未有此怪！」占云：「有客鬼索食，可殺狗，並甘果酒飯，于庭中祀之，可得無他。」其家如師言，鬼果大得食。自此後恆作怪，友鬼之教也。

Trick-or-Treat

Nan Chao Song Dynasty (420-479CE) Liu Yi-Qing (403-444CE) "You Ming Lu"

A ghost who just died was weak and exhausted. He saw a friend who had been dead for twenty years, yet was rather strong. The two of them greeted each other. The friend said, "How come you became like this?" He answered, "I am starving. Teach me some method to get food." The friend said, "It is of no problem. You can haunt the houses of people, who will definitely be very scared and offer you food."

Then the new ghost went to the east side of the village where a family, who had strong belief in Buddhism, lived. On the west side of their house was a mill, and the ghost went working on the mill like the living did. The host of the family said to his sons, "Buddha pitied our poor conditions and sent a ghost to help with the mill." Then they sent more wheat to the mill for the ghost to grind. At dusk, the ghost had already ground several hundred liters of the wheat, and was too exhausted to stay. The ghost scolded his friend, "Why did you lie to me?" The friend said, "Just go out again, you must receive something." Then the new ghost went back to the west side of the village where there lived a family who believed in Daoism. There was a tool for husking grain. The ghost went to work, husking grain like the living did. The Taoist family said, "Yesterday a ghost helped someone's family, and now it comes to help us. We must hurry and send more grain for it to husk." Moreover, the maids were ordered to help sift the grain. The ghost worked until the evening and became exhausted without receiving any food. He came back in the night and was very angry at his friend, saying, "We are relatives, different from others, why did you lie to me? I had worked for two families yet I was offered nothing, not even the slightest share of food." The friend said, "You are unlucky, that's all. The two families have their religious beliefs and it would be difficult to startle them. Now go and look for common families to stir up trouble, and you should not work in vain."

The new ghost then again went into the village and found a family. There was a bamboo fence in front of their house. The ghost went through the gate and saw a group of women gathering and eating in front of the window. As he walked into the yard, he found a white dog and held it up in the air, spinning it. The family saw this and became scared, saying "This had never happened before." The divinator said, "An intruder ghost came for food. You can kill the dog and in the yard offer fruits, wine and rice as a sacrifice for the ghost. Then there will be no more troubles." The family followed the instructions and the ghost finally got plenty food. Ever since then, he haunted people's houses just as his ghost friend had taught him.

五、鬼朋友請吃飯 南朝 宋·劉義慶:《幽明錄》卷六

晉升平元年,任懷仁年十三,為臺書佐。鄉里有王祖復為令史,恆寵之。懷仁已十五、六矣,頗有異意。祖銜恨,至嘉興,殺懷仁,以棺殯埋於徐祚田頭。

祚夜宿息田上,忽見有冢,至朝、中、暮三時,輒分以祭之。呼云:「田頭鬼!來就食。」至瞑眠時,亦云:「來伴我宿。」如此積時,後忽見形,云:「我家明當除服❸作祭,祭甚豐厚,君明隨去。」祚云:「我是生人,不當相見。」鬼云:「我自當隱君形。」

---

❸ 除服 : After one passes away, their relatives must wear thick white clothing, similar to a potato sack. According to the relation between relatives, this clothing should be worn between three months to three

祚便隨鬼去，計行食頃，便到其家。家大有客，鬼將祚上靈座，大食滅。闔家號泣，不能自勝，謂其兒還。見王祖來，便曰：「此是殺我人，猶畏之！」便走出，祚即形露。家中大驚，具問祚，因敘本末。遂隨祚迎喪，鬼便斷絕。

The Returned Favor

Nan Chao Song Dynasty (420-479CE) Liu Yi-Qing (403-444CE) "You Ming Lu"

During the Jin Dynasty（晉）（265-420CE）, Ren Huai-Ren（任懷仁）served as the magistrate's assistant in the central government at the age of 13. Wang Zu（王祖）, a fellow townsman and official, liked to fool around with Huai Ren sexually. When Huai-Ren was about 15 or 16 years old, he wanted to break off this uncommon affair with Wang（王）. Yet Wang bore grudge against Huai-Ren and murdered him as soon as they reached the area of Jia Xing（嘉興）. Wang placed Hui-Ren's body in a coffin and buried him in a man named Xu Zuo's（徐祚）field.

At night Zuo（祚）rested in the field and suddenly saw a tomb. Later he offered a share of his food in front of the tomb

---

years. When the mourning period has been fulfilled, the clothing can than be removed.

in the morning, noon and evening, calling out, "Ghost by the field, come and eat!" When Zuo was about to sleep at night, he would say, "Come and accompany me while I sleep." This went on for a long time. Later the ghost suddenly appeared and said, "The mourning period has ended and there will be an offering of abundant sacrifices tomorrow at my home, come with me tomorrow." Zou replied, "I am a living human and should not go there and reveal myself." The ghost said, "I will help you to become invisible."

Zuo then followed and reached the ghost's home within a short moment. The house was full of guests and the ghost brought Zuo to the altar and ate all the food. The family could not help but cry at the sight, thinking that their son had returned.When the ghost saw Wang Zu come, it said, "He is the one that killed me. I am still afraid of him." Then he ran out, and the figure of Zuo appeared in front of his family, who were all very shocked. Zuo told them everything in detail after being inquired by the family. They then followed Zuo to move their son's coffin back, and the ghost never appeared again afterwards.

六、放心不下的鬼丈夫

南朝　宋・劉義慶：《幽明錄》卷二

庾崇者，建元中江州溺死。爾日即還家，見形一如平生。多在妻樂氏室中。妻初恐懼，每呼諸從女作伴，於是鬼來漸疏。時或暫來，輒恚罵曰：「貪與生者接耳，反致疑惡，豈副我歸意邪？」從女在內紡績，忽見紡績之具在空中，有物撥亂，或投之於地。從女怖懼皆去，鬼即常見。

有一男才三歲，就母求食。母曰：「無錢，食那可得？」鬼乃淒愴，撫其兒頭曰：「我不幸早逝，今汝窮乏；愧汝念汝，情何極也！」忽見將二百錢置妻前，云：「可為兒買食。」

如此經年，妻轉貧苦不立。鬼云：「卿既守節，而貧苦若此，直當相迎耳！」未幾，妻得疾亡，鬼乃寂然。

The Spirit of the Worried Husband

Nan Chao Song Dynasty (420-479CE) Liu Yi-Qing (403-444CE) "You Ming Lu"

During the Jian Yuan（建元）（343-344CE）period, a man named Yu Chong（庾崇）had drowned to death in Jiang State（江州）. On the same day his spirit returned home and showed as his figure from before. He mostly stayed in his wife Yue's（樂）room. In the beginning, his wife was frightened and asked her cousins to keep her company. Thus, gradually his spirit appeared less often. Sometimes when he came back he would yell at her, "You would rather have contact with the living, and instead, are afraid and dislike me. Is this a fair way to treat me after my concern for you?" The cousins, who were spinning cotton into yarn, suddenly saw the spinning machines and tools float up into the air. Everything was in a mess and some objects were thrown onto the floor. They became scared and left. Ever since then the spirit showed up more often.

They had a son, who was about three years old, asking his mother for food. His mother said, "We have no money. Where can we get food from?" The spirit grievously stroked his son's head, saying, "I unfortunately died early leaving you poor. I am sorry and worry about you. The pain has torn up my heart." Suddenly they saw him put two hundred dollars in front of his wife and he said, "You can buy some food for our son."

After a year, the wife had become poorer and poorer, and was not able to support the family. The spirit said, "You have preserved widowhood, yet you had become so poor. Now I am going to bring you here with me." Not long after, the wife died of disease and the spirit did not show up anymore.

七、醉鬼中了鬼計　　東晉·干寶：《搜神記》卷十六

　　瑯琊秦巨伯，年六十，嘗夜行飲酒，道經蓬山廟。忽見其兩孫迎之，扶持百餘步，便捉<u>伯</u>頸著地，罵：「老奴，汝某日捶我，我今當殺汝！」<u>伯</u>思惟某時信捶此孫。<u>伯</u>乃佯死，乃置<u>伯</u>去。

　　<u>伯</u>歸家，欲治兩孫。兩孫驚惋，叩頭❹言：「為子孫，寧可有此！恐是鬼魅，乞更試之。」<u>伯</u>意悟。數日，乃詐醉，行此廟間。復見兩孫來，扶持<u>伯</u>。<u>伯</u>乃急持，鬼動作不得。達家，乃是兩偶人也。<u>伯</u>著火炙之，腹背俱焦坼。出著庭中，夜皆亡去。<u>伯</u>恨不得殺之。

　　後月餘，又佯酒醉夜行，懷刀以去。家不知也。極夜不還。其孫恐又為此鬼所困，乃俱往迎<u>伯</u>，<u>伯</u>竟刺殺之。

Drunken Mishap

Dong Jin Dynasty(317-420CE) Gan Bao（？-336CE) "Sou Shen Ji"

Qin Ju-Bo（秦巨伯）of Lang Ye（瑯琊）was sixty years old. One night after drinking, as he passed Peng Shan Temple（蓬

---

❹　叩頭 Kowtow: The highest form of respect in Chinese etiquette used to show one's obedience or used to apologize or plea for forgiveness from a severe mistake. It is the act of kneeling down and placing one's hands and forehead on the ground. When used an apology, one must knock his/her forehead on the ground.

山廟）he saw his two grandsons coming towards him. They took his arms and helped him along for about a hundred paces. They then seized him by the neck and threw him to the ground. "Old slave!" they swore at him, "You beat us the other day, so today we are going to kill you." 伯（Bo）remembered that he had indeed beaten the boys at some time. He then pretended to be dead, and his grandsons left him there.

When he got home he decided to punish them. Shocked and distressed, they got down on their hands and knees and kowtowed. "How could we, your grandsons, do such a thing?" they protested. "It must have been ghosts. Please further investigate."

A few days later the old man pretended to be drunk and walked past the temple again. Once more the two grandsons came to take his arms, and this time he seized them so that they could not escape and they turned into ghosts. When he got home, the two ghosts had transformed into wooden puppets. Bo burnt them till their backs and bellies were scorched and cracked. Then he left them in the courtyard, yet that night the two scorched puppets escaped. Bo regretted not killing them in the first place.

One month later, the old man pretended to be drunk and went out at night again, taking a knife with him. His family did not know his whereabouts. As it was very late in the night and Bo was not yet back, his grandsons feared the ghosts had caught him again. So they went out to look for him. Yet this time the old man hacked his own grandsons to death, thinking they were the two ghosts attacking him again.

八、小心有鬼　東晉·干寶：《搜神記》卷十六

　　吳興施續，為尋陽督，能言論。有門生，亦有理意，常秉無鬼論。忽有一黑衣白袷客來，與共語，遂及鬼神。移日，客辭屈，乃曰：「君辭巧，理不足。僕即是鬼，何以云無？！」問：「鬼何以來？」答曰：「受使來取君，期盡明日食時。」

　　門生請乞酸苦。鬼問：「有人似君者否？」門生云：「施續帳下都督，與僕相似。」便與俱往，與都督對坐。鬼手中出一鐵鑿，可尺餘，安著都督頭，便舉椎打之。都督云：「頭覺微痛。」向來轉劇，食頃便亡。

Beware of Ghost

Dong Jin Dynasty(317-420CE) Gan Bao (？-336CE) "Sou Shen Ji"

Shi Xu（施續）of Wu Xing（吳興）served as the governor—general of Xun Yang （尋陽） and was good at debating. A subordinate of his was also intelligent, always holding the theory that there were no ghosts in the world. Suddenly, a man dressed in black wearing a white cap came to talk with the subordinate. They discussed supernatural beings. After a long period of time, the man in black retorted saying, "You are eloquent yet lack reason and sense in your theories. I am a ghost! Why do you insist that there aren't any ghosts at all?" The subordinate then asked him, "Well then, Ghost, what your reason for being here?" The ghost answered, "I have been ordered to take your life! You will die tomorrow morning!"

Grief-stricken, the subordinate asked the ghost for mercy. The ghost asked, "Is there anyone who looks like you?" The subordinate answered, "A subordinate-governor of Shi Xu looks similar to me." Then the two went together and sat across from the governor. The ghost took out a sharp iron chisel, about one foot long, put it on the governor's head, and hit it with a hammer. The governor said, "My head hurts a little." Later his headache became more serious and intense, and soon he died.

九、鬼打架 　南朝 宋·劉義慶：《幽明錄》卷四

　　建德民虞敬上廁，輒有一人授草，手內與之，不睹其形。如此非一過。

後至廁，久無送者，但聞戶外鬥聲。窺之，正見死奴與死婢爭先進草，奴適在前，婢便因後搗之，由此輒兩相擊。食頃，<u>敬</u>欲出，婢奴陣勢方未已，乃屬聲叱之，奄如火滅。自是遂絕。

Toilet Paper

Nan Chao Song Dynasty (420-479CE) Liu Yi-Qing (403-444CE) "You Ming Lu"

Every time Yu Jing（虞敬）of Jian De County（建德縣）went to the lavatory, somebody always handed him toilet paper from outside. Though it had happened more than once, he never got to see the face or figure of that person.

Later, he went to the lavatory and no one gave him toilet paper for a long time. He only heard some noise of people fighting. Looking out, he saw a dead servant and maid fighting to give him paper. The servant got ahead and the maid beat him from behind. The two of them kept fighting endlessly. Soon, Jing（敬）wanted to come out from the lavatory, yet their fighting had not ended. Jing then scolded and yelled to them loudly, and they suddenly disappeared like flames being distinguished. They were gone for good.

十、鬼婦設局殺妾　無名氏：《志怪》

　　永嘉中，黃門將張禹曾行經大澤中。天陰晦，忽見一宅門大開。
禹遂前至廳事。有一婢出問之，禹曰：「行次遇雨，欲寄宿耳。」
婢入報之，尋出，呼禹前。

　　見一女子年三十許，坐帳中，有侍婢二十餘人，衣服皆燦麗。
問禹所欲，禹曰：「自有飯，唯須飲耳。」女敕取鐺與之，因燃火
作湯，雖聞沸聲，探之尚冷。女曰：「我亡人也，塚墓之間無以相
共，慚愧而已。」因歔欷告禹曰：「我是任城縣孫家女，父為中山
太守，出適頓丘李氏。有一男一女，男年十一，女年七歲。亡後，
李氏幸我舊使婢承貴者。今我兒每被捶楚，不避頭面。常痛極心髓！
欲殺此婢，然亡人氣弱，須有所憑。託君助濟此事，當厚報君。」
禹曰：「雖念夫人言，緣殺人事大，不敢承命！」婦人曰：「何緣令
君手刃？唯欲因君為我語李氏家，說我告君事狀。李氏念惜承貴，
必做禳除。君當語之，自言能為厭斷之法。李氏聞此，必令承貴蒞
事，我因伺便殺之。」禹許諾。

　　及明而出，遂語李氏，具以其言告之。李氏驚愕，以語承貴，
大懼，遂求救於禹。既而禹見孫氏自外來，侍婢二十餘人，悉持刀
刺承貴，應手仆地而死。未幾，禹復經過澤中，此人遺婢送五十匹
雜綵以報禹。

Set Up by the Deceased

Anonymous"Zhi Guai"

One day, during the Yong Jia (永嘉) era (307-317CE), the general of Yellow Gate (黃門), Zhang Yu (張禹) passed by a large pond, the sky became dark, and suddenly he saw a mansion's door open. He then walked into the hall where a maid came out and asked if there was anything she could help with. Yu (禹) said, "It is raining and I wanted to stay here for a night." The maid went to report to her master and came back immediately to invite Yu into a room.

He saw a woman, about thirty years old, sitting inside a curtain with more than twenty maids, dressed well, awaiting beside her. The woman asked what Yu needed. Yu answered, "I have rice, so drinking water is all I need." The woman ordered the maid to give him a pot and build a fire to boil water. Although he heard the sound of boiling water, he could not feel the heat of water from the pot. The woman said, "I'm dead. I feel embarrassed that there is nothing to offer you in the tomb." Then she said in tears, "I am the daughter of the Sun (孫) family in Ren Cheng County (任城縣). My father is the chief magistrate of Zhong Shan (中山). I married Li (李) of Dun Qiu (頓丘) and gave birth to one daughter and one son. My son is eleven years old and my daughter is seven. After I died, Li took my maid, Cheng-Gui (承貴), as his concubine. She often beat my children with sticks, which has been an unbearable pain in my heart. I want to kill the maid yet my breath is rather weak and I need to depend on someone else. I need you to help me with this and I will repay your effort well." Yu said, "Though I have sympathy for you, murder is a big thing. I can not agree on your request." The woman said, "How could I ask you to kill someone? I just need you to tell the Li family about it. Li cherished and worried about Cheng-Gui so he would definitely hold a ceremony to dispel the misfortune. You can tell them that you are able to vanquish evil spirits. When Li heard this, he will have Cheng-Gui come to the ceremony and I can kill her then." Yu then agreed.

Yu then left at dawn and went to Li and telling Li everything his dead wife said. Li was shocked and told Cheng-Gui about it. They were both frightened and asked for Yu's help. Then Yu saw Sun coming from the outside with more than twenty maids, all of them holding knives to kill Cheng-Gui , who then suddenly fell down to the floor and died. Before long, Yu passed by the pond again and the dead wife sent her maids to give him fifty bolts of various kinds of silk as a gift to repay his effort.

十一、幽靈馬車　　東晉‧陶潛：《搜神後記》卷三

　　宋時有諸生遠學，其父母燃火夜作，兒忽至前，嘆息曰：「今我但魂爾，非復生人。」父母問之，兒曰：「此月初病，以今日某時亡。今在琅琊任子成家，明日當殮，來迎父母。」父母曰：「去此千里，雖復顛倒，那得及汝？」兒曰：「外有車來，但乘之，自得至矣。」

　　父母從之，上車。忽若睡，比雞鳴，已至所在。視其駕乘，但魂車木馬。遂與主人相見，臨兒悲哀。問其疾消息，如言。

Ghost Carriage

Dong Jin Dynasty (317-420CE) Tao Qian (365-427CE) "Sou Shen Hou Ji"

During the Song Dynasty（宋代）(420-479CE), a student went to a faraway place to study. While his parents were working in the night by the candlelight, the son came to them and sighed, "I am now only a ghost, and am not living anymore." The parents asked him what happened and he said, "I was sick at the beginning of this month and died sometime today. Now my body is in the house of Ren Zi-Cheng（任子成）in Lang Ye（琅琊）, and is to be encoffined tomorrow. I come here to take you there."His parents replied, "Lang Ye is extremely far away from here, we cannot make it even if we hurried as best as we could." The son said, "A carriage is coming outside, you only have to get on the carriage and you can be there in time."

His parents agreed and got on the carriage, where they felt sleepy and dreamy. They then heard a rooster's call and they had reached the place where their son's body was. The carriage carrying them was a ghost carriage with wooden horses, given to the dead during the funeral. Then the parents met the host, and mourned by their son's body. They inquired about their son's illness, and it was exactly like their son had said.

十二、鬼知音　晉·荀氏：《靈鬼志》

嵇康燈下彈琴，忽有一人長丈餘，著黑單衣，革帶。康熟視之，乃吹火滅之，曰：「恥與魑魅爭光！」

嘗行，去洛數十里❺，有亭❻名月華，投此亭，由來殺人。中散心神蕭散，了無懼意。至一更，操琴，先作諸弄，雅聲逸奏，空中稱善。中散撫琴而呼之：「君是何人？」答云：「身是故人，幽沒於此。聞君彈琴，音曲清和，昔所好，故來聽耳。身不幸非理就終，形體殘毀，不宜接見君子。然愛君之琴，要當相見，君勿怪惡之。君可更作數曲。」中散復為撫琴，擊節，曰：「夜已久，何不來也？形骸之間，復何足計！」乃手挈其頭，曰：「聞君奏琴，不覺心開神悟，恍若暫生。」遂與共論音聲之趣，辭甚清辯。謂中散曰：「君試以琴見與。」乃彈〈廣陵散〉。便從受之，果悉得。中散先所受引，殊不及。與中散誓：「不得教人！」

天明，語中散：「相與雖一遇於今夕，可以遠同千載。於此長絕，不勝悵然！」

---

❺　里 li：The character li is a traditional Chinese measuring unit of distance. Its length is close to half a kilometer.

❻　亭 station：A guard station with a two-story building, established in a suburban area. The first floor is used to provide shelter for travelers overnight, and the second floor is used as the office for local officers.

Ghost Musical

Jin Dynasty (266-420CE) Xun "Ling Gui Zhi"

One night while Ji Kang（嵇康）(223-262CE) was playing the Gu Qin（古琴）❼ under a lantern's light, a man, over ten feet tall, wearing a black gown with a leather belt suddenly appeared. Carefully examining the man, Kang（康）blew out the light and said, "I disdain to share the light with ghosts."

One time Kang went out and stayed in a station called Yue Hua（月華）, tens of kilometers away from Luo Yang（洛陽）. The travelers who stay at this station often die of unknown reasons. Kang's mind was free and easy, feeling no fear at all. At one o'clock in the morning, he started playing the Gu Qin（古琴）. He first played some elegant and graceful songs, and heard some compliments coming from the air. Kang, playing the Gu Qin, asked, "Who are you?" It answered, "I am a dead person that was buried here. I heard you playing the Gu Qin. The songs you played were so brisk and harmonious, just like what I used to enjoy, so I'm here to listen. I died of a tragic accident and my body had been destroyed. It wouldn't be proper to let you see me. However,

---

❼ 古琴 Gu Qin : A plucked seven-stringed Chinese musical instrument. It has traditionally been favored by scholars.

after falling in love with your music, I would like to meet you. Please don't be disgusted with my figure. Would you please play a few more songs?" Kang then continued to play and the ghost clapped with the rhythm. Kang said, "It is very dark now. Why don't you come forward? As far as appearances, there is no need to make a big fuss over it." Then the ghost, holding his head in his hands, appeared and said, "When I listen to your songs, I become cheerful and happy, as if I were alive again." Then he discussed with Kang the essence of music. He talked in good order and with good reasoning. He asked Kang, "Would you lend me the Gu Qin for a while?" Then he played *Guang Ling Tune*（廣陵散）, and Kang learned it from him. All the songs Kang had learned before were no better than it. The ghost made a pact with Kang that he could never teach anyone the masterpiece.

At dusk, he told Kang, "Although we only shared one evening together, yet it is of important significance as if we had spent a thousand years together. I have to bid farewell to you now. I can't help but feel sorrowful."

十三、鬼新娘要渡河　東晉・干寶：《搜神記》卷五

淮南全椒縣有丁新婦者，本丹陽丁氏女，年十六，適全椒謝

家。其姑嚴酷，使役有程，不如限者，仍便笞捶。不可堪，九月七日乃自經死。遂有靈響，聞於民間，發言於巫祝曰：「念人家婦女，作息不倦，使避九月七日，勿用作事！」

吳平後，其女幽魂思鄉欲歸。永平元年九月七日，見形，著縹衣，戴青蓋，從一婢，至牛渚津求渡。有兩男子共乘船捕魚，仍呼求載。兩男子笑，共調弄之，言：「聽我為婦，當相渡也。」丁嫗曰：「謂汝是佳人，而無所知。汝是人，當使汝入泥死；是鬼，使汝入水。」便卻入草中。

須臾，有一老翁乘船載葦，嫗從索渡。翁曰：「船上無裝，豈可露渡，恐不中載耳。」嫗言：「無苦。」翁因出葦半許，安處著船中，徑渡之，至南岸。臨去，語翁曰：「吾是鬼神，非人也，自能得過，然宜使民間粗相聞知。翁之厚意，出葦相渡，深有慙感，當有以相謝者。若翁速還去，必有所見，亦當有所得也！」翁曰：「媿燥濕不至，何敢蒙謝！」翁還西岸，見兩男子覆水中。進前數里，有魚千數，跳躍水邊，風吹至岸上。翁遂棄葦，載魚以歸。

於是丁嫗遂還丹陽，江南人皆呼為丁姑。九月七日不用作事，咸以為息日也。今所在祠之。

The Testament of the Ghostess

Dong Jin Dynasty (317-420CE)Gan Bao (？-336CE) "Sou Shen Ji"

The daughter of Ding（丁）from Dan Yang（丹陽），at the age of sixteen was married to Xie（謝）from Quan Jiao（全椒）.

Her mother-in-law was ruthless and harsh on her, assigning her every task with strict requirement. If she could not finish them in time, she would be whipped. Unable to sustain the suffering, she hung herself on the seventh day of September. Later, mysterious sounds occurred within the society. She then announced through the witches, "I sympathize for the women who work endlessly and would like them to rest on the seventh day of September."

After the Kingdom of Wu (228-280CE) had been diminished, Ding's daughter, now a nostalgic ghost, wished to return to her homeland. On the seventh day of September, she appeared wearing blue clothes and a black veil, accompanied by a maid, in search of a ship to cross the river at the Niu Zhu Dock (牛渚津). She called upon two men fishing together to help her and her maid cross the river. The men laughed, flirting with her, saying. "If you will be my wife, I will carry you across the river." Ding said, "I thought you were good men, yet you did not know what is good for you. As humans, I curse you to fall into mud and die; as ghosts, I curse you to drown to death." She then left and went into the tussock.

Soon, an old man on a boat carrying reeds came, and when asked by Ding to help her cross the river, he said, "My boat has no cover for protection, how can I take you two across the river? I'm afraid it wouldn't be suitable to carry the both of you." Ding said, "Don't worry about it."The old man then removed half of the reeds and cleared a space for Ding and her maid to ride comfortably. They crossed the river and reached the south bank. As Ding was leaving, she said to the old man, "I'm a ghost, not human, and am capable of crossing the river by myself. However, I wish people to know about it. You are very kind to remove the reeds for me. I really don't deserve this. I will thank you for what you did. Please go back now and you will definitely see something to repay you for your great deeds." The old man said, "I am ashamed of my bad treatment towards you. How can I accept your reward?" When the old man returned to the west bank, he saw two men dead, floating in the water. After continuing on for some distance, he found more than one thousand fish jumping on the riverside. They were carried onto the riverbank by the wind. The old man then abandoned his reeds, gathered the fish and left.

Then Ding returned to Dan Yang. The people of Jiang Nan (江南) called her Ding the Fairy (丁姑). Women did not perform any housework on the seventh day of September which later became labeled as the day of rest. Nowadays, people still worship Ding the Fairy.

十四、病鬼上門求診　宋·吳均撰·《續齊諧記》

　　錢塘徐秋夫善治病，宅在湖溝橋東。夜聞空中呻吟聲甚苦。秋夫起，至呻吟處問曰：「汝是鬼邪？何為如此？饑寒須衣食邪？抱病須治療邪？」鬼曰：「我是東陽人，姓斯名僧平。昔為樂游吏，患腰痛死。今在湖北，雖為鬼，苦亦如生。為君善醫，故來相告。」秋夫曰：「但汝無形，何由治？」鬼曰：「但縛茅作人，按穴鍼之，訖，棄流水中可也。」秋夫作茅人，為鍼腰目二處，并復薄祭，遣人送後湖中。及暝，夢鬼曰：「已差，并承惠食，感君厚意。」

　　秋夫宋元嘉六年為奉朝請。

The Voodoo Doll

Nan Chao Song Dynasty (420-479CE) Wu Jun (469-520CE) "Xu Qi Xie Ji"

　　Xu Qiu-Fu（徐秋夫）of Qian Tang（錢塘）was good at curing diseases. He lived on the east side of Hu Gou Bridge （湖溝橋）. One night he heard someone moaning in pain, so he got up and went to where the sound was coming from, asking, "Are you a ghost? What happened to you? Are you hungry or cold? Do you need clothes or food, or do you moan because you are sick and need to be cured?" The ghost said, "My name is Si Seng-Ping（斯僧平）from Dong Yang（東陽）.

I was the administrator of the Royal Playground when I was alive. I died of lumbago. Today I reside in Hu Bei（湖北）, and although I am a ghost, I still suffer from the same pain. You are good at curing diseases, so I come to you for help." Qiu-Fu （秋夫）said, "Yet you have no figure. How can I cure you?" The ghost said, "Make a doll similar to human figure out of couch grass and use acupuncture on it. Afterwards, throw the doll into flowing water and that's it." Qiu-Fu then made a doll and used acupunctured on the two points of his loins. After a simple ceremony, he had the doll thrown into the lake. During that night, he dreamt of the ghost coming to him saying, "I have recovered from the illness. Thank you for kindly giving me food in the ceremony, I appreciate your benevolence."

Qiu-Fu served in the government during the Song Dynasty（宋代） (420-479CE).

主題八：動物緣

Theme 8: Animal Encounters

Living in this beautiful world with all other creatures, we humans are not the initial origin of all living objects, nor do we have the ability to fly, swim, or be stronger than all other creatures. However we have accumulated wisdom to create civilization thus building an empire dominated by humans, holding other creatures at our command. Based on the human-centric ideology, people claim to each other that "Humans are the soul of the universe." From a positive point of view, this human-oriented ideology prompts humans to progress and always be on top. On the contrary, it may also drive human to exploit other living creatures from gaining a commanding position.

Animals help humans with farming, fishing, hunting, and transportation which from this derive relationships between animals and humans built off of mutual trust and love mostly due to their dependence on each other in daily life and shared emotions. As a result, many Chinese folktales were written about this relationship between humans and animals. In addition, the Confucian school advocates braveness, loyalty, benevolence, friendly affections and repayment of gratitude through an analogy on animal ethical behavior where "tigers, as fierce as they are, do not eat their own children," "the unconditional parental love of cows," "goats kneeling down for drinking milk," and "crows crying at night for their children to return." However, mankind's interpretations on animal behavior are not acknowledged by the animal kingdom, for such values only exist in human society.

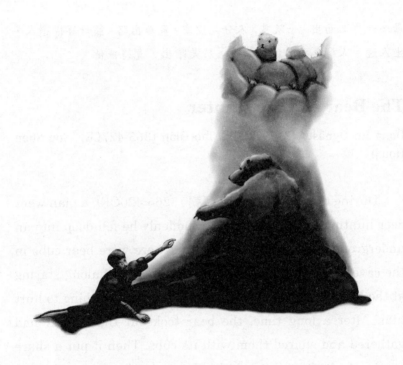

一、熊媽媽的愛心　　晉‧陶潛：《搜神後記》卷九

晉升平中，有人入山射鹿。忽墮一坎，窅然深絕。內有數頭熊子。須臾，有一大熊來，瞪視此人。人謂必以害己。良久，出藏果，分與諸子。末後作一分，置此人前。此人飢甚，於是冒死取啖之。既而轉相狎習。

熊母每旦出，覓果食還，輒分此人，賴以延命。熊子後大，其母一一負之而出。子既盡，人分死坎中，窮無出路。熊母尋復還入，坐人邊。人解其意，便抱熊足，於是躍出，竟得無他。

The Bear and the Hunter

Dong Jin Dynasty (317-420CE) Tao Qian (365-427CE) "Sou Shen Hou Ji"

During the Jin Dynasty（晉朝）(265-420CE), a man went deer hunting in the mountains. Suddenly he fell deep into an underground cave with no way out. There were bear cubs in the cave, and soon afterwards a big bear came along staring at the hunter. The hunter thought the bear was going to hurt him. After a long time, the bear took out the fruit it had gathered and shared them with its cubs. Then it put a share of the fruit in front of the hunter. The hunter, being extremely hungry, risked his life eating the fruit. Later he grew familiar and closer with the bear.

Everyday the mother bear left to forage for food, and when it returned, it would share them with the hunter, who relied and survived upon it. After the cubs became bears, the mother bear carried them out of the cave one by one. When all the bears had left, the hunter assumed that he would die in the cave, having not being able to find his way out. Soon the mother bear came back and sat by the hunter. He then understood, clung onto the feet of the bear and was carried out of the cave safe and sound.

二、滅火救主的義犬　　東晉·干寶：《搜神記》卷二十

　　孫權時，李信純，襄陽紀南人也。家養一狗，字曰「黑龍」，愛之尤甚，行坐相隨，飲饌之間，皆分與食。忽一日，於城外飲酒大醉，歸家不及，臥於草中。遇太守鄭瑕出獵，見田草深，遣人縱火蓺之。信純臥處，恰當順風。犬見火來，乃以口拽純衣，純亦不動。臥處比有一溪，相去三、五十步，犬即奔往，入水濕身，走來臥處。周迴以身灑之，獲免主人大難。

　　犬運水困乏，致斃於側。俄爾，信純醒來，見犬已死，遍身毛濕。甚訝其事。覩火蹤跡，因爾慟哭。聞於太守。太守憫之，曰：「犬之報恩甚於人。人不知恩，豈如犬乎！」即命具棺槨衣衾葬之。今紀南有義犬塚，高十餘丈。

The Firefighting Dog
Dong Jin Dynasty (317-420CE) Gan Bao (？-336CE) "Sou Shen Ji"

During the Three Kingdom（三國）time period when Sun（孫）(182-252CE) was in power, lived a man named Li Xin-Chun（李信純）of Ji Nan（紀南）. Xin-Chun（信純）had a dog named "Black Dragon" that he loved deeply, bringing it with him wherever he went, even sharing food with it. One day, Xin-Chun was drunk outside the city and could not make it home, falling into the brushwood. The magistrate, Zheng Xia （鄭瑕）, happened to go out hunting and passed by the brushwood. He ordered his men to burn the brushwood. The wind's direction was blowing towards the direction where Xin-Chun slept. The dog saw the fire and pulled Xin-Chun's clothes with its mouth, yet he remained still. A stream ran thirty to fifty steps away from where he slept. The dog ran toward it, drenched its body in the stream, and came back to Xin-Chun, shaking and sprinkling the water around it's master. Xin-Chun then finally escaped the fire.

The dog became exhausted during the rescue and died by Xin-Chun's side. Soon Xin-Chun woke up and saw his dog, drenched and dead. He was rather astonished by this event, and as he found remnants of the fire, he became moved to tears. When the magistrate heard about this event, he felt sorry for the dog and said, "A dog's gratitude is superior to that of a human. If people do not know how to repay the kindness from one another, then people are inferior to dogs!" Then he ordered to prepare a coffin and clothes for the burial of the dog. Nowadays in Ji Nan, there is a tomb, about thirty feet tall, of the loyal dog.

三、救救我家的母老虎 東晉・干寶：《搜神記》卷二十

　　蘇易者，盧陵婦人，善看產，夜忽為虎所取。行六、七里❶，至大壙，厝易置地，蹲而守。見有牝虎當產，不得解，匍匐欲死，輒仰視。易怪之，乃為探出之，有三子。生畢，虎負易還。再三送野肉於門內。

The Tiger and the Midwife

Dong Jin Dynasty(317-420CE) Gan Bao (？-336CE) "Sou Shen Ji"

Su Yi（蘇易）, a woman in Lu Ling（盧陵）, was an excellent midwife. One night she was carried off by a tiger, and after walking for three or four kilometers, she was placed on the ground in a big cave and the tiger squat down beside guarding over her. Yi（易）saw a mother tiger about to give birth yet the delivery was not successful. The mother tiger was struggling on the ground, dying. The mother tiger held up its head and looked at Yi, who then went over to help it deliver three cubs. After the delivery, the original tiger carried Yi back. The tiger then often sent game meat to the door of her house.

---

❶ 里 li：The character li is a traditional Chinese measuring unit of distance. Its length is close to half a kilometer.

四、通風報信的鸜鵒 南朝 宋·劉義慶：《幽明錄》卷三

晉司空桓豁在荊州，有參軍剪五月五日鸜鵒舌，教令學語，遂無所不名，與人相問。顧參軍善彈琵琶，鸜鵒每立聽移時，又善能效人語笑聲。司空大會吏佐，令悉效四坐語，無不絕似。有參佐齆鼻，語難學，學之不似，因納頭於甕中以效焉，遂與齆者語聲不異。

主典人於鸜鵒前盜物，參軍如廁，鸜鵒伺無人，密白主典人盜某物，參軍銜之而未發。後盜牛肉，鸜鵒復白，參軍曰：「汝云盜肉，應有驗。」鸜鵒曰：「以新荷葉裹，著屏風後。」檢之果獲，痛加治。而盜者患之，以熱湯灌殺。參軍為之悲傷累日，遂請殺此人，以報其怨。司空言曰：「原殺鸜鵒之痛，誠合治殺。不可以禽鳥故，極之於法。」令止五歲刑也。

The Mynah Informant

Nan Chao Song Dynasty (420-479CE) Liu Yi-Qing (403-444CE) "You Ming Lu"

During the Jin Dynasty（晉朝）(265-420CE), while the Minister of Justice, Huan Huo（桓豁）（320-377CE）was governing the Jing State（荊州）, an officer of military affairs trimmed the tongue of his own mynah and taught it how to speak. The mynah learned how to say all kinds of things and was able to greet people. Staff officer Gu（顧）was an expert in playing the pipa ❷, and the mynah always stood beside him listening for a long time. The mynah was also good at imitating the voices of everyone. When the Minister summoned his subordinates, he asked the mynah to imitate the tones of those present, and the mynah did so without a single mistake. One subordinate spoke with a heavy nasal tone, which was difficult to imitate. The mynah then put its head into a jug and spoke identically to the voice of that subordinate with the nasal congestion.

One day, a keeper stole things in front of the mynah, and when the officer was in the bathroom with no one around, the mynah secretly told him what happened. The officer did not expose this event to anyone. Later the keeper stole beef and the mynah again reported it to the officer, who said, "You said he stole beef. Then there must be some proof." The mynah responded, "The beef was wrapped by fresh lotus leaves and hidden behind a screen." After checking it out the officer found evidence just as expected, and the keeper was seriously punished. Holding a grudge toward this, the keeper killed the mynah in boiling water. The officer grieved for the mynah for several days and asked for revenge by killing the keeper. The

---

❷ 琵琶 pipa: A kind of stringed musical instrument made of wood similar to the lute.

Minister said, "The keeper should be sentenced to death with the cruelty he had done to the mynah. Yet we could not decree capital punishment to a person for killing a bird." He then decreed a five-year sentence to the keeper.

五、大象報拔刺之恩　　南朝 宋·劉敬叔：《異苑》卷三

　　始興郡陽山縣有人行田，忽遇一象，以鼻捲之。遙入深山，見一象，腳有巨刺。此人牽挽得出，病者即起，相與躑陸，狀若歡喜。前象復載人，就一污濕地，以鼻掘出數條長牙，送還本處。

　　彼境田稼常為象所困，其象俗呼為「大客」。因語云：「我田稼在此，恆為大客所犯，若念我者，勿復見侵。」便見躑躅，如有馴解。於是一家業田，絕無其患。

The Elephant's Gratitude

Nan Chao Song Dynasty (420-479CE) Liu Jing-Shu（？-468CE）"Yi Yuan"

A man in Shi Xing County（始興郡）went for work upon his field and suddenly came across an elephant. The elephant curled him up with its trunk and walked into the mountains. The man saw another elephant with a large thorn in the sole of its foot, and he pulled it out with great effort. The injured elephant then got on its feet and stomped the ground, as if in great joy. The previous elephant carried the man to a low swamp, and dug out some ivory with its nose, and then sent him back to where they had originally met.

The crops in the fields were often damaged by elephants, which had been given the name "Da Ke(大客)"(big visitor) by locals. The man then told the elephant, "These are my fields, which are always being damaged by Da Ke . If you take me into consideration, please do not harm my crops anymore." Then he saw the elephant stomp its feet, as if it had understood what he said. Consequently, the elephants no longer damaged his crops in the fields.

六、忠狗與蟒蛇　南朝　宋·劉義慶：《幽明錄》卷二

　　晉太興二年，吳人華隆好弋獵，畜一犬，號曰:「的尾」，每將自隨。隆後至江邊，被一大蛇圍繞固身，犬遂咬蛇死焉，而隆僵仆，無所知矣。

　　犬彷徨嘷吠，往復路間，家人怪其如此，因隨犬往，隆悶絕委地，載歸家，二日乃蘇。隆未蘇之間，犬終不食。自此，愛惜同於親戚焉。

The Loyal Dog and The Python

Nan Chao Song Dynasty (420-479CE) Liu Yi-Qing (403-444CE) "You Ming Lu"

During the Jin Dynasty（晉朝）（265-420CE），Hua Long（華隆）of Wu（吳）was fond of hunting. He had a dog named "Di Wei(的尾)", that he took everywhere he went. Later when Long（隆）went to the riverside and was encountered by a huge python that wrapped tightly around his body. His dog rushed towards the python and bit it to death, and Long lied face down on the ground unconscious.

The dog barked in a flurry and ran back and forth on the road. Long's family members found it strange so they followed the dog and saw Long laying on the ground in a coma. They brought Long back home and it was not until two days later that Long regained consciousness. The dog did not eat anything when Long was in a coma. Ever since then they treated the dog as if it were one of their family members.

七、忠狗突圍襲敵　東晉·陶潛：《搜神後記》卷九

會稽句章民張然，滯役在都，經年不得歸。家有少婦，無子，惟與一奴守舍，婦遂與奴私通。然在都養一狗，甚快，名曰：「烏龍」，常以自隨。

後假歸，婦與奴謀，欲得殺然。然及婦作飯食，共坐下食。婦語然：「與君當大別離，君可強啖。」然未得啖，奴已張弓撥矢當戶，須然食畢。

然涕泣不食，乃以盤中肉及飯擲狗，祝曰：「養汝數年，吾當將死，汝能救我否？」狗得食不啖，惟注睛舐脣視奴。然亦覺之。奴催食轉急，然決計，拍膝大呼曰：「烏龍，與手！」狗應聲傷奴。奴失刀仗倒地，狗咋其陰，然因取刀殺奴。以婦付縣，殺之。

The Betrayal

Dong Jin Dynasty (317-420CE) Tao Qian (365-427CE) "Sou Shen Hou Ji"

Zhang Ran（張然）of Kuai Ji（會稽）served in the capital and could not go home for many years. He had a young wife and servant at home, but no children. His wife had an affair with the servant. Ran（然）had a dog, called "Wu Long"（烏龍）. The dog was agile, and Ran often took it with him.

Later he had time off and went back home. His wife and servant planned to kill Ran. While Ran was cooking with his wife, his wife said, "We are about to part for a long time. Eat some more." Before Ran had even eaten a single bite, his servant at the door prepared a bow and arrow, waiting to shoot him when he finished his meal.

Ran's eyes were full of tears as he could not eat, so he gave the food to his dog, to which he prayed, "I have had you for so many years and now I will die. Can you save my life?" Even upon giving food the dog didn't eat, he just licked his lips and stared at the servant. Ran saw this and suddenly came up with a plan. As the servant urged Ran to eat, Ran patted his knee, shouting, "Go on Wu Long, sick him!" As soon as it heard the order, the dog then quickly injured the servant. The servant dropped his bow and arrow on the ground and the dog bit his genitals. Ran then drew his knife and killed the servant. He handed his wife over to the magistrate, who sentenced her to death sentence.

八、烏龜來救溺　　東晉·陶潛：《搜神後記》卷十

　　晉咸康中，豫州刺史毛寶戍邾城。有一軍人，於武昌市見人賣一白龜子，長四、五寸，潔白可愛，便買取持歸，著甕中養之。日漸大，近欲尺許。其人憐之，持至江邊，放江水中，視其去。

　　後邾城遭石季龍攻陷，毛寶棄豫州，赴江者莫不沈溺。於時所養龜人被鎧持刀，亦同自投。既入水中，覺如墮一石上，水裁至腰。須臾，游出。中流視之，乃是先所放白龜，甲六、七尺。既抵東岸，出頭視此人，徐游而去。中江猶回首視此人而沒。

The Turtle Comes to the Rescue

Dong Jin Dynasty (317-420CE) Tao Qian (365-427CE) "Sou Shen Hou Ji"

During the Jin Dynasty（晉朝）(265-420CE）, Mao Bao（毛寶）, the chief governor of Yu State（豫州）was garrisoned at Zhu City（邾城）. A soldier saw someone selling a baby turtle, about ten centimeters long, white and adorable, in Wu Chang City（武昌市）. He bought the turtle and kept it in an earthen jar. Day by day the turtle got bigger, eventually growing twenty-two centimeters long. Out of pity, the man brought the turtle to the riverside and released it into the river, watching as it swam away.

Shi Ji-Long（石季龍）later evaded Zhu City , and Mao Bao abandoned the city. The escaping troops jumped into the river and drowned to death. The man who kept the turtle, wearing a suit of armor and holding a saber, jumped into the river like everyone else. When he fell into the river, he felt as if he had fallen onto a big stone where the river was only waist deep. The man slowly crossed the river. When he was halfway across he looked into and found the white turtle he once released, whose shell was already more than one meter long. When the man reached the bank, the head of the turtle emerged from the water and stared at the man, and then slowly swam away. Upon reaching the middle of the river, the turtle turned back with a glance, than immerged into the water.

主題九：我變我變我變變變

Theme 9: Transfigurations

In this theme humans undergo abnormal changes to their bodies which include: Detachable body parts and the transplantation from one to another, spirits leaving the human body, and the ability to become invisible and conceal oneself. The unusual concept of this phenomenon of the human body in these stories has exceeded the normal state of our physical form. Even progressive modern plastic surgery techniques are unable to accomplish instant face or leg exchange.

Literature is a language that can express a deep hidden cultural meaning through a short simple text. Lively animated scenes of transfiguration are just the surface of these strange stories, the core meaning sublimely points to the culture connotation. During the Wei-Jin Dynasties, an aesthetic perception of the human body arouse, especially within the intellectual class. Sense of beauty has set in adoration for the handsome and aversion for the ugly. Furthermore, Chinese have contacted with foreigners from the Middle East and North West during this period with frequent international exchanges. Due to difference in appeals and enmities against each other, the foreigners have been deemed ugly at the time. Other stories associate with the bizarre habitual behavior of the ethnic groups in China.

Popularity of Buddhism and Taoism has also provided the stories with religious backgrounds. Deriving from preachers applying conjuring tricks claiming to have supernatural powers to attract a larger audience are stories describing magic and invisibility. Therefore, for thousands of years Buddhism and Taoism have played a major role in impacting Chinese Folk Literature.

一、換臉　南朝 宋·劉義慶：《幽明錄》卷四

河東賈弼，小名翳兒，具譜究世譜。義熙中，為琅邪府參軍。夜夢有一人，面魋皰，多鬚、大鼻、睅目，請之曰：「愛君之貌，欲易頭，可乎？」弼曰：「人各有頭面，豈容此理！」明晝又夢，意甚惡之，乃於夢中許易。

明朝起，自不覺，而人悉驚走藏，云：「那漢何處來？」琅邪王大驚，遣傳教呼視，弼到，琅邪遙見，起還內。弼取鏡自看，方

知怪異。因還家，家人悉驚入內，婦女走藏，曰：「那得異男子？！」彌坐，自陳說良久，并遣人至府檢問，方信。

後能半面啼，半面笑；兩手各捉一筆，俱書，辭意皆美；此為異也，餘并如先。俄而<u>安帝</u>崩，<u>恭帝</u>立。

Facelift dream

Nan Chao Song Dynasty (420-479CE) Liu Yi-Qing (403-444CE) "You Ming Lu"

Jia Bi（賈弼）of He Dong（河東）, nicknamed Yi-E（翳兒）, was an expert in the field of genealogy. During the East Jin Dynasty（東晉）(317-420CE), he served as an officer in Duke Lang Ye's government. One night he dreamt of a man who had pimples covering his face, a bushy beard, big nose and squinty eyes, pleading, "I like your face, can I exchange mine with yours?" Bi（弼）replied, "Everyone has his own look. It is nonsense to say such a thing like that!" The next morning Bi dreamt of him again. Bi extremely detested this man, so in his dream he promised to exchange faces to avoid the man's harassment.

The next morning when Bi woke up he found nothing strange, yet when people saw him they all ran away in fear, saying, "Where did this man come from?" The duke of Lang

Ye was rather astonished and sent people to summon Bi. As soon as Duke Lang Ye saw Bi coming from a distance, he got up and returned to his room. It wasn't until Bi looked at himself in the mirror that he knew something strange had happened.

Bi then went home. His family members were so frightened that as soon as they saw Bi they went in the house to avoid him. Women ran to hide, saying, "Where did this ugly man come from?" Bi sat down as it took him a long time to explain what had happened. He also sent people to the Lang Ye Palace to ask for proof in order for his family members to believe him.

Later he could only cry on one side of his face, and smile on the other. When he held a brush pen in each of his hands, he was able to write two beautiful articles at the same time. Besides these changes that took place, everything else remained the same as before. Soon Gong Emperor（恭帝 386-421CE）succeeded after the demise of An Emperor（安帝 382-419CE）.

二、移植了一雙飛毛腿

南朝 宋・劉義慶：《幽明錄》卷二

晉元帝世有甲者，衣冠族姓，暴病亡。見人將上天詣司命，司命更推校，算歷未盡，不應枉召，主者發遣令還。甲尤腳痛，不能行，無緣得歸。主者數人共愁，相謂曰：「甲若卒以腳痛不能歸，我等坐枉人之罪。」遂相率具白司命。司命思之良久，曰：「適新召胡人康乙者，在西門外，此人當遂死，其腳甚健，易之，彼此無損。」主者承敕出，將易之，胡形體甚醜，腳殊可惡，甲終不肯。主者曰：「君若不易，便長決留此耳。」不獲已，遂聽之。主者令二人並閉目，俄忽，二人腳已互易矣。仍即遣之。

豁然復生，具為家人說。發視，果是胡腳，叢毛連結，且胡臭。甲本士，愛翫手足，而忽得此，了不欲見。雖獲更活，每惆悵，殆如欲死。旁人見，識此胡者死猶未殯，家近在茄子浦。甲親往視胡尸，果見其腳著胡體，正當殯歛，對之泣。

胡兒並有至性，每節朔，兒並悲思，馳往抱甲腳號咷；忽行路相逢，便攀援啼哭。為此，每出入時，恆令人守門，以防胡子。終身憎穢，未嘗恬視，雖三伏盛暑，必復重衣，無暫露也。

Hairy Feet Transplant

Nan Chao Song Dynasty (420-479CE) Liu Yi-Qing (403-444CE) "You Ming Lu"

During the Jin Dynasty（晉朝）（265-420CE）, a person of gentry suddenly died of a disease. He was taken to be judged by the Deified Judge of Life, who then found that the man's life had not been fulfilled and concluded that they shouldn't have summoned upon him. Officers in charge of this event then were ordered to send him back, however the man complained that his feet were too painful to walk home. Those in charge were worried, all saying, "If the man can not go back because of the pain in his feet, we will commit a crime of doing the man wrong." They then reported this to the Judge, who thought for a long time then said, "Kang Yi（康乙）, a barbarian, had just been summoned and is outside the West Gate, and is about to die. His feet are rather strong. If we exchange his feet with the man's, it will do no harm." The officers then accepted and went out to exchange their feet.

However, since the body of Kang Yi was very ugly, his feet were so grotesque that the man would not agree to accept them. The officers said, "If you don't want to exchange your feet, you will have to stay here forever." He then stopped resisting and agreed. The two were asked to shut their eyes, and their feet exchanged instantly. Then the man was sent back.

After the man had revived he told his family about what had happened. He pulled up his pant legs, exposing the hairy and smelly feet of the barbarian. As a scholar, the man liked to take good care of his hands and feet, now with such ugly feet, he couldn't bear to look at them. Even though he was granted the opportunity to live again, he always felt frustrated and depressed wanting to die. Someone around him that knew the barbarian told the man that the barbarian had not been encoffined yet, and his house was near Qie Zi Pu （茄子浦）. The man himself then visited the barbarian, and there he found his very own feet on the dead body about to be encoffined. He cried at the feet.

The children of the barbarian practiced filial piety ❶ and during festivals, they would go to the man's house and cry to

---

❶ 孝順 Filial Piety：A form of etiquette in which a child must show respect, obedience, and well treatment towards their parents.

the man's feet to mourn over their father's death. Sometimes when they met the man on the road, they would grab him, weeping and wailing endlessly. Because of this, the man ordered servants to help him avoid the children. He hated his feet for the rest of his life, and never looked at them in delight. Even during the hot summer days of June, he would wear two layers of clothes to cover up his feet.

三、頭殼飛走了　東晉·干寶：《搜神記》卷十二

秦時，南方有落頭民，其頭能飛。其種人部有祭祀，號曰「蟲落」，故因取名焉。

吳時，將軍朱桓得一婢，每夜臥後，頭輒飛去，或從狗竇，或從天窗中出入，以耳為翼。將曉復還。數數如此，傍人怪之。夜中照視，唯有身無頭。其體微冷，氣息裁屬。乃蒙之以被。

至曉頭還，礙被，不得安，兩三度墮地，噫咤甚愁，體氣甚急，狀若將死。乃去被，頭復起，傅頸。有頃，和平。桓以為大怪，畏不敢畜，乃放遣之。既而詳之，乃知天性也。時南征大將，亦往往得之。又嘗有覆以銅盤者，頭不得進，遂死。

A Head of its Own

Dong Jin Dynasty (317-420CE) Gan Bao (? -336CE) "Sou Shen Ji"

During the Chin Dynasty（秦朝）（259 BCE-195BCE）, there lived a tribe in the south. The heads of the people in the tribe were able to fly. The tribe has a ceremony called "Chong Luo"（蟲落）, this is where they got their name from. During Wu's （吳）Regime, General Zhu Huan（朱桓）had received a maid. Every night after going to bed, using her ears as wings, her head would fly out of the house from the dog's entrance or from the ceiling window and return at dawn. Happening frequently, others found this to be strange. In the middle of the night, they used a candle's light to check on her, and found only her body without a head. Her body temperature was cold and her breath was weak. They then completely covered her entire body with a quilt.

At dawn, the head returned, yet was not able to connect to its original position due to hindrance from the quilt. The head dropped to the floor for several times and sighed worriedly. Her breath became heavy as if about to die. When the others saw this, they quickly removed the quilt, and the head flew up and sat upon the neck. Soon her breath became calm. Huan （桓）thought this was very odd, and being frightened did not dare to keep her as a maid, so she was dismissed. Afterwards he understood the situation, realizing this was habitual behavior of her people. The generals who went to war in the south often took people from that tribe as servants. And once, a man used a copper plate to cover one's neck, and the head could not return to the body, so this person died.

四、斷舌魔術　東晉・干寶：《搜神記》卷二

晉永嘉中，有天竺胡人，來渡江南。其人有數術，能斷舌、復續、吐火，所在人士聚觀。將斷時，先以舌吐示賓客。然後刀截，血流覆地。乃取置器中，傳以示人。視之，舌頭半舌猶在。既而還，取含續之，坐有頃，坐人見舌則如故，不知其實斷否。

其續斷，取絹布，與人各執一頭，對剪，中斷之。已而取兩斷合視，絹布還連續，無異故體。時人多疑以為幻，陰乃試之，真斷絹也。

其吐火，先有藥在器中，取火一片，與黍糖合之，再三吹呼，已而張口，火滿口中，因就蒸取以炊，則火也。又取書紙及繩縷之屬投火中，眾共視之，見其燒蒸了盡。乃撥灰中，舉而出之，故向物也。

Magic

Dong Jin Dynasty (317-420CE) Gan Bao (？-336CE) "Sou Shen Ji"

During the Jin Dynasty（晉朝）（265-420CE）, a man from India came to Jiang Nan（江南）. He was able to perform magic like cutting his tongue, reconnection of objects, and fire spitting. Wherever he went, people all crowded around him and watched his performances. When performing the trick of cutting his tongue, he would first stick out his tongue to show spectators, than cut it off having blood dripping down to the ground. He put the cut off tongue in a vessel and showed it to the spectators one by one. The other half of his tongue remained in his mouth. After everyone saw the cut-off tongue, he then held it in his mouth and spliced it back together. Everyone saw his tongue return to its original shape, as if never been cut off before.

Then he performed the trick of reconnecting objects. First, he took a piece of silk cloth and had someone hold the other end. He folded the cloth and cut it. Then he put the two cut pieces of cloth together and they reconnected as if they had never been cut. Many then had doubts thinking it was a trick, but after secret examination, they found the cloth had really been cut.

When performing the fire spitting trick, he put gunpowder in a vessel and lit it on fire, and than mixed it with malt sugar. He took several deep breaths, opened his mouth quickly, and it was full of fire. He then threw paper, rope, and fabrics into the fire. Everybody watched as everything burnt to ashes. Afterwards he fiddled with in the ashes and pulled out everything he had thrown in before in its original form.

五、恐怖洗澡法　東晉・陶潛：《搜神後記》卷二

　　晉大司馬桓溫，字元子。末年，忽有一比丘尼，失其名，來自遠方，投溫為檀越尼。才行不恒，溫甚敬待，居之門內。

　　尼每浴，必至移時。溫疑而窺之。見尼裸身，揮刀，破腹出臟，斷截身首，支分臠切。溫怪駭而還。及至尼出浴室，身形如常。溫以實問，尼答曰：「若逐凌君上，形當如之。」時溫方謀問鼎，聞之悵然，故以戒懼，終守臣節。尼後辭去，不知所在。

The Appalling Bath

Dong Jin Dynasty (317-420CE) Tao Qian (365-427CE) "Sou Shen Hou Ji"

　　During the Jin Dynasty（晉朝）（265-420CE），Huan Wen（桓溫）（312-372CE）served as the Chief General. During his late years, a Buddhist nun, who's name was unknown, suddenly came to him. The nun was highly trained so Wen（溫）treated her well and respectfully, having her stay in his house.

Every time the nun bathed, she always took a long time. Wen felt strange about this, so he secretly watched as she took a bath. He saw the nun naked, holding a knife in hand, slice open her belly taking out her internal organs and cut off her head and body parts, than chop them into pieces. Frightened by the sight, Wen backed off. When the nun came out of the bathroom, her body was back to normal. Wen told her what he saw and asked her about it, and the nun answered, "If someone overcomes the emperor their body would become this way." At that time Wen was intending to overthrow the emperor. After hearing the nun's warning, he grew disappointed and upset, becoming extremely cautious. In the end, he held his integrity and remained a courtier. Later, the nun left with no one knowing where she went.

六、鵝籠裡的書生　南朝 宋・吳均：《續齊諧記》

　　陽羨許彥，于綏安山行，遇一書生，年十七、八，臥路側，云腳痛，求寄鵝籠中。彥以為戲言。書生便入籠，籠亦不更廣，書生亦不更小，宛然與雙鵝並坐，鵝亦不驚。彥負籠而去，都不覺重。

　　前行息樹下，書生乃出籠，謂彥曰：「欲為君薄設。」彥曰：「善。」乃口中吐出一銅奩子，奩子中具諸餚饌，珍羞方丈。其器皿皆銅物，氣味香旨，世所罕見。酒數行，謂彥曰：「向將一婦人自隨，今欲暫邀之。」彥曰：「善。」又於口中吐一女子，年可十五、六，衣服綺麗，容貌殊絕，共坐宴。

俄而書生醉臥，此女謂彥曰：「雖與書生結妻，而實懷怨。向亦竊得一男子同行，書生既眠，暫喚之，君幸勿言。」彥曰：「善。」女子於口中吐出一男子，年可二十三、四，亦穎悟可愛，乃與彥敘寒溫。

書生臥欲覺，女子口吐一錦行障遮書生，書生乃留女子共臥。男子謂彥曰：「此女子雖有心，情亦不甚。向復竊得一女人同行，今欲暫見之，願君勿洩。」彥曰：「善。」男子又於口中吐一婦人，年可二十許，共酌戲談甚久。聞書生動聲，男子曰：「二人眠已覺。」因取所吐女人，還納口中。

須臾，書生處女乃出，謂彥曰：「書生欲起。」乃吞向男子，獨對彥坐。然後書生起，謂彥曰：「暫眠遂久，君獨坐，當悒悒邪？日又晚，當與君別。」遂吞其女子、諸器皿，悉納口中，留大銅盤，可二尺廣，與彥別，曰：「無以藉君，與君相憶也。」

彥太元中，為蘭臺令史，以盤餉侍中張散。散看其銘，題云是永平三年作。

The Extraordinary Student

Nan Chao Song Dynasty (420-479CE) Wu Jun (469-520CE) "Xu Qi Xie Ji"

Xu Yan（許彥）of Yang Xian（陽羨）hiked in the Sui An

（綏安）area and came across a student, about 17 or 18 years old, lying on the roadside saying that his feet hurt, asking to be carried in Yan's（彥）goose cage. Yan originally thought it was a joke, but still allowed the student to enter the cage. The cage did not grow in size and the student did not become smaller. The student bent over and next to the two geese, which did not seem to be bothered by the student. Yan then carried the cage without it feeling the heavy at all.

After some distance they rested under a tree. The student came out from the cage and said, "I would like to prepare some food for you." "Okay" Yan replied. The student then from his mouth spit out a lunchbox made of bronze, with various kinds of food and wine. The delicacies spread out for ten square feet with dining utensils made of bronze. The food was extraordinarily delicious, rarely seen in the world. After drinking some wine, the student said to Yan, "I have brought a girl with me and would like to invite her to come out." Yan said, "Okay." An extremely beautiful girl in a glamorous dress, around the age of 15 or 16, came out from the student's mouth and sat down to eat with them.

Soon, the student was drunk. The girl then told Yan, "Though I am married to the student, I really resent him from the bottom of my heart. I have brought a man with me, and since the student has fallen into sleep, I'd like to bring him out. I hope you won't tell my husband about this." "Okay. Yan replied. The girl then spat out an adorable, bright man about 23 or 24 years of age, who then chatted with Yan.

When the drunken student was about to wake up, the girl spat out a screen made of samite to cover the student and herself, and the two slept together behind it. The man told Yan, "Though the girl has affection for me, she is not a very sincere person; I have brought a girl with me, and now I want to have her come out. I hope you will not tell the others." Yan said, "Okay." Then the man spat out a woman about 20 some years old, and they drank, played, and chatted together for a long period of time. After hearing some movement from the student, the man said, "The two have woken up." So he swallowed down the woman he had just spat out. Soon, the girl came out from the screen, and told Yan, "The student is about to get up." Then she swallowed down the man, and sat across from Yan.

The student then got up and told Yan, "I had slept for too long and left you here alone, I assume you must be very bored. It has been rather dark, and I should say goodbye." Then he swallowed the girl, utensils and everything else. He left a big bronze plate about two feet wide and said farewell to Yan, "I have nothing to repay you for your kindness. Take this as memorabilia."

During the Tai Yuan（太元）era（376-396CE）in the Jin（晉朝）Dynasty, Yan served as an official in the Royal Library. He offered the bronze plate as a gift to Zhang San（張散）, the Emperor's advisor. San（散）looked at the inscription on the plate and found out that it was made during the age of the Ming Emperor（明帝）（28-75CE）in the Han Dynasty（漢朝）.

七、隱形人　東晉・干寶：《搜神記》卷一

　　介琰者，不知何許人也。住建安方山。從其師白羊公、杜受玄一無為之道，能變化隱形。嘗往來東海，暫過秣陵，與吳主相聞。吳主留琰，乃為琰架宮廟。一日之中，數遣人往問起居。琰或為童子，或為老翁；無所食啗，不受飼遺。

　　吳主欲學其術，琰以吳主多內御，積月不教。吳主怒，敕縛琰，著甲士引弩射之。弩發，而繩縛猶存，不知琰之所之。

The Invisible Man

Dong Jin Dynasty (317-420CE) Gan Bao（？-336CE）"Sou Shen Ji"

A man named Jie Yan（介琰）lived in Fang Shan（方山）of Jian An（建安）. He followed his masters Bai Yang Gong（白羊公）and Du（杜）, learning the ability to change his appearance and the ability to become invisible. He once went to Dong Hai（東海）passing through Mo Ling（秣陵）to visit the King of Wu（吳）. The king of Wu persuaded him to stay and built him a temple. Several times a day, the king sent servants to look after him. Sometimes Yan（琰）transformed into a child, and sometimes an old man. He ate nothing and accepted none of the gifts from the King.

The King wanted to learn his magic arts, but since the king had many concubines, for several months his request was turned down. The king was furious and ordered to have Yan tied up and shot by the palace guards. However, as the crossbow was shot, Yan disappeared though the ropes without a trace.

八、神魂顛倒　南朝 宋·劉義慶：《幽明錄》卷五

鉅鹿有龐阿者，美容儀。同郡石氏有女，曾內覩阿，心悅之。未幾，阿見此女來詣阿，阿妻極妒，聞之，使婢縛之，送還石家，中路遂化為煙氣而滅。婢乃直詣石家說此事。石氏之父大驚曰：「我女都不出門，豈可毀謗如此！」

阿婦自是常加意伺察之。居一夜，方值女在齋中，乃自拘執，以詣石氏。石氏之父見之，愕眙，曰：「我適從內來，見女與母共作，何得在此？」即令婢僕於內喚女出，向所縛者奄然滅焉。父疑有異，故遣其母詰之。女曰：「昔年龐阿來廳中，曾竊視之，自爾

彷彿即夢詣阿，及入戶，即為妻所縛。」石曰：「天下遂有此奇事！
夫精神所感，靈神為之冥著，滅者蓋其魂神也。」

　　既而女誓心不嫁。經年，<u>阿妻</u>忽得邪病，醫藥無徵，阿乃授幣
<u>石氏女</u>為妻。

Head Over Heels

Nan Chao Song Dynasty (420-479CE) Liu Yi-Qing (403-444CE) "You Ming Lu"

Pang E（龐阿）of Ju Lu（鉅鹿）was a handsome man. A girl from the same country saw him once and fell head over heels for him. Soon afterwards, E（阿）saw the girl had come to visit him. E's wife was an extremely jealous woman. When she heard of this event she sent her maids to tie the girl up, sending her back home. Halfway back, the girl turned into a wisp of smoke and disappeared. The maids came to the girl's home and told her father, who became very surprised saying, "My daughter never left the house. How could you defame her like this?"

Ever since then E's wife started keeping her eye out for the girl. One night, she came across the girl in the study room and tied the girl up on her own, taking the girl to her father. The father was astounded when he saw her, and said, "I just came from the house and saw my daughter there doing house chores with her mother. How could she be here?" He immediately asked the maids to bring out his daughter, and the girl who was tied up vanished all of the sudden. The father suspected something strange so he had his wife question their daughter. The daughter confessed saying, "There was a time when E came into the hall and I spied on him secretly. Since then, as if in a dream, I went to visit E. When I entered through the door, I was tied up by his wife..." Her father assumed, "Can there be such a thing in this world! When one is in deep love, one will find its way. Even the soul was called upon by affection and showed its figure. I suppose that the one who disappeared must be her soul."

Since then the girl swore that she would not marry. One year later, the wife of E was inflicted with a strange illness and no cure could save her. E then presented a betrothal gift and married the girl.

九、金蟬脫殼的丈夫　東晉·陶潛：《搜神後記》卷三

宋時有一人，忘其姓氏，與婦同寢。天曉，婦起出後，其夫尋亦出外。婦還，見其夫猶在被中眠。須臾，奴子自外來，云：「郎求鏡。」婦以奴詐，乃指牀上以示奴。奴云：「適從郎間來。」於

是馳白其夫。夫大愕，便入。與婦共視，被中人高枕安寢，正是其
形，了無一異。慮是其神魂，不敢驚動；乃共以手徐徐撫牀，遂冉
冉入席而滅。夫婦惋怖不已。

少時，夫忽得疾，性理乖錯，終身不癒。

Two in One

Dong Jin Dynasty (317-420CE) Tao Qian (365-427CE) "Sou Shen Hou Ji"

During the Song Dynasty（宋代）（420-479CE），a man, whose last name was unknown, slept with his wife in the same bed. In the morning his wife got up leaving the bedroom, and he followed afterwards. When his wife went back to the bedroom, she found her husband still in bed. Soon, a servant came from outside and said, "The master wants a mirror." Assuming the servant was lying, the wife pointed to her husband in bed. The servant said, "I just got back from the master." Then the wife quickly rushed to report this to her husband. He was rather astonished and came into the house, checking with his wife. The man in bed was sleeping quite peacefully and looked exactly like the husband. They did not dare to wake up the man in bed, thinking that it might be the spirit of the husband. Then the two gently rubbed the quilt, and the man in bed sank into the bed mat and disappeared. The couple became extremely terrified.

Soon, the husband sickened with a disease that made him cranky and ill-tempered, and for the rest of his life he was never cured.

主題十：醫病怪譚

Theme 10: Mystical Cures

Illness and disease are probably the major threat to mankind's existence. The Chinese characters sick（疾）、witch（巫）、medicate（醫）have appeared in Oracle bone scripts（甲骨文）over 5000 years ago, thus indicating that the treatment for illnesses have already existed and been practiced in ancient China. Throughout the world many cultures have someone responsible for treating such illnesses. In early times, cure practitioners were similar to shamons or sorcerers, and within the Chinese culture, it was believed that many forms of sickness derived from evil.

Coming along with the development of civilizations was the division between the evolution of shamans and doctors. It wasn't until the end of the Han Dynasty（漢朝）that this became distinct. However, after the Han Dynasty, during the Wei Jin Nan Bei Dynasties （魏晉南北朝）, due to the lack of the doctors and inadequate diagnosis knowledge, mystical cures were still used to treat or prevent illnesses.

Before the invention of the microscope, it was believed that viruses were groups of evil spirits similar to an army spreading throughout the world. Many thought that being able to control the virus' troops, meant being able to control illnesses or plaques. In Chinese tradition, the "Wen Shen（瘟神）God of Plaque", has the authority to allow viruses to spread or die off. Because of this, the Chinese have many folk customs involving worship and sacrifice to the God of Plaque and the use of many diverse attempts to find cures for illnesses.

Other than mysterious treatments, medications emerge in these mythical stories, such as the famous Hua Tuo（華佗）pioneering general anesthesia for surgical operations. Besides anesthesia, Hua Tuo also applies antiphlogistic on wounds to prevent inflammation. As for the use of medicinal materials, there are records of using python's gall bladder to cure eye illness, live spiders to cure stomach ache, platycodon decoction to cure rabies, even the use of white horse urine and the skull of the dead. All in all, people at that time spare no effort ruminating on how to prevent and cure illness to eliminate the threats for others. Despite ridiculous prescriptions and conjectures, the courageous attempts show a light of hope in the field of medication

一、蛇膽治眼疾　東晉·干寶：《搜神記》卷十一

顏含字宏都，次嫂樊氏，因疾失明。醫人疏方，須蚺蛇膽，而尋求備至，無由得之。含憂歎累時。

嘗畫獨坐，忽有一青衣童子，年可十三、四，持一青囊授含。含開視，乃蛇膽也。童子逡巡出戶，化成青鳥飛去。得膽藥成，嫂病即愈。

The Cure of the Python

Dong Jin Dynasty (317-420CE) Gan Bao (？-336CE) "Sou Shen Ji"

The wife of Yan Han's（顏含）second oldest brother was inflicted with an illness losing her eyesight. The prescription the doctor gave required the gall bladder of a python, which was unattainable anywhere. Han（含）worried about this for a long time.

One day while he sat alone, a boy dressed in blue around the age of 13 or 14 years old, came with a blue bag and gave it to Han. Han opened it and found the gall bladder of a python. Then the boy immediately went out the door, transformed into a blue bird, and flew away. After receiving the gall bladder, the medicine was made and his sister-in-law recovered shortly after.

二、神醫華佗動手術　東晉·干寶：《搜神記》卷三

沛國華佗，字元化，一名旉。瑯邪劉勳為河內太守，有女年幾二十，苦腳左膝裡有瘡，癢而不痛。瘡愈，數十日復發。如此七、八年。迎佗使視。佗曰：「是易治之。當得稻糠黃色犬一頭，好馬二匹。」以繩繫犬頸，使走馬牽犬，馬極輒易。計馬走三十餘里❶，犬不能行。復令步人拖曳，計向五十里。

乃以藥飲女，女即安臥，不知人。因取大刀，斷犬腹近後腳之前。以所斷之處向瘡口，令二、三寸停之。須臾，有若蛇者從瘡中出，便以鐵椎橫貫蛇頭。蛇在皮中動搖良久，須臾不動，乃牽出，長三尺許，純是蛇，但有眼處，而無瞳子，又逆鱗耳。以膏散著瘡中，七日愈。

Hua Tuo Works Miracles

Dong Jin Dynasty (317-420CE) Gan Bao (？-336CE) "Sou Shen Ji"

---

❶　里 li : The character li is a traditional Chinese measuring unit of distance. Its length is close to half a kilometer.

Hua Tuo（華佗）（145-208CE）of Pei County（沛國），nicknamed Yuan-Hua（元化）or Fu（尃），was proficient in the medical field. Another man named Liu Xun（劉勳）of Lang Ye（瑯邪）served as the magistrate of He Nei County （河內郡）. Liu's（劉）daughter, about twenty years old, suffered from a fester in her left knee that tickled but had no pain. Many days after recovering, her wound had a relapse. This pattern continued on for seven or eight years. Liu invited Hua Tuo to examine his daughter's injury. Tuo（佗）said, "This is easy to cure. It requires a yellow dog and two good horses." He then tied the dog around its neck with a rope and had the horses take turns dragged the dog while running. The horses had been reckoned to have run for more than fifteen kilometers, and the dog could no longer walk. Next, in addition he had someone drag the dog. The dog moved a total of about twenty five kilometers.

Then he gave the potion of medicine to Liu's daughter, who fell into a deep sleep after drinking it. He took a broadsword and chopped off the dog's rear leg. Then he laid the dog's wound next to the girl's at a distance of two or three inches. Shortly after, something similar to a snake crawled out from the girl's wound. He immediately thrust an awl into the head of the snake, which wriggled for a long time before stopping still. He then pulled the snake out of the wound. It had the length of sixty centimeters. It was purely a snake, but its eyes had no pupils and its scales grew in the opposite direction. He applied medicine on the wound, and the girl recovered after seven days.

三、棺材裡的矛與弓箭　東晉・干寶：《搜神記》卷三

　　信都令家，婦女驚恐，更互疾病，使輅筮之。輅曰：「君北堂西頭有兩死男子：一男持矛，一男持弓箭；頭在壁內，腳在壁外。持矛者主刺頭，故頭重痛，不得舉也；持弓箭者主射胸腹，故心中懸痛，不得飲食也。晝則浮游，夜來病人，故使驚恐也。」

　　於是掘其室中，入地八尺，果得二棺。一棺中有矛，一棺中有角弓及箭。箭久遠，木皆消爛，但有鐵及角完耳。乃徙骸骨，去城二十里❷埋之。無復疾病。

The Spell of the Coffin

Dong Jin Dynasty (317-420CE) Gan Bao (？-336CE) "Sou Shen Ji"

　　In the magistrate of Xin Du County's（信都郡）house, all the women were scared and panic-stricken, for they all got sick one after another. They had Guan Lu（管輅）to divine

---

❷　里 li：The character li is a traditional Chinese measuring unit of distance. Its length is close to half a kilometer.

about this event. Lu（輅）said, "In the west side of the north hall are two dead men. One has a spear in hand, and the other a bow and arrow. Their heads are in the wall with their feet sticking out. The one with the spear thrusts towards the head, so people feel heavy and painful headaches, not being able to lift up their heads. The one with the bow and arrow aims towards the chest and stomach, so people feel pain in their heart and are not able to eat. The two ghosts wander around during the day and make people sick in the night. This is why your family feels scared."

Then they dug up the room and found two coffins eight feet under the ground. In one coffin was a spear, and in the other a bow and arrow decorated with horns. The wooden part of the arrows had been rotten due to its antiquity, while the iron part and the horns remained. They removed the skulls of the dead men and buried them ten kilometers away from the city. They never got sick again.

四、恐怖藥方死人頭 南朝 宋·劉義慶：《幽明錄》卷四

庾宏為竟陵王府佐，家在江陵。宏令奴無患者載米餉家，未達三里，遭劫被殺，尸流泊查口村。時岸傍有文欣者，母病，醫云：「須得髑髏屑，服之即差。」欣重賞募索。有鄰婦楊氏見無患尸，因斷

頭與欣。

欣燒之，欲去皮肉，經三日夜不焦，眼角張轉。欣雖異之，猶惜不棄。因刮耳頰骨與母服之，即覺骨停喉中，經七日而卒。尋而楊氏得疾，通身洪腫，形如牛馬。見無患頭來罵云：「善惡之報，其能免乎？」楊氏以語兒，言終而卒。

Deadly Prescription

Nan Chao Song Dynasty (420-479CE) Liu Yi-Qing (403-444CE) "You Ming Lu"

Yu Hong（庚宏）, a subordinate of Duke Jing Ling（竟陵王）, lived in Jiang Ling（江陵）. He sent his servant, Wu-Huan（無患）, to take rice back to his home. When he only had three kilometers left in his journey, Wu-Huan was robbed and murdered. His body drifted down the river to Cha Kou village（查口村）. By the shore lived a man named Wen Xin（文欣）, whose mother was sick and was told by the doctor that she needed the minced skull of a dead man to cure the illness. Xin（欣）offered a heavy reward for the skull. His neighbor, Mrs. Yang,（楊）saw the body of Wu-Huan and cut off the head to give to Xin.

Xin burnt the skull, hoping to remove the flesh and meat. After being cooked for three days and three nights, the head still would not burn and its eyes could still open and roll. Even though Xin felt this was strange, he was reluctant to give up. Then he cut off the flesh near the ear and cheek and gave it to his mother. As soon as his mother swallowed it, she felt as if a bone was stuck in her throat, and died after seven days. Soon after, Mrs. Yang also fell sick and her body swelled up like a horse or cow. She saw the head of Wu-Huan come scolding her saying, "You can never escape karma and punitive judgment." Mrs. Yang told her son what happened and died right after.

五、馬尿與鱉的病理實驗

東晉・陶潛：《搜神後記》卷三

　　昔有一人，與奴同時得腹瘕病，治不能愈。奴既死，乃剖腹視之，得一白鱉，赤眼，甚鮮明。乃試以諸毒藥澆灌之，并內藥於鱉口，悉無損動。乃繫鱉於牀腳。

　　忽有一客來看之，乘一白馬。既而馬溺濺鱉，鱉乃惶駭，欲疾走避溺，因繫之不得去，乃縮藏頭頸足焉。病者察之，謂其子曰：「吾病或可以救矣。」乃試取白馬溺以灌鱉上，須臾，便消成數升水。病者乃頓服升餘白馬溺，病豁然愈。

The Horse That Brought Hope

Dong Jin Dynasty (317-420CE) Tao Qian (365-427CE) "Sou Shen Hou Ji"

A long time ago, a man and his servant were inflicted with a disease that caused a tumor in the stomach and could not be cured. After his servant died, the man cut open his servant's stomach to examine it and found a white soft-shell turtle with bright red eyeballs. Then he tried to kill the turtle by feeding it many kinds of poison, however the turtle was not affected at all. Then he tied the turtle to the foot of the bed.

All of the sudden, a guest riding a white horse came to visit him. Then the white horse peed on the floor and the urine splashed the turtle. The turtle became very scared and wanted to elude the urine, but was not able to being tied up. Then the turtle drew back its head, neck, and feet. The man with the illness observed the turtle's reaction and told his son, "Maybe I can be cured." Then he tried sprinkling the white horse's urine on the turtle, and after a while, the turtle dissolved into water. The man then drank more than one liter of urine from the white horse, and recovered shortly after.

主題十一：異形現身記

Theme 11: Stories of Exorcism

Why do spirits appear? Where do they come from? Are they ominous or suggesting good fortune? How can we identify spirits in order to subjugate or exorcize them? These questions, along with their answers are the foundation of this theme.

The origin of spirits lies between two concepts; one is that the sequence of the Five Elements is out of order, and the other comes from the concept of an object turning into a monster after living for a long period of time. Chinese traditional philosophers believe that "Qi"(氣)is the composing element of the universe, and "Qi" consists of the five elements: wood, fire, earth, metal, and water, which are the so-called "Wu-Xing."（五行）"Qi" is in the state of motion and thus generates the changes of aggregation and dispersion. The objects form because of the aggregation of "Qi," yet when Qi disperses, an objects appearance may vanish while it's "Qi" continues to recycle. From the aspect of circulation of "Qi" which composes the universe, the objects have the features of exchanging and interacting with each other. Moreover, due to the constant movement of "Qi", the objects also keep on changing and influencing others.

Under normal circumstances, every object has their own Qi and it runs regularly and harmoniously. Yet when the movement of Qi becomes irregular, or when an object lives too long, an unusual phenomenon occurs. These evil spirits that have lived for a long time mostly are malicious to humans. To vanquish these spirits requires courage to fight them directly, or relies on Taoist rituals, incantation, or ceremonial instruments to drive out evil spirits. The steps of subjugating spirits or demons include locating, unveiling, exorcizing or killing them.

In the rituals of either wizardry or religions, exorcism technically seems to be strange or deliberately mystifying. Yet in the deeper cultural connotation, people trying to perform different kinds of magical behavior may not necessarily be the result from their ignorance or arrogance; instead, it may be that people are trying to transcend the limits of human powers and conquer weakness and fear. The process of exorcism is both a horrifying and rejoicing experience, for all the participants long for a salvation from this suffering.

"Evil Spirits" may be a conjecture originating from the fear of unknown danger. Therefore once there is fear in the world, the imagination of "evil" becomes prevalent among people. For ordinary people, one method to overcome evil spirits is to stay calm and be courageous, or in addition, some may hire an outside priest to perform special rituals in order to regain one's peace. As far as whether or not exorcism practices are truly authentic, the answer relies on the perspective of observers.

一、套話捉妖計　東晉・干寶：《搜神記》卷十八

安陽城南有一亭，夜不可宿，宿輒殺人。書生明術數，乃過宿之。亭民曰：「此不可宿！前後宿此，未有活者。」書生曰：「無苦也。吾自能諧。」遂住廨舍，乃端坐誦書，良久乃休。

夜半後，有一人，著皂單衣，來往戶外，呼「亭主！」，亭主應諾，「見亭中有人耶？」答曰：「向者有一書生，在此讀書。適休，似未寢。」乃喑嗟而去。須臾，復有一人，冠赤幘者，呼「亭主！」，問答如前，復喑嗟而去。既去，寂然。

書生知無來者，即起，詣向者呼處，效呼「亭主！」。亭主亦應諾。復云：「亭中有人耶？」亭主答如前。乃問曰：「向黑衣來者誰？」曰：「北舍母豬也。」又曰：「冠赤幘來者誰？」曰：「西舍

老雄雞父也。」曰:「汝復誰耶?」曰:「我是老蝎也。」於是書生密,便誦書至明,不敢寐。

天明,亭民來視,驚曰:「君何得獨活?!」書生曰:「促索劍來!吾與卿取魅。」乃握劍至昨夜應處,果得老蝎,大如琵琶,毒長數尺。西舍得老雄雞父。北舍得老母豬。凡殺三物,亭毒遂靜,永無災橫。

The Imitator

Dong Jin Dynasty (317-420CE) Gan Bao (?-336CE) "Sou Shen Ji"

On the south side of An Yang (安陽) city stood a lodge where no one would stay for the night; if anyone did, he or she would end up murdered. One student proficient in Daoist techniques, came to seek accommodation in the lodge, but was refused by the lodge manager who said, "You can not stay over night. No one has survived after staying one night in this lodge." The student said, "Don't worry about it. I have a solution." He then stayed in the guest room and read for a long time before going to bed.

After midnight, a man in a long black robe came to the outside of the lodge, calling for the host. The host replied, and the man in the black robe said, "Have you seen who is staying in the lodge?" The host said, "There is a student reading here.

He just went to bed but has not fallen asleep yet." Then the man in the black robe sighed and left. Soon a man wearing a red bandana came and asked the same question as the man in black robe. The host gave him the exact same answer as before, and the man with the red bandana sighed and left. After leaving the night was silent.

The student knew that no one else would come, so he came to the area where the previous two men were and imitated them calling for the host. The host replied, and the student said, "Is there anyone staying in the lodge?" The host replied with the same answer as before. The student continued to ask, "Who was the man in the black robe?" The host said, "He's the sow in the north side of the guest room." "What about the one with the red bandana?" "He's the old rooster in the west side of the guest room," the host answered. The student then asked, "And who are you exactly?" "I am an old scorpion," the host replied. Then the student became quiet, and instead of going to bed, he read until morning arrived.

As the sun rose the lodge manager became surprised, "How did you survive?" The student said, "Find me a sword quickly. We have to catch the beasts together." Then the student, with a sword in his hand, went to where he was talking with the host the previous night and caught the old scorpion, which was as big as a pipa ❶ with an extremely long tail. He then went to the west side of the lodge to catch the old rooster, and then to the north side to catch the sow. After killing the three beasts, there were no more disasters in the lodge.

二、布袋收狐妖　東晉・干寶：《搜神記》卷三

韓友字景先，盧江舒人也。善占卜，亦行京房厭勝之術。劉世則女病魅積年，巫為攻禱，伐空冢故城間，得狸、鼉數十，病猶不差。

友筮之，命作布囊，俟女發時，張囊著窗牖間。友閉戶作氣，若有所驅。須臾間，見囊大脹，如吹，因決敗之。女仍大發。

友乃更作皮囊二枚，沓張之，施張如前，囊復脹滿。因急縛囊口，懸著樹，二十許日，漸消。開視，有二斤狐毛。女病遂差。

The Exorcism Bags

Dong Jin Dynasty (317-420CE) Gan Bao（？-336CE)"Sou Shen Ji"

　　Han You（韓友）of Lu Jiang（盧江）was good at divination, as well as the Jing Fang（京房）（77-37BCE）School's exorcism

---

❶　琵琶 pipa: A kind of stringed musical instrument similar to a lute.

techniques. The daughter of Liu Shi Ze（劉世則）had been suffering for years from being possessed by evil spirits. Her father had a wizard hold a ritual to exorcise her in a graveyard in an abandoned town. The wizard expelled more than ten foxes and Chinese alligators. Yet she was not cured.

You（友）divined for her and had someone make a fabric bag. When the girl's spirit was possessed, he set the bag by the window-side. He closed all the doors and windows, and waved his hands in the air as if driving something away. He watched as the bag swelled up as if being inflated with air. Then the bag exploded and the girl became more enraged.

You then used two other leather bags as a double layer and put them by the window-side just like before. Once again the bags swelled up and he quickly tied up the opening and hung the bags on a tree. After twenty-some days, the bags gradually shrank in size. When he opened the bags, he found three kilograms of fox hair. The girl was then cured.

三、捉妖達人　東晉・干寶：《搜神記》卷二

　　壽光侯者，漢章帝時人也。能劾百鬼眾魅，令自縛見形。其鄉人有婦為魅所病，侯為劾之，得大蛇數丈，死於門外；婦因以安。又有大樹，樹有精，人止其下者死，鳥過之亦墜。侯劾之，樹盛夏

枯落，有大蛇長七、八丈，懸死樹間。

　　章帝聞之，徵問，對曰：「有之。」帝曰：「殿下有怪，夜半後，常有數人，絳衣披髮，持火相隨。豈能劾之？」侯曰：「此小怪，易消耳。」帝偽使三人為之。侯乃設法，三人登時仆地無氣。帝驚曰：「非魅也！朕相試耳。」即使解之。

The Master Exorcist

Dong Jin Dynasty (317-420CE) Gan Bao (？-336CE) "Sou Shen Ji"

During the Han Dynasty（漢朝）（202BCE-220CE）, a man called Shou Guang-Hou（壽光侯）was able to perform the arts of exorcism, and order evil spirits to tie themselves up and appear. The wife of a man from Hou's（侯）hometown was possessed by an evil spirit. Hou performed an exorcism on her, capturing a snake which was several meters long. He killed the snake outside their house, and the woman became peaceful and well. In addition there was a tree with spirits. Anyone who stopped under the tree would end up dead, even birds flying by would fall to their death. Hou exorcised the tree during midsummer, and the tree dried and withered, and a snake more than fifteen meters long hung on the tree and dead.

The Emperor Zhang（章帝）（58-88.CE）heard rumors of

Hou and called upon him for inquiry. Hou replied to the Emperor saying the stories were all true. The Emperor then said, "There are demons in the palace. After midnight, there are often several people dressed in red with hair in disarray, holding torches while following each other one by one. Are you able to subdue them?" Hou answered, "These are small demons and are easy to deal with." The Emperor then ordered three people to disguise themselves as the demons. Hou set an altar and practiced magic there. The three immediately fell to the ground breathless. Shocked, the Emperor said, "They are not ghosts! I just wanted to test your magic abilities." Then he ordered Hou to release them at once.

四、新娘中邪了　　南朝　宋·劉義慶：《幽明錄》卷五

宋高祖永初中，張春為武昌太守，時有人嫁女，未及升車，忽便失性。出外毆擊人乘，云己不樂嫁俗人。巫云是邪魅，乃將女至江際，擊鼓，以術祝治療。

春以為欺惑百姓，刻期須得妖魅。後有一青蛇來到巫所，即以大釘釘頭。至日中，復見大龜從江來，伏前。更以赤朱書背作符，更遣去入江。至暮，有大白鼉從江中出，乍沈乍浮，向龜隨後催逼。鼉自分死，冒未先入幔與女辭決。女慟哭，云失其姻好。自此漸差。

或問巫曰：「魅者歸于何物？」巫云：「蛇是傳通，龜是媒人，

鼉是其對。所獲三物，悉是魅。」春始知靈驗。

The Possessed Bride

Nan Chao Song Dynasty (420-479CE) Liu Yi-Qing (403-444CE) "You Ming Lu"

During the Song Dynasty（宋代）（420-479CE）, Zhang Chun（張春）served as chief magistrate of Wu Chang County （武昌郡）. There was a family whose daughter was about to marry. When the daughter was ready to enter the carriage, she lost her senses and attacked the people outside saying that she didn't want to marry an ordinary man. The sorcerer believed that she was affected by some evil spirit, and took her to the riverside. He beat a drum and cured her with his sorcery.

Chun（春）thought the sorcerer was cheating the common people, so he demanded the sorcerer to catch the demon within a limited period of time. Then a green snake crawled out and the sorcerer instantly ran a big nail through its head. At noon, a giant turtle emerged from the river and rested on the ground. The sorcerer then wrote a spell on the turtle's back with red ink and drove it back into the river. When night fell, a giant white alligator came from the center of the river, bobbing up and down, with the turtle chasing after it. The alligator assumed it was going to die, so it crawled and ventured into the tent to bid farewell with the daughter. The daughter was heart-broken and cried that she had lost her good husband. Since then her condition improved.

Some asked the sorcerer, "Which beast was the evil spirit?" The sorcerer said, "The snake was a messenger, the turtle a matchmaker, and the alligator was her match. The three creatures were all evil spirits." It was then that Chung realized that the sorcery was effective.

主題十二：感天動地

Theme 12: Touching the Heavens and Earth

Stories in this theme feature extraordinary reactions of human beings' when encountered by undesired misfortune. The sources of detriment are triggered by natural disasters, war, bandits, governmental issues, the Emperor's order and the threat from wild animals. Therefore, characters in this theme's stories are forced to face a terrible fate of death, some being sacrificed in order to conquer the threat of survival for themselves or for the community, and through their courage along with strategic maneuvers are able to overcome the crisis at hand and gain back their opportunity of life. In most situations common people, when faced with these extremities, are overwhelmed and unable to change the obvious outcome. However, because of their strong persistence the heavens and the earth were deeply moved and come to aid and assist the characters after their death.

The stories in this theme also touch base on the legends of iron-smelting in ancient China. While iron is abundant underneath the earth, it exists naturally in the form of mineral instead of metal. The history of iron-smelting in China dates back to 600 BCE, which is two thousand years earlier than other countries thanks to its suitable quality and better furnaces. Legend has it that Mo-Ye （莫邪）, the wife of Gan-Jiang （干將）, jumped into a boiling furnace to increase the temperature of it, which has successfully improved the technology of iron-smelting. Due to its finer sharpness and fortitude, ironware replaced bronze as weapons. Therefore, Gan Jiang's execution was probably not the result of his delayed delivery of the swords, but rather the Emperor's fear of the forging techniques being leaked to other nations.

The story of the virtuous widow Zhou Qing （周青） epitomizes the injustice existing at that time. As a widow, she is the lowest of minorities and is accused of murdering her mother-in-law, who is unable to bear the suffering of her illness and decides to commit suicide. Before the execution of Zhou Qing, she vehemently curses god, the earth, and local people. Her tragic misfortune has moved the heaven and her innocence is eventually vindicated by a blizzard as a sign of the heaven's sympathy. Writer Guan Han Qing 關漢卿 （1210？-1300？CE）of Yun Dynasty（元朝）（1271-1368CE） produced a masterpiece called "The Injustice to Dou E"（竇娥 冤）based on the story of Zhou Qing. The play was translated into French one hundred years ago and was spread throughout Europe. "Snow in June"（六月雪）is one of the famous Chinese opera's based on this story.

一、彭娥走山　南朝 宋·劉義慶：《幽明錄》卷二

晉永嘉之亂，郡縣無定主，強弱相暴。宜陽縣有女子，姓彭，名娥，父母昆弟十餘口，為長沙賊所攻。時娥負器出汲於溪，聞賊至，走還。正見塢壁已破，不勝其哀，與賊相格。賊縛娥驅出溪邊，將殺之。

溪際有大山，石壁高數十丈，娥仰天呼曰：「皇天寧有神不？我為何罪，而當如此！」因走向山，山立開，廣數丈，平路如砥。群賊亦逐娥入山，山遂隱合，泯然如初，賊皆壓死山裡，頭出山外。

娥遂隱不復出。娥所捨汲器化為石，形似雞，土人因號曰石雞山，其水為娥潭。

Peng E and the Landslide

Nan Chao Song Dynasty (420-479CE) Liu Yi-Qing (403-444CE)
"You Ming Lu"

During the Yong Jia Rebellion（永嘉之亂）(307-312CE), there were no consistent officials governing in the counties, so the strong and the fierce bullied the small and weak. In Yi Yang County（宜陽縣）was a woman named Peng E（彭娥）. Her family of over ten people had all been killed by bandits from Chang Sha（長沙）. At the time of the murder, E（娥）was taking a container to the stream to collect water. When she heard the bandits arrive, she ran back home immediately. As she returned she found the wall surrounding the village had already been breached. Unable to restrain her grief, she fought with the bandits, who trussed her up and took her to the bank of the stream in an attempt to kill her.

There was a mountain by the stream with a cliff more than one hundred meters high. E shouted up to the heavens, "Is there any justice? What wrong have I done to deserve such torment?" Then she ran quickly towards the cliff, which immediately split several meters wide, and a smooth road opened in front of her. The bandits followed E through the split in the cliff of the mountain walls. The walls closed together and the bandits were all crushed in the cliff, with their heads sticking out.

E then hid in the mountain and never came out again. The container she carried turned to stone having the shape similar to a rooster. The locals then called the mountain "Stone Rooster Mountain,"（石雞山）and its lake was named "E Pool"（娥潭）.

二、無頭將軍的笑傲告別

東晉・干寶：《搜神記》卷十一

漢武時，蒼梧賈雍為豫章太守，有神術。出界討賊，為賊所殺，失頭，上馬回，營中咸走來視雍。雍胸中語曰：「戰不利，為賊所傷。諸君視有頭佳乎？無頭佳乎？」吏涕泣曰：「有頭佳。」雍曰：「不然，無頭亦佳。」言畢，遂死。

The General's Dignified Farewell

Dong Jin Dynasty (317-420CE) Gan Bao (？-336CE) "Sou Shen Ji"

During the Han Dynasty（漢朝）(202B.C.E-220CE), Jia Yong（賈雍）of Cang Wu（蒼梧）served as the chief magistrate of Yu Zhang（豫章）. He had extraordinary abilities. On a punitive expedition across the country's boarder to capture rebels, Yong（雍）was killed and lost his head; yet still, he mounted his horse and returned to camp headless. All the soldiers in the camp came to see Yong. Yong spoke from his chest saying, "The battle is not going well. I have been hurt severely by the rebels. Soldiers! Is it better to have a head, or is it better without?" The soldiers cried out, "It is better to have a head." "No, it is good to be without a head," said Yong, who died instantly.

三、干將莫邪與俠客　東晉・干寶：《搜神記》卷十一

　　<u>楚干將莫邪</u>為楚王作劍，三年乃成。王怒，欲殺之。劍有雌雄。其妻重身當產，夫語妻曰：「吾為王作劍，三年乃成。王怒，往必殺我。汝若生子是男，大，告之曰：『出戶望南山，松生石上，劍在其背。』」於是即將雌劍，往見<u>楚王</u>。王大怒，使相之：「劍有二，一雄一雌。雌來，雄不來。」王怒，即殺之。

　　<u>莫邪</u>子名<u>赤比</u>，後壯，乃問其母曰：「吾父所在？」母曰：「汝父為<u>楚王</u>作劍，三年乃成。王怒，殺之。去時囑我：『語汝子：出戶望南山，松生石上，劍在其背。』」於是子出戶南望，不見有山，

但覩堂前松柱下，石砥之上，即以斧破其背，得劍。日夜思欲報楚王。

王夢見一兒，眉間廣尺，言：「欲報讎！」王即購之千金。兒聞之，亡去。入山行歌。客有逢者，謂：「子年少，何哭之甚悲耶？」曰：「吾干將莫邪子也。楚王殺吾父，吾欲報之！」客曰：「聞王購子頭千金，將子頭與劍來，為子報之。」兒曰：「幸甚！」即自刎，兩手捧頭及劍奉之，立僵。客曰：「不負子也。」於是屍乃仆。

客持頭往見楚王，王大喜。客曰：「此乃勇士頭也！當於湯鑊煮之。」王如其言。煮頭三日三夕，不爛。頭踔出湯中，瞋目大怒。客曰：「此兒頭不爛，願王自往臨視之，是必爛也。」王即臨之。客以劍擬王，王頭隨墮湯中。客亦自擬己頭，頭復墮湯中。三首俱爛，不可識別。乃分其湯肉葬之，故通名「三王墓」。今在汝南北宜春縣界。

The Legend of Gan-Jiang Mo-Ye and the Knight

Dong Jin Dynasty (317-420CE) Gan Bao（？-336CE）"Sou Shen Ji"

Gan-Jiang Mo-Ye（干將莫邪）took three years to forge swords for the King of Chu（楚）. The king was furious at the delay and intended to kill him. At that time, Gan-Jiang's wife, was about to give birth, so Gan-Jiang told her "I took three years to make swords for the king. He is angry with that and will kill me when I approach him. If you give birth to a boy, tell him after he grows up, 'Stand outside the house and look at the southern hill, where there is a pine tree growing on a rock, a sword is on its back.'" Then Gan-Jiang took the female sword to the king. The king flew into a rage and had the sword examined. The man examining the sword said, "There are two swords, one male and the other female. The female sword is here, yet the male sword is not." The king was angry so he killed Gang- Jiang.

Mo-Ye's son was named Chi-Bi（赤比）. After he grew up, he asked his mother, "Where is my father?" "Your father had made swords for the king, spending three years to forge them. The king was angry with that and killed him. Your father urged me to tell you, 'Stand outside the house and look at the southern hill, where there is a pine tree growing on a rock, a sword is on its back.'"She answered him. However, the son didn't see any mountain when he looked out from the house, but he saw that there was a column made of pinewood with a whetstone in front of the hall. He chopped down the column with an axe and retained the sword. Day and night he thirsted to take revenge on the king.

The king had a dream of a broad-foreheaded boy telling him, "I shall have revenge!" Therefore, the king then offered a bounty of one thousand units of gold for the boy's head. When

Chi-Bi heard this, he ran away and hid in the mountains. A knight passed, hearing Chi-Bi wail grievously and said, "You are so young. Why do you cry with so much sorrow?" Chi-Bi replied, "I am the son of Gan-Jiang Mo-Ye. The king of Chu killed my father. I want to take revenge for his death." The knight said, "I have heard that the king offered an award for your head. Turn over your head and sword and I will help you take revenge on your father's death." Chi-Bi then accepted saying, "I am blessed," and took his own life. He handed his head and sword to the knight and stood there still. The knight told him, "I won't fail you." Then Chi-Bi's body fell to the ground.

The knight took the head to the king of Chu. The king was full of joy. The knight said, "This is a head of a brave man, you should cook it with a wok." The king did so, but the head wouldn't soften after three days of cooking. It often leaped out from the boiling water and stared at the king furiously. The knight told the king, "In order for the head to soften you must come to look at him in person." Then the king immediately went to inspect, and the knight sliced the king's head which dropped into the wok. Then the knight also sliced his own head into the wok. In the end, the three heads were all boiled down and couldn't be recognized at all. The remains in the wok were buried at the Grave of the Three Kings (三王墓),

which is now at the border of Yi Chun County（宜春縣）, the
north of Ru Nan（汝南）.

四、少女英雄斬巨蟒　　東晉・干寶：《搜神記》卷十九

　　東越閩中，有庸嶺，高數十里。其西北隰中，有大蛇，長七、
八丈，大十餘圍，土俗常病。東冶都尉及屬城長吏，多有死者。祭
以牛羊，故不得福。或與人夢，或下諭巫祝，欲得啗童女十二、三
者。都尉令長，並共患之。然氣屬不息。共請求人家生婢子，兼有

罪家女養之。至八月朝祭，送蛇穴口。蛇出，吞嚙之。累年如此，已用九女。

爾時預復募索，未得其女。將樂縣李誕家，有六女，無男，其小女名寄，應募欲行，父母不聽。寄曰：「父母無相，惟生六女，無有一男，雖有如無。女無緹縈濟父母之功，既不能供養，徒費衣食，生無所益，不如早死。賣寄之身，可得少錢，以供父母，豈不善耶？」父母慈憐，終不聽去。寄自潛行，不可禁止。

寄乃告請好劍及咋蛇犬。至八月朝，便詣廟中坐。懷劍，將犬。先將數石米餈，用蜜麨灌之，以置穴口。蛇便出，頭大如囷，目如二尺鏡。聞餈香氣，先啗食之。寄便放犬，犬就嚙咋，寄從後斫得數創。瘡痛急，蛇因踊出，至庭而死。寄入視穴，得其九女髑髏，悉舉出，詫言曰：「汝曹怯弱，為蛇所食，甚可哀愍。」於是寄女緩步而歸。

越王聞之，聘寄女為后，拜其父為將樂令，母及姊皆有賞賜。自是東冶無復妖邪之物。其歌謠至今存焉。

The Heroine that Killed the Python

Dong Jin Dynasty (317-420CE) Gan Bao (？-336CE) "Sou Shen Ji"

Around the central area of Min（閩）in Dong Yue（東越）was a tall mountain called Yong Mountain（庸嶺）. The northwest side of the mountain had a swamp where there lived an anaconda that was 15-16 meters in length. The local residents feared this anaconda seriously. Many officials died of disease, so they offered cattle and lamb as a sacrifice to the anaconda to avoid disasters. However, this was all done in vain. The anaconda then expressed his desire of eating twelve or thirteen year old virgins through messages in common people's dreams, or by communicating with a sorcerer. The officials were very concerned, and the plague was not suppressed yet. So they recruited and raised the girls of the servant maids and criminals to offer to the anaconda. In the beginning of August, the girl was sent to the cave of the anaconda as a sacrifice. The anaconda crawled out from the cave and swallowed the girl down. They followed this method to offer sacrifice to the anaconda every year, and there had been nine girls who were sacrificed.

When time came to recruit more girls, there weren't any available for sacrifice. Li Dan (李誕) of Jiang Le County (將樂縣) had six daughters but no son. The youngest daughter named Li Ji (李寄), was recruited and ready to set out, however, her parents would not let her go. The girl said to her parents, "Our household environment is no good, my parents only giving birth to six daughters and no sons. Although being here, I have no provisions for the family. I am not able save my father away from sufferings like Ti Ying（緹縈）❶ , nor could I care after my parents. I just waste the food and clothing and would rather die early. If I were to be sold we could gain some money for provision. Wouldn't that be great?" Ji's（寄）parents cherished her and could not let her go no matter what.

Ji then acted secretly and left without her parents able to do anything about it. She sought for a sharp sword and a dog that could bite snakes. In the beginning of August, Ji went and sat at the altar in front of the cave with a sword and the dog. She made a huge rice ball weighing almost one hundred kilograms, filled with honey, and placed it outside of the cave. The anaconda then crawled out from the cave. Its head was as big as a barn, and its eyes were like a mirror that was fifty centimeters in diameter. It smelled the aroma of the rice ball and started to swallow it down. After the anaconda ate, Ji sent the dog out, which sprung at the anaconda and snapped at it. Ji then followed behind and slashed the anaconda with great strength. The anaconda was seriously injured and in extreme pain. It twisted around on the ground, jumped out from the

---

❶ 緹縈 Ti Ying : A famous daughter from the Han Dynasty who practiced filial piety. She devoted herself to be a slave in order to reduce her father's punishment.

cave landing front of the altar, and died. Ji went into the cave and found the skull of the nine girls sacrificed previously. She moved the skull out and sighed, "You are too wimpy, and that's why you got eaten by the anaconda. What a pity." Then she took her time walking back home.

The king of Dong Yue heard about this event and married Ji, who became queen, and her father became the magistrate of Jiang Le County, while her mother and sisters were also rewarded. After that, no monster ever appeared in the Dong Yue area. Songs sung of the girl are still being passed down to this day.

五、孝婦行刑前的詛咒　東晉‧干寶：《搜神記》卷十一

漢時，東海孝婦養姑甚謹。姑曰：「婦養我勤苦，我已老，何惜餘年，久累年少。」遂自縊死。其女告官云：「婦殺我母！」官收繫之，拷掠毒治。孝婦不堪苦楚，自誣服之。時于公為獄史，曰：「此婦養姑十餘年，以孝聞徹，必不殺也。」太守不聽。于公爭不得理，抱其獄詞，哭於府而去。

自後郡中枯旱，三年不雨。後太守至，于公曰：「孝婦不當死，前太守枉殺之，咎當在此。」太守即時身祭孝婦冢，因表其墓。天立雨，歲大熟。

　　長老傳云：「孝婦名<u>周青</u>。<u>青</u>將死，車載十丈竹竿，以懸五旛，立誓於眾曰：『<u>青</u>若有罪，願殺，血當順下；<u>青</u>若枉死，血當逆流！』既行刑已，其血青黃，緣旛竹而上標，又緣旛而下云。」

Curse of the Filial Widow

Dong Jin Dynasty (317-420CE) Gan Bao (？-336CE) "Sou Shen Ji"

　　During the Han Dynasty（漢朝）（202BCE-220CE），a married woman conformed to filial piety ❷ devoted herself into taking care of her mother-in-law. Yet her mother-in-law thought to herself, "It has been toilsome for my daughter-in-law to take care of me. I am old now. Why should those few remaining days of my life become the burden of the young?" Then she hung herself and committed suicide. The mother-in-law's daughter filed a lawsuit against the daughter-in-law, accusing her of murdering her mother. The daughter-in-law was then taken into custody and tortured by officials in order to get her to confess her crime. She couldn't bear the torment so she confessed to murdering her mother-in-law. At the time, a law officer named Yu（于）said, "This widow has been taking care of her mother-in-law for

---

❷ 孝順 Filial Piety：A form of etiquette in which a child must show respect, obedience, and well treatment towards their parents.

more than ten years. Her virtue of filial piety is publicly known. She would never kill her mother-in-law." The chief magistrate did not accept his argument. Failing to appeal for the wife, Yu carried her confession and left the office in bitter tears.

From then on there was a drought in the county. For three consecutive years not a single raindrop fell. Then the succeeding chief magistrate arrived in the county, and Yu said, "A wife of filial piety should not have been executed. The former chief magistrate wrongly accused her. This is probably the reason that we have a drought!" The chief magistrate then went to the widow's tomb to offer a sacrifice at once, and established a statue representing her filial piety and proving her innocence. It started to rain immediately, and the locals received a large harvest at the end of the year.

The elders used to say, "When the widow Zhou Qing （周青）was about to be executed, on the prisoner's chariot carried a ten-meter-tall bamboo stick that hung five flags ❸ on it. The wife vowed in front of the public announcing, 'If I am guilty, I am willing to die, and my blood will drip down along my body. Yet if I am wronged, my blood will flow in the opposite direction.' And after she was executed, her blood, which was

---

❸ 旛 Fan：Flags used to summon on the spirit of the dead.

blue and yellow, flowed up the flagstick to its top and dripped down along the flag."

主題十三：幽明即時通

Theme 13: Messages Through Dreams

Just like grass which sprouts in the spring and withers in the winter, human beings also conform to this natural cycle of life and death; however, humans unlike plants are overcome by affections and attachments to our loved ones when faced with death. Once someone dies, their family and friends may not be able to recover from the pain of losing a beloved one. The living cannot let go of the dead, while the dead, full of regret, are helplessly distraught. Thus the wishes of the dead can only be carried out by the living, relying on passing messages through dreams. Meanwhile, the living are also concerned about the dead, worrying about their situation after death. Upon another's death, the imagination and thoughts of coldness, hunger, incarceration, darkness, dampness, and pain come naturally to the mind of the living, which make them believe that the dead are in need of their help. Such extraordinary messages appear under this mental state.

Stories in this theme feature the extraordinary communication through dreams among the living and the dead. Most of the messages are from the dead asking their living family or friends for help. Some messages are from the dead sending their news of death and the funeral date, and other messages are used to inform the living of thoughts left unsaid. In rare situations, some messages are warnings from the dead of the livings invasions towards them.

When death falls upon one, through this kind of communication, both the dead and the living may be able to fulfill their duties of human relations, making amend for the lost and continuing on with their lives.

一、結髮認屍　　南朝 宋·劉義慶:《幽明錄》卷三

　　<u>晉太元</u>初,<u>符堅</u>遣將<u>楊安</u>侵<u>襄陽</u>。其一人於軍中亡,有同鄉人扶喪歸,明日當到家。死者夜與婦夢曰:「所送者非我尸。倉樂面下者是也。汝昔為我作結髮猶存,可解看便知。」

　　迨明日,送喪者果至。婦語母如此,母不然之。婦自至<u>南豐</u>,細檢他家尸,髮如先,分明是其手迹。

Search of the Braids

Nan Chao Song Dynasty (420-479CE) Liu Yi-Qing (403-444CE)
"You Ming Lu"

During the Jin Dynasty（晉朝）（265-420CE）, in the Qin Kingdom（秦國）（350-394CE）King Fu Jian（苻堅）（338-385CE）sent his general, Yang An（楊安）, to invade Xian Yang（襄陽）. One soldier died during the war. His body was carried by his fellow townspeople headed towards home.

The night before arrival, the dead man told his wife in her dream, "The body carried back is not mine. The body under the ship deck is. The braids you made for me are still intact and you can untie them to check." The next day, the body carried had arrived just as expected. His wife told her mother-in-law about her dream the night before, yet her mother-in-law did not agree with her.

His wife then went to Nan Feng（南豐）herself, carefully examining other bodies for her mate and finally came across one with hair braids exactly as the ones she had made for her husband.

二、幫鬼搬家　東晉‧干寶：《搜神記》卷十六

　　漢南陽文穎，字叔長，建安中為甘陵府丞。過界止宿，夜三鼓時，夢見一人跪前，曰：「昔我先人，葬我於此，水來淊墓，棺木溺，漬水處半，然無以自溫。聞君在此，故來相依。欲屈明日暫住須臾，幸為相遷高燥處。」鬼披衣示穎，而皆沾濕。穎心愴然，即寤，語諸左右，曰：「夢為虛耳，亦何足怪！」

　　穎乃還眠。向寐復夢見，謂穎曰：「我以窮苦告君，奈何不相愍悼乎？」穎夢中問曰：「子為誰？」對曰：「吾本趙人，今屬汪芒氏之神。」穎曰：「子棺今何所在？」對曰：「近在君帳北十數步，水側枯楊樹下，即是吾也。天將明，不復得見，君必念之！」穎答曰：「諾。」忽然便寤。

　　天明可發，穎曰：「雖云夢不足怪，此何太適！」左右曰：「亦何惜須臾，不驗之耶？」穎即起，率十數人將導，順水上，果得一枯楊，曰：「是矣。」掘其下，未幾，果得棺。棺甚朽壞，半沒水中。穎謂左右曰：「向聞於人，謂之虛矣。世俗所傳，不可無驗。」為移其棺，葬之而去。

Moving the Dead

Dong Jin Dynasty (317-420CE) Gan Bao (？-336CE) "Sou Shen Ji"

During the Han Dynasty（漢朝）（202BCE-220CE），Wen Ying（文穎）from Nan Yang（南陽）served as an official of Gan

Ling County（甘陵郡）. When he traveled to the border of the county, he stopped to set up camp for the evening. At midnight, he dreamt of a man kneeling down in front of him saying, "I was buried here by my family, however, water has eroded my tomb and the coffin is sitting halfway in the water. I am not able to keep warm. I heard that you are around, so I come to you in reliance. Would you please temporarily wait to leave, and tomorrow help move me to a higher-elevated, dryer area?" The ghost raised its clothes up, showing that they were all soaked. Ying(穎)felt sad for the ghost so and woke up from his dream. He told his retinue about his dream, yet they replied, "Dreams are not real. There is no need to feel bewildered?" Ying then went back to bed.

Just as he fell asleep, the ghost told Ying, "I have explained my difficulties with you, why don't you have sympathy for me?" Ying asked the ghost in his dream, "Who are you?" And the ghost said, "I was originally from Zhao（趙）, but now I belong to the god of Wang Mang（汪芒）." Ying asked, "Where is your coffin?" The ghost said, "It is close, just ten or more steps northward from your tent, under a withered poplar tree by the riverside. It is almost dawn, so I can't stay anymore. Please have sympathy for me." Ying then agreed and he suddenly woke up.

The sun had risen and they were able to continue on their way, but Ying still worried about the ghost and said, "Although dreaming is nothing peculiar, the dream is too clear to be unreal." His retinue replied, "If so, why hesitate? Let's go check it out!" Ying then set out, leading more than ten men and went up along the river. They found the withered poplar tree, and Ying said, "Here it is." They dug deep and found a coffin, which was seriously eroded and soaking halfway in the water. Ying told the others, "I used to think the mysterious things others told me weren't true. Yet now I know that those folktales were not made up." Then he moved the coffin for the ghost, reburied it, and left.

三、非常關說　東晉・干寶：《搜神記》卷十六

　　蔣濟字子通，楚國平阿人也。仕魏，為領軍將軍。其婦夢見亡兒，涕泣曰：「死生異路。我生時為卿相子孫，今在地下為泰山伍伯，憔悴困苦，不可復言。今太廟西謳士孫阿，見召為泰山令，願母為白侯，屬阿，令轉我得樂處。」言訖，母忽然驚寤。

　　明日以白濟。濟曰：「夢為虛耳。不足怪也！」日暮，復夢，曰：「我來迎新君，止在廟下。未發之頃，暫得來歸。新君明日日中當發，臨發多事，不復得歸。永辭於此。侯氣彊，難感悟，故自

訴於母。願重啟侯，何惜不一試驗之。」遂道阿之形狀，言甚備悉。
天明，母重啟濟：「雖云夢不足怪，此何太適適。亦何惜不一驗之。」

　　濟乃遣人詣太廟下，推問孫阿，果得之，形狀證驗，悉如兒言。
濟涕泣曰：「幾負吾兒！」於是乃見孫阿，具語其事。阿不懼當死，
而喜得為泰山令，惟恐濟言不信也，曰：「若如節下言，阿之願也。
不知賢子欲得何職？」濟曰：「隨地下樂者與之。」阿曰：「輒當奉
教。」乃厚賞之。言訖，遣還。

　　濟欲速知其驗，從領軍門至廟下，十步安一人，以傳消息。辰
時傳阿心痛，巳時傳阿劇，日中傳阿亡。濟曰：「雖哀吾兒之不幸。
且喜亡者有知。」後月餘，兒復來，語母曰：「已得轉為錄事矣。」

The Unusual Lobbyist

Dong Jin Dynasty (317-420CE) Gan Bao（？-336CE）"Sou Shen Ji"

Jiang Ji （蔣濟）of Chu（楚）was the general of the central
army during the Wei dynasty（魏國）（220-265CE）. One night
his wife dreamed of their dead son telling her in tears, "Life
and death are two different paths. When alive, I was a
member of an aristocratic family. Now I am just an
anonymous escort of Tai Mountain ❶ （太山）in hell. I feel

---

❶　太山 Tai Mountain : Ancient Chinese believed that when one dies they
　　then would live below Tai Mountain under the rule of the dead. The chief
　　of this region is Master Tai Mountain.

languished with hardships beyond words description. On the west of the Imperial Ancestral Temple lives a singer named Sun E（孫阿）, who has been appointed to the chief magistrate of Tai Mountain. Please report this to father to ask E（阿）to transfer me to some other easy post." After he had finished speaking, his mother suddenly woke up.

The next day she explained what happened to Ji（濟）, who said, "Dreams are mere illusions. It's not worth making a fuss over." When night fell, the mother once again dreamt of her dead son telling her, "I come here to greet the newly-appointed chief magistrate. Before departure, I am temporarily able to return home for a while. The magistrate will be leaving tomorrow at noon and by that time I will be too busy to come back. Now I bid farewell to you. My father's Qi（氣）is so strong I cannot come close to him, so I come to you Mother. I wish you could explain to him once more. Why hesitate, I wish father could go and confirm this!" Then he described the figure and appearance of E in detail to his mother.

When morning came, the mother again explained what happened to Ji. "Though dreams are mere illusions, the dream I had is too clear and obvious to ignore. Why don't you just give it a try?" Ji then sent people to the Imperial Ancestral Temple and found E, whose figure and appearance corresponded to the description from his son. Tears dropped on Ji's cheeks. He said, "I almost failed to accomplish my son's wish." Then he summoned E and told him about the story in detail. E was not afraid that he would die, instead he was happy to hear that he would become the chief magistrate of Tai Mountain after his death. Only was he afraid that Ji's words were not true. E then said, "If it is just like you say, than I am willing. What job does your son want to transfer to?" Ji said, "The easier the better." E promised him.

After granting E abundant rewards, Ji sent him back. Wanting to know the outcome immediately, Ji set one man every ten steps from the main gate of his place to the Imperial Ancestral Temple to report the latest news to him.

In the morning there was news saying that E felt pain in his heart, and after several hours, this pain became more acute. By noon one reported the death of E. Ji said, "Though I pity my son's misery, I felt gratified that we still have a connection." After more than one month, his son came back again and told his mother that he had been appointed as the clerk's assistant.

四、朋友再見　東晉·干寶：《搜神記》卷十一

漢范式，字巨卿，山陽金鄉人也。一名汜。與汝南張劭為友，

劭字元伯，二人並遊太學。後告歸鄉里，式謂元伯曰：「後二年當
還，將過拜尊親，見孺子焉。」乃共剋期日。

後期方至，元伯具以白母，請設饌以候之。母曰：「二年之別，
千里結言，爾何相信之審耶？」曰：「巨卿，信士；必不乖違。」
母曰：「若然，當為爾醞酒。」至期果到。升堂拜飲，盡歡而別。

後元伯寢疾甚篤，同郡郅君章、殷子徵晨夜省視之。元伯臨終，
歎曰：「恨不見我死友。」子徵曰：「吾與君章，盡心於子，是非死
友，復欲誰求？」元伯曰：「若二子者，吾生友耳；山陽范巨卿，
所謂死友也。」尋而卒。

式忽夢見元伯，玄冕垂纓，屣履而呼曰：「巨卿，吾以某日死，
當以爾時葬，永歸黃泉。子未忘我，豈能相及？」式恍然覺悟，悲
歎泣下，便服朋友之服，投其葬日，馳往赴之。

未及到而葬已發引。既至壙，將窆，而柩不肯進。其母撫之曰：
「元伯，豈有望耶？」遂停柩。移時，乃見素車白馬，號哭而來。
其母望之曰：「是必范巨卿也！」既至，叩喪言曰：「行矣，元伯！
死生異路，永從此辭！」會葬者千人，咸為揮涕。式因執紼而引，
柩於是乃前。式遂留止冢次，為修墳樹，然後乃去。

Bidding Farewell

Dong Jin Dynasty (317-420CE) Gan Bao（？-336CE) "Sou Shen Ji"

During the Han Dynasty（漢朝）（202BCE-220CE），a man
named Fan Ju-Qing（范巨卿）studied together with his friend

Zhang Yuan-Bo（張元伯）in the Imperial Academy. One time they took leave to go home, Ju-Qing（巨卿）told Yuan-Bo（元伯）, "I'll return in two years, and at that time I will visit your parents and your children." They then fixed upon a date.

When the appointed day approached, Yuan-Bo told his mother about Ju-Qing's soon to be visit and asked her to prepare a meal for his friend. Yet his mother said, "It has been two years since you two separated, and it's only a mere agreement verbally, how can you be sure of his visiting?" Yuan-Bo replied, "Ju-Qing is a scholar who keeps his promise. He will not break the appointment with me." His mother then said, "In that case, I will then make wine for him." When the day came, Ju-Qing arrived. Yuan-Bo invited Ju-Qing to enter the living room and greet his mother. They had a great time remembering past time memories, and then Ju-Qing departed.

Later Yuan-Bo fell ill and was in critical condition. His fellow countrymen Zhi（郅）and Yin（殷）came day and night in concern. Yuan-Bo sighed with his last breath, "It's a shame that I cannot see my best friend." Yin said, "Zhi and I devote ourselves to taking care of you, and if we are not your best friends, then who else could be?" Yuan-Bo replied, "You are my excellent friends, yet Ju-Qing is my eternal friend." Soon he passed away.

Suddenly Ju-Qing dreamed of Yuan-Bo wearing a black cap which was not tied up and walking in his shoes untidily as if in a hurry. Yuan-Bo called out, "Ju-Qing! I have passed away and will be buried at certain time. I will be perpetually be owned by the Land of the Dead! You have not forgotten me, have you? Can you attend my funeral?" Ju-Qing then woke up and sighed in tears. He quickly got up, got dressed in mourning clothes ❷ , and rode to Yuan-Bo's house making it there the day of the funeral.

The coffin had been taken to the grave before Ju-Qing arrived. When they were about to bury it, the coffin could not be moved forward. Yuan-Bo's mother stroked the coffin and asked, "Son, are you expecting someone to come?" Then they stopped the process. Soon there came a plain carriage with white horses ❸ and people crying out loud. Yuan-Bo's mother saw this in the distance, and said, "It must be Fan Ju-Qing." When Ju-Qing arrived, he caressed the coffin, saying in tears,

---

❷ 孝服 : After one passes away, their relatives must wear a thick white clothing, similar to a potato sack. According to the relation between relatives, this clothing should be worn between three months to three years. Between friends, a sparse fabric is tied as a belt to represent friendship.

❸ 素車白馬 : During a funereal service, the color of the carriage must be plain and horses white as a sign of sympathy for the lost one.

"Let's go now Yuan-Bo! We are separated by the crossroads of life and death. Farewell to you." There were one thousand people attending the funeral and everyone was moved by this scene. Ju-Qing then took the rope ❹ connected to the coffin and led it forward. The coffin then moved. Ju-Qing stayed at the grave, trimmed the nearby hedges, and planted trees around it before he left.

五、尿出了人命　南朝 宋·劉義慶：《幽明錄》卷三

　　桓大司馬鎮赭圻時，有何參軍晨出，行於田野中，溺死人髑髏上。還，晝寢，夢一婦人語云：「君是佳人，何以見穢污？暮當令知之！」

　　是時有暴虎，人無敢夜行者。何常穴壁作溺穴。其夜，趨穴欲溺，虎怒溺，嚙斷陰莖，即死。

Death by Urination

Nan Chao Song Dynasty (420-479CE) Liu Yi-Qing (403-444CE) "You Ming Lu"

---

❹　紼 Fu : Originally Fu is a long rope which is used to suspend the coffin into the grave, subsequently becoming a symbol of mourning the dead, especially for close friends.

While the great general Huan Wen（桓溫）（312-373CE）was stationed at Zhe Qi（赭圻）, staff officer He（何）made his rounds in the fields. He urinated on the skull of a dead person. Later when he got back and took a nap, he dreamt of a woman saying, "You are a good man. How can you lay waste to people like that? I will teach you a lesson tonight!"

There was a fierce tiger around the area, so people did not dare to go out at night. The staff officer often drilled a hole in the wall so that he could pee outside through the hole. That night, while he was peeing through the hole, the tiger became enraged from the smell of the urine and bit off his penis. He died on the spot.

主題十四：恐怖特區

Theme 14: Horror Zone

Humans throughout their entire life cannot live without occupying residential and foreign space, or their life would become unimaginably desolate. Therefore, in one's life, searching for residential space requires traveling throughout foreign lands in order to find an area that serves as a form of protection and gives human beings a sense of security from inhabitancy. Due to the chaos and major migration during the Wei-Jin Nan-Bei dynasties（魏晉南北朝）, people encountered several peripheral places such as deserted houses, ancient tombs and battlefields covered with dead bodies. When a person comes in contact with this kind of environment, in their minds they may make an association between this unfamiliar area and horror, distrust, violence and suspicions bringing about thoughts of life threatening circumstances. This fear may drive humans to examine on these mysterious areas and happenings.

Stories in this theme depict situations of the panic resulting from the place or the imaginations of places out of the panic-stricken minds. There are stories like people going on an pilgrimage to celestial places only to find the "celestial valley" is, in twist of events, in fact a "snake canyon"; soldiers who died in a battlefield still waking up in the middle of the night to fight, having no idea that the war is over; and sometimes haunted houses would return to a peaceful state through the house owner's calmness, while sometimes the owner would die in the haunted house and all would return to peace. The fun of these stories lies in these scenes and incidents, which also reflects human's rich imagination of space.

一、飛仙谷 　西晉・張華：《博物志》卷十

　　天門郡有幽山峻谷，而其上人有從下經過者，忽然踴出林表，狀如飛仙，遂絕跡。年中如此甚數，遂名此處為仙谷。有樂道好事者，入此谷中，洗沐以求飛仙，往往得去。

　　有長生意思人，疑必妖怪。乃以大石自墜，牽一犬入谷中，犬復飛去。

　　其人還告鄉里，募數十人，執杖揭山草，伐木，至山頂觀之，遙見一物長數十丈，其高隱人，耳如簸箕。格射刺殺之。所吞人骨

積此左右，已成封，蟒開口廣丈餘，前後失人，皆此蟒氣所噏上。
於是此地遂安穩無患。

The Gateway to Heaven

Xi Jin Dynasty (266-316CE) Zhang Hua (232-300CE) "Bo Wu Zhi"

In the Tian Men County（天門-heaven's gate 郡）stood lofty mountains with a deep canyon. When people passed through the canyon, some of them would suddenly soar up into the air, shooting up-out of the woods with the appearance similar to a fairy, and then disappear. Such cases had happened several times, so people called this area "Celestial Canyon." Those who admired the Taoist arts of becoming an immortal fairy went into the canyon bathing themselves ❶ in order to become a fairy, leaving never to return.

A man with apt strategy suspected that it must be the demon spirits that were doing all the tricks. Therefore he used a big stone to bring him down to the bottom of the canyon taking a dog along with him. As expected, the dog soared up into the air.

---

❶ 洗沐 : In Taoist belief, one must cleanse their body and change into clean clothes before offering sacrifices to represent a clean body and mind, showing they are pious to the gods.

The man went back and told his fellow villagers what had happened. He then recruited dozens of people, each of them carrying blades, cutting down weeds and trees around the mountain. Later they went to the top of the mountain to observe the canyon. From afar they saw a serpent object over ten meters in length with its front standing as tall as a human and two ears as big as sieves. People then aggressively worked together to kill the beast. The bones of the men the beast had eaten were piled up nearby, forming a mound. The beast's mouth could open about two-meters wide. The missing people around this period of time had all been eaten by this humungous beast. After they had killed the serpent, there was no more trouble around the area.

二、鬼廁所　　東晉·陶潛:《搜神後記》卷七

　　宋襄城李頤,其父為人不信妖邪。有一宅,由來凶不可居,居者輒死。父便買居之。多年安吉,子孫昌熾。為二千石❷,當徙家之官。

---

❷　二千石:The monthly salary of a government official equal to 50,000kg of grain. This is a high-ranking official's income in ancient China.

臨去，請會內外親戚。酒食既行，父乃言曰：「天下竟有吉凶否？此宅由來言凶，自吾居之，多年安吉，乃得遷官，鬼為何在？自今已後，便為吉宅。居者住止，心無所嫌也。」

語訖，如廁，須臾，見壁中有一物，如卷席大，高五尺許，正白。便還取刀斫之，中斷，化為兩人；復橫斫之，又成四人！便奪取刀，反斫殺<u>李</u>。持至坐上，斫殺其子弟。凡姓<u>李</u>者必死，惟異姓無他。

<u>頤</u>尚幼在抱。家內知變，乳母抱出後門，藏他家，止其一身獲免。<u>頤</u>字<u>景真</u>，位至<u>湘東</u>太守。

Bathroom Bloodbath

Dong Jin Dynasty (317-420CE) Tao Qian (365-427CE) "Sou Shen Hou Ji"

During the Song Dynasty（宋代）(420-479CE), there lived a man named Li Yi（李頤）of Xiang Cheng（襄城）. His father did not believe in the supernatural. There was a house that had never been auspicious for any man to reside, anyone who lived inside would end up dead. Li Yi's father bought this house to live in. They lived many years in this house safely with much fortune and many offspring. Later, Li Yi's father was promoted to a high-ranking governmental position and was getting ready to move out to go to work.

When the time came for the family to move, his father held a banquet inviting relatives to enjoy a meal together. After all the food and wine had been brought out to the table, Li Yi's father spoke," Is there really good or bad fortune in heaven or earth? This house had always been said to be unlucky, but ever since I moved in we lived many years peacefully with a lot of fortune, even able to receive a promotion. Where are the ghosts now? From today on this house is an auspicious house. Anyone living here shouldn't feel worried!"

When finished speaking, he left to go to the bathroom. After a short period of time, he saw on the bathroom wall a strange object similar to a rolled-up rug in size, over one meter high and completely white. He immediately went back to get a knife to cut this strange object. As he chopped through the center of the object it unexpectedly turned into two people. He then again cut across horizontally and they turned into four people. Next, one of the strange objects took the knife, turned it around and chopped, killing Li Yi's father. They even carried the knife to the dinning area, killing all of his offspring.

At that time Yi（頤）was still an infant. In order to survive the crisis, his nanny held him and snuck out from the back door to hide him in someone else's house. Yi was the only survivor in this tragedy. He later served as Chief Magistrate in Xiang Dong County（湘東郡）.

三、誤入險境　南朝 宋・祖沖之：《述異記》

南康縣營民<u>區敬之</u>，<u>宋元嘉元年</u>，與息共乘舫，自縣泝流，深入小溪。幽荒險絕，人跡所未嘗至。夕登岸，停止舍中。<u>敬之</u>中惡猝死，其子然火守屍。

忽聞遠哭聲，呼「阿舅」，孝子驚疑；俯仰間，哭者已至。如人長大，被髮至足，髮多被面，不見七竅，因呼孝子姓名，慰唁之。孝子恐懼，遂聚薪以然火。此物言：「故來相慰，當何所畏，將須然火？」

此物坐亡人頭邊哭，孝子於火光中竊窺之。見此物以面掩亡人面，亡人面須臾裂剝露骨。孝子懼，欲擊之，無兵仗。須臾，其父屍見白骨連續，而皮骨都盡。竟不測此物是何鬼神。

Wrong Turn
Nan Chao Song Dynasty (420-479CE) Zu Chong-Zhi (429-500CE) "Shu Yi Ji"

A resident in Nan Kang County（南康縣）named Ou Jing-Zhi（區敬之）was on a boat with his son going upstream. They traveled to an extremely dangerous remote section of the stream where no one else had ever set foot before. Halfway through their travels they went ashore at dusk to stop and rest. However Jing-Zhi（敬之）was afflicted with a virulent disease and died right away. His son, watching over his father's body, built a fire.

Then he heard someone crying and shouting, "A-Jiu!（阿舅-uncle）" He was extremely terrified as the one crying came to him. With the same height as a human being and hair covering the face draping down to its feet, it called the name of the son and extended its condolence. Horrified, the son piled up more firewood on the fire. It said, "I came all the way to share my sympathy with you, why are you so scared, why must you build such a fire?" It then sat beside the head of the body, crying.

The son secretly observed him with the dim light from the fire, and saw it use its face to cover the dead father's face. The skin on the father's face suddenly peeled open exposing the bones. The son was scared, and though he wanted to attack it, he had no weapons. Soon the skin on his father's dead body was completely gone, exposing a white skeleton. He could never figure out what kind of ghost it was.

主題十五：死去又活來

Theme 15: Revival

In traditional Chinese philosophy, life is the combination of the flesh and the soul, both of which are composed of "Qi" （氣）." *The Book of Rites"* （禮記）❶ records that "The soul ascends to heaven, while the body stays on earth." The soul belongs to "Yang Qi"（陽氣）and is of light weight, so it rises to the heavens, while the flesh is "Yin Qi"（陰氣）having heavy weight, so it belongs to the earth. When an organism is alive, its flesh and soul are as one, and when the body dies, the flesh and soul separate. When one dies, the body remains on earth and the soul will ascend to heaven. According to this theory, death has two directions: the body remains on the ground, usually where it is buried, unable to move freely; and

---

❶ 禮記 Book of Rights : A book edited in the Han Dynasty（漢朝）by scholars in a Confucius school. Its contents define social status and etiquette.

the soul is brought to "heaven", "Tai Mountain " （太山）, or "hell" for final judgment. Usually the soul has much more mobility than the body. Based on the concept above, there are two ways of revivals in the stories of this theme: the soul interceding with heaven's judge, or from being rescued from one's coffin after a false accusation of death. When the soul returns to its body, they recombine as one and the dead revive.

Stories in this theme include people drunken or in a coma being recognized as dead and then returning to consciousness, people receiving a misjudgment by hell and then being released, people bribing the judge's ghost subordinates to avoid death, or more sentimentally, the judge sympathizing with the dead and sending them back to take care of their children. The plots in these stories, besides acting as a reflection of a wish for survival, also reveal the terrible judgment of death along with the corruption and abuse of judicial law during the Wei-Jin Nan-Bei Dynasties （魏晉南北朝）.

一、醉死一千天　東晉‧干寶：《搜神記》卷十九

　　狄希，中山人也，能造千日酒，飲之千日醉。時有州人姓劉，名玄石，好飲酒，往求之。希曰：「我酒發來未定，不敢飲君。」石曰：「縱未熟，且與一杯，得否？」希聞此語，不免飲之。復索曰：「美哉！可更與之。」希曰：「且歸，別日當來，只此一杯，可眠千日也！」石別，似有怍色。至家，醉死。家人不之疑，哭而葬之。

　　經三年，希曰：「玄石必應酒醒，宜往問之。」既往石家，語曰：「石在家否？」家人皆怪之，曰：「玄石亡來，服已闋矣。」希驚曰：「酒之美矣，而致醉眠千日，今合醒矣！」乃命其家人，鑿塚破棺看之。

　　塚上汗氣徹天，遂命發塚！方見開目張口，引聲而言曰：「快哉！醉我也！」因問希曰：「爾作何物也？令我一杯大醉，今日方醒！日高幾許？！」墓上人皆笑之，被石酒氣衝入鼻中，亦各醉臥三月。

Potent Wine

Dong Jin Dynasty (317-420CE) Gan Bao (？-336CE) "Sou Shen Ji"

　　Di Xi（狄希）of Zhong Shan（中山）brewed wine that could make people drunk for a thousand days. Liu Xuan-Shi（劉玄石），a heavy drinker in the region, asked for some of this

liquor. "It has just been brewed and has not settled yet," Xi
（希）told him. "I dare not offer you any." "Even if the wine is
not ready, can I still have one cup?" begged Xuan-Shi（玄石）.
Xi couldn't refuse and gave him one cup of wine. "Excellent!
Please let me have another cup!" But Xi rejected him saying,
"You had better go home now and come back again some
other time. Just this one cup will make you drunk for a
thousand days." Xuan-Shi was embarrassed and left. When
he reached home, he became a dead drunk. His family
suspected he was dead, wept, and buried him.

Three years later Xi said to himself, "Xuan-Shi must
have recovered by now from the wine. I must go and see
him." He went to Xuan-Shi's house and asked, "Is Xuan-Shi
home?" The family felt strange. "He is dead," they said. "The
three-year-mourning period is over. ❷ " Xi was shocked and
replied, "Ah, my fine wine sent him to sleep for a thousand
days. But now he should be awake." He told Xuan-Shi's
family to go and check on the tomb.

While they arrived at the tomb, they saw vapor emitting
from Xuan-Shi's grave and Xi ordered them to dig out the

---

❷ 服喪期滿：After one passes away, their relatives must wear a thick white
clothing, similar to a potato sack. According to the relation between
relatives, this clothing should be worn between three months to three
years.

grave. They found Xuan-Shi with his eyes and mouth open, yawning in a long voice, "Wonderful! I have never been so drunk!" And he asked Xi, "What is that brew of yours? A single cup made me so drunk that I am just waking up today! What time is it?" All the people around the grave laughed at him. Sniffing the wine on Xuan-Shi's breath, they all fell into a drunken stupor for three whole months.

二、爽死了　南朝 宋·劉義慶：《幽明錄》卷五

　　有人家甚富，止有一男，寵恣過常。遊市，見一女子美麗，賣胡粉，愛之，無由自達，乃託買粉。日往市，得粉便去，初無所言。積漸久，女深疑之……明日復來，問曰：「君買此粉，將欲何施？」答曰：「意相愛樂，不敢自達，然恆欲相見，故假此以觀姿耳。」女悵然有感，遂相許以私，尅以明夕。

　　其夜，安寢堂屋，以俟女來。薄暮果到，男不勝其悅，把臂曰：「宿願始伸於此！！」歡踊遂死。女惶懼，不知所以，因遁去，明還粉店。

　　至食時，父母怪男不起，往視，已死矣。當就殯斂。發篋笥中，見百餘裹胡粉，大小一積。其母曰：「殺吾兒者，必此粉也！」入市遍買胡粉，次此女，比之，手跡如先。遂執問女曰：「何殺我兒？！」女聞嗚咽，具以實陳。父母不信，遂以訴官。女曰：「妾豈復恡死？乞一臨尸盡哀。」縣令許焉。徑往，撫之慟哭曰：「不幸致此，若

魂而靈，復何恨哉！」男豁然更生，具說情狀。遂為夫婦，子孫繁
茂。

Deadly Ecstasy

Nan Chao Song Dynasty (420-479CE) Liu Yi-Qing (403-444CE)
"You Ming Lu"

There once was an extremely wealthy family of which only had one, spoiled son. One day when he wandered into the market, he saw a beautiful woman selling cosmetic powders. He fell in love with her at first sight, yet he did not know how to tell her of his affection. He pretended that he wanted to buy the cosmetic powder, going to the market everyday and leaving right after he bought the powder without saying a word. As time went by, the woman grew suspicious of him. The next day as the man arrived, the woman asked, "Mister, how are you using this powder?" "I secretly like you yet I don't know how to tell you. I wanted to see your beauty so I came to buy your powder," he replied. The woman was touched so she secretly agreed to date him the next evening.

The next evening, the man lied on his bed, waiting for the woman. Then the woman came, and the man, not able to control his excitement, grabbed her hand and said, "I've been holding on to this dream for so long, and now it finally comes true!" He jumped up in excitement and suddenly died. The girl was shocked and did not know what to do, so she left, returning to the powder shop the next day.

When it was time for breakfast, the man's parents found it strange that their son did not wake up yet, so they went to check on him, finding his dead body. Then they prepared a funeral for him. The mother opened the bamboo basket in her son's room and found in it more than one hundred packs of cosmetic powder, piled together. She said, "My son's death must be related to these powders." Then she went to the market to buy different cosmetic powders to match one by one with her son's. When she arrived at the woman's shop, she bought one pack of comestic powder, comparing it to her son's, she found that the woman's powder had the same wrapping on the pack as the powder in her son's basket. Then she caught the woman and questioned her, "Why did you kill my son?" When the woman heard this she started weeping and explained everything that happened. The parents of the man did not believe it so they went to court.

The woman told the court, "I'm not reluctant to die. I only wish I could send my condolence beside his body." The magistrate allowed her to do so. The woman went directly to the mourning hall and touched his body, crying, "This was a misfortune. If we can meet again in life after death, then I have no sorrows." The man then suddenly revived, and told everybody what had happened in detail. Afterwards, the two got married and had many children.

三、死裡求生有暗盤 　東晉‧陶潛：《搜神後記》卷四

　　襄陽李除，中時氣死，其婦守屍。至於三更，崛然起坐，搏婦臂上金釧甚遽。婦因助脫，既手執之，還死。婦伺察之。

　　至曉，心中更暖，漸漸得蘇。既活，云：「為吏將去，比伴甚多，見有行貨得免者，乃許吏金釧，吏令還，故歸取以與吏，吏得釧，便放令還，見吏取釧去。」

　　後數日，不知猶在婦衣內。婦不敢復著，依事咒埋。

The Golden Bracelet

Dong Jin Dynasty (317-420CE) Tao Qian (365-427CE) "Sou Shen Hou Ji"

A man named Li Chu（李除）of Xiang Yang（襄陽）died of an epidemic disease. His wife guarded over his body. At midnight, he suddenly popped up into a sitting position and with great effort, wrested the golden bracelet from his wife's arm. His wife then helped to take the bracelet off. Shortly after Li got the bracelet, and died again. His wife watched beside him closely.

At dawn, his heart got warmer and he gradually regained consciousness. After reviving he said, "I was taken away by the ghost officials, there were many people around. I saw some bribe the officials and their death sentences were remitted. I promised to give the officials your golden bracelet and they sent me back here to get it. After receiving the bracelet they released me. I saw the ghost officials take away the golden bracelet."

After several days, surprisingly, the bracelet was still inside his wife's clothes. His wife dared not to wear it again. Then they buried it according to folk custom ❸.

四、推薦替死鬼　　南朝 宋・劉義慶：《幽明錄》卷四

　　北府索盧貞者，本中郎荀羨之吏也。以晉太元五年六月中病亡，經一宿而蘇。云見羨之子粹，驚喜曰：「君算未盡，然官須得三將，故不得便爾相放……君若知幹捷如君者，當以相代！」盧貞

---

❸ 咒埋：In Chinese ancient times, it is believed that the dead live underground. When one wants to make an offering to the dead, the Chinese custom is to bury the item underground and speak, explaining the purpose of the offering.

即舉龔穎，粹曰：「穎堪事否？」盧貞曰：「穎不復下己！」粹初令盧貞疏其名，緣書非鬼用，粹乃索筆自書之。盧貞遂得出。

　　忽見一曾鄰居者，死亡七、八年矣，為泰山門主，謂盧貞曰：「索都督獨得歸邪？」因囑盧貞曰：「卿歸，為謝我婦，我未死時，埋萬五千錢於宅中大牀下。我乃本欲與女市釧，不意奄終，不得言於女、妻也。」盧貞許之。

　　及蘇，遂使人報其妻，已賣宅移居武進矣。因往語之，仍告買宅主，令掘之，果得錢如其數焉。即遣其妻與女市釧。

　　尋而龔穎亦亡，時軰共奇其事。

The Scapegoat from Hell

Nan Chao Song Dynasty (420-479CE) Liu Yi-Qing (403-444CE) "You Ming Lu"

Suo Lu-Zhen（索盧貞）of Bei Fu ❹（北府）was originally a subordinate of General Xun Xian-Zhi(荀羨之). He died of an illness, and after one night, revived to life. He said that he met Xun Cui（荀粹）, the son of Xun Xian-Zhi. Cui（粹）said astoundingly, "Your life time has not ended yet! However, we are in need of three generals here so we cannot let you go just like that. If you happen to know any person who is as

---

❹　北府 Bei Fu：Another name for the ministry of national defense in the Jin Dynasty.

competent as you are, then we can switch the two of you."
Lu-Zhen(盧貞)then immediately recommended Gong Ying(龔
穎) to him. Cui asked, "Is Ying (穎) capable of the job?" "Ying
is no less talented than me," answered Lu-Zhen. At first, Cui
had Lu-Zhen write down Ying's name, but since ghost's
writing is different from the living, Cui took the pen and
wrote it down himself. Then Lu-Zhen was released.

He then saw a former neighbor, who had been dead for
seven or eight years and was in charge of the affairs of the
arrivals and departures in hell. The neighbor said, "Are you
allowed to go back now, Officer Lu-Zhen?" Then he exhorted
Lu-Zhen, "When you get back, please apologize to my wife for
me. I once buried fifteen hundred dollars under the bed in our
house, and it was supposed to be the money for buying a
golden bracelet for my daughter. Yet I died unexpectedly and
did not tell my wife and daughter about the money." Lu-Zhen
promised him.

After reviving, he sent someone to tell the information to
the neighbor's wife. However their house was sold and the
family had moved to Wu Jing County (武進縣). He then went
to Wu Jing to tell them, and in addition informed the current
owner of their house about it, asking for the permission to dig
out the money. To no surprise, they received the exact
amount of money that was said. The money was returned to

the wife and used to buy the golden bracelet for their daughter.

Soon after, Gong Ying died and people were amazed by this event.

五、鬼判官開恩　南朝 宋·劉義慶：《幽明錄》卷三

琅邪人姓王，忘名，居錢塘。妻朱氏，以太元九年病亡，有二孤兒。王復以其年四月暴死，三日而心下猶暖，經七日方蘇。

說初死時，有二十餘人，皆烏衣，見錄，錄去到朱門白壁，狀如宮殿。吏朱衣素帶，玄冠介幘，或所被著，悉珠玉相連結，非世間儀服。

復將前，見一人長大，所著衣狀如雲氣。王向叩頭，自說：「婦已亡，餘孤兒尚小，無依，奈何？」便流涕。此人為之動容，云：「汝命自應來，以汝孤兒，特與三年之期。」王又曰：「三年不足活兒。」左右有一人語云：「俗尸何痴！此間三年，是世中三十年。」因便送出。

又三十年，王果卒。

Mercy of the Ghost Judge

Nan Chao Song Dynasty (420-479CE) Liu Yi-Qing (403-444CE) "You Ming Lu"

In the Jin Dynasty（晉朝）（317-420CE）, a man named Wang（王）from Lang Ye（琅邪）lived in Qian Tang（錢塘）. His wife died of a disease and left him with two sons. Wang then had a sudden death in April of the same year.

For three days his heart remained warm, and on the seventh day, Wang revived. He explained to others that in the beginning of his death, over twenty people dressed completely in black arrested him and brought him to a place that looked like a palace with white walls and a red gate. Officials inside were wearing red clothes with plain silk belts and their hair was tied back in a bandana underneath a black cap ❺. Some officials wore delicate clothes with pearls and jade decorations never seen before in the human world.

He continued forward and saw a tall man wearing clothes glorious like the clouds in the sky. Wang knelt down and kow-towed ❻, saying in tears, "My wife is dead and my sons are still young with nobody to raise them. What are they to

---

❺ 朱衣素帶，玄冠介幘：The formal dress code of the officials in the Jin Dynasty.

❻ 叩頭 Kowtow: The highest form of respect in Chinese etiquette used to show one's obedience or used to apologize or plea for forgiveness from a severe mistake. It is the act of kneeling down and placing one's hands and forehead on the ground. When used an apology, one must knock his/her forehead on the ground.

do?" With a tinge of emotion, the man said, "This is your destiny. However, in concern for your children, I will give you three more years!" "But three years is not enough for me to raise my children," Wang said. One of the tall man's subordinates spoke, "How stupid you dead people are! Three years in hell is equal to thirty years in the world of mortals." Then Wang was sent out and lived for another thirty years.

六、開棺救死　東晉‧干寶：《搜神記》卷十五

　　晉咸寧二年十二月，琅邪顏畿字世都，得病，就醫張瑳使治，死於張家。棺斂已久，家人迎喪，旐每繞樹木而不可解。人咸為之感傷。引喪者忽顛仆，稱畿言曰：「我壽命未應死，但服藥太多，傷我五臟耳。今當復活，慎無葬也！」其父拊而祝之曰：「若爾有命，當復更生，豈非骨肉所願？今但欲還家，不爾葬也。」旐乃解。

　　及還家，其婦夢之曰：「吾當復生，可急開棺！」婦便說之。其夕，母及家人又夢之。即欲開棺，而父不聽。其弟含，時尚少，乃慨然曰：「非常之事，自古有之。今靈異至此，開棺之痛，孰與不開相負！」父母從之，乃共發棺，果有生驗，以手刮棺，指爪盡傷，然氣息甚微，存亡不分矣。於是急以綿飲瀝口，能咽，遂與出之。

　　將護累月，飲食稍多，能開目視瞻，屈伸手足，然不與人相當。不能言語，飲食所須，托之以夢。如此者十餘年，家人疲於供護，

不復得操事。<u>含</u>乃棄絕人事，躬親侍養，以知名州黨。後更衰劣，
卒復還死焉。

Coffin Coma

Dong Jin Dynasty (317-420CE) Gan Bao（？-336CE) "Sou Shen Ji"

During the Jin Dynasty（晉朝）（317-420CE），a man named Yan Ji（顏畿）was inflicted with an illness and died in the house of Doctor Zhang Cuo（張瑳）. After his body was encoffined for a period of time, his family took the coffin home. A flag ❼ was tangled with the trees and couldn't be separated. The scene of it saddened everyone. One person who carried the coffin suddenly fell over, saying that Ji（畿）spoke to him saying, "I am not dead. I had taken too much medicine which had harmed my internal organs. Now I can revive, so please do not bury me." His father, stroked the coffin and said, "If you are not dead, then come back. Isn't this what I, as a father, would hope for? Now let us go home, and we will not bury you." Then the flag was released from the trees.

After they got home, Ji's wife dreamed of him telling her, "I am about to revive. Now, immediately open the coffin!" His

---

❼　旐 Zhao：A flag in front of the coffin used to lead the coffin when moving it during a funeral.

wife then told others about it. That night, his mother and other family members had the same dream. When they were about to open the coffin, his father disagreed. His younger brother, Han（含）, who was still very young, sighed with emotion, "There have been unusual things happening before and now, it is rather occult. Though it is a grief to open the coffin, compared with the regret of not opening it, what is less harmful?" The parents then agreed and opened the coffin together. There was evidence of life just as expected. Ji had scratched the coffin and his fingernails were all damaged. His breath was so weak that it was hard to tell whether he was dead or alive. Then they quickly soaked cotton in water and dripped water into his mouth. He was able to swallow water, so they then moved him out of the coffin.

After being taken care of for several months, he was eating more and more, and was able to open his eyes and stretch his limbs. However, he could not communicate with other people. Even though he could not speak, he sent messages about his need of eating and drinking through dreams. It went on like this for more than ten years, and his family had been taking care of him exhaustedly, not able to do other things. Han also gave up his normal life to take care of his brother, and was respected and highly praised in the region. Yet Ji got weaker and weaker, and in the end, passed away.

七、陰錯陽差大劈棺　　東晉·干寶：《搜神記》卷十五

漢建安四年二月，武陵充縣婦人李娥，年六十歲，病卒，埋於城外，已十四日。娥比舍有蔡仲，聞娥富，謂殯當有金寶，乃盜發冢求金。以斧剖棺。斧數下，娥於棺中言曰：「蔡仲，汝護我頭！」仲驚遽，便出走。會為縣吏所見，遂收治。依法，當棄市。

娥兒聞母活，來迎出，將娥回去。武陵太守聞娥死復生，召見，問事狀。娥對曰：「聞謬為司命所召，到時得遣出。過西門外，適見外兄劉伯文，驚相勞問，涕泣悲哀。娥語曰：『伯文，我一日誤為所召，今得遣歸，既不知道，不能獨行，為我得一伴否？又我見召在此已十餘日，形體又為家人所葬埋，歸當那得自出？』伯文曰：『當為問之。』即遣門卒與戶曹相問：『司命一日誤召武陵女子李娥，今得遣還。娥在此積日，尸喪又當殯殮，當作何等得出？又女弱獨行，豈當有伴耶？是吾外妹，幸為便安之。』答曰：『今武陵西界，有男子李黑，亦得遣還，便可為伴。兼敕黑過娥比舍蔡仲，發出娥也。』於是娥遂得出，與伯文別。伯文曰：『書一封，以與兒佗。』娥遂與黑俱歸。事狀如此。」

太守聞之，慨然歎曰：「天下事真不可知也！」乃表以為：「蔡仲雖發冢，為鬼神所使，雖欲無發，勢不得已，宜加寬宥。」，詔書報可。太守欲驗語虛實，即遣馬吏於西界推問李黑，得之，與娥語協。乃致伯文書與佗。佗識其紙，乃是父亡時送箱中文書也。表文字猶在也，而書不可曉。乃請費長房讀之，曰：「告佗，我當從府君出案行部，當以八月八日日中時，武陵城南溝水畔頓，汝是時必往！」

到期，悉將大小於城南待之。須臾果至。但聞人馬隱隱之聲，詣溝水，便聞有呼聲曰：「佗來，汝得我所寄李娥書不耶？」曰：「即得之，故來至此。」伯文以次呼家中大小，久之，悲傷斷絕，曰：「死生異路，不能數得汝消息。吾亡後，兒孫乃爾許大！」良久，謂佗曰：「來春大病，與此一丸藥，以塗門戶，則辟來年妖癘矣。」言訖忽去，竟不得見其形。

至來春，武陵果大病，白日皆見鬼，唯伯文之家，鬼不敢向。
費長房視藥丸曰：「此方相腦也。」

The Accidental Grave Robbery

Dong Jin Dynasty (317-420CE) Gan Bao（？-336CE) "Sou Shen Ji"

During the Han Dynasty（漢朝）（202BCE-220CE），in Wu Ling（武陵），an old woman named Li E（李娥）around sixty years old, died from a disease and was buried outside the city for fourteen days. Li's neighbor, Cai Zhong（蔡仲），heard that E（娥）was wealthy and wanted to rob the grave, assuming that there must be many valuable objects inside. As he chopped at the coffin with an axe, from inside the coffin E said, "Watch my head, Cai Zhong!" Hearing her speak, Zhong（仲）quickly ran away frightened. One official of the County happened to witness everything, so he brought Zhong to justice. According to the law, he had to be executed in the public market.

The son of E heard his mother had revived, so he came to take her back. The director of Wu Ling County heard about the revival and summoned upon E to inquire about what had happened.　E answered, "It was a mistake that the official in charge of life and death called upon me. I was set free when I got there. I then bumped into my cousin Liu Bo-Wen (劉伯文) when I passed by the West Gate (西門). He consoled me with astonishment. I said in tears, 'Bo-Wen (伯文), I was summoned here by mistake, and am now set free. Yet I do not know the way back and I can't walk alone. Would you find me a companion? I have been here for more than ten days and my body was buried already. How could I get out when I go back?' Bo-Wen said, 'I will help ask for you.' Bo-Wen then reported to the official in charge of household registration saying, 'The woman Li E was summoned by mistake and is set free now. She has been here for some time and her body has already been buried. How can she get out of this mess? Moreover, she is an old woman and could not walk alone can you find her a companion? She is my cousin so please help make some arrangements.' The official answered, 'A man named Li Hei (李黑) in western Wu Ling is also returning back to the earth and could keep her company. I will order Hei (黑) to go to the house of Cai Zhong, who is the neighbor of E, so the coffin could be opened and E could be set free.' When I was ready to go back, I bade farewell to Bo-Wen, who said, 'I have a letter for my son, Tuo (佗).' Hei and I then went back together. This is roughly what happened."

The County Director sighed as he heard the story, saying, "We could never expect such a thing would happen. Fact is stranger than fiction." Then he filed a report to his supervisors, in which he wrote, "Although Cai Zhong is a grave robber, he was driven by the forces of the supernatural. In no circumstance could he restrain not to dig out the grave. He should be forgiven." The verdict was then approved. The County Director wanted to verify the story the woman told, so he sent a knight to inquire with Li Hei, who lived in the western Wu Ling. The information he got corresponded with Li E's words. After that the director transferred the letter from Bo-Wen to Tuo. Tuo recognized the paper which was the commendation ❽ stored in the coffin when his father was buried. Although the text was still on paper, but his father's writing was unrecognizable. Because of this, they had Fei Chang-Fang（費長房）read the letter. Fei explained, "This letter says, 'I am going to go on an inspection tour with the magistrate. At noon of August 8th, we will rest on the canal in the southern side Wu Ling. You must be there at that time.'"

When time came, Tuo took his family and waited beside the South Gate of the castle. Shortly after, his father arrived. They saw nothing but heard the sound of people and horses approaching, as soon as the cavalry reached the canal, they

---

❽ A text which used to compliment the dead, it is stored in a box with the coffin.

heard a voice call for Tuo, "Tuo! Come here! Did you get the letter Li E transferred for me?" Tuo answered, "Yes, that's why I am here." Bo Wen called his family members' name one by one, and after a long period of time, said sadly, "Life and death are two different worlds. I cannot hear news about you very often. My offspring have all grown up since I passed away." After a long pause, he told Tuo, "There is going to be an epidemic disease spreading next spring. I give you this medicine. Rub it on the door to avoid the disease." Bo-Wen's figure couldn't be seen at all during the conversation, and he left suddenly.

The next spring, an epidemic disease spread as expected. Ghosts were seen even during the daylight, yet only the house of Bo-Wen was not haunted. Carefully examining the pill, Fei Chang-Fang said, "This medicine is made of the brain of Fang Xiang ❾, a celestial animal."

---

❾ 方相 Fang Xiang : In ancient Chinese, people believe there is a monster which lives underground eating the bodies of the dead. Fang Xiang is the only animal that can oppose the monster.

主題十六：死亡預告

Theme16: Omen of Death

As the law of nature, the fact that life comes along with death is acknowledged by human beings, we live therefore we die. However, in the turbulent age of Wei-Jin Nan-Bei Dynasties, death is a great threat that casts shadows all over the earth. Apart from the death caused by ageing or disease, the likes of epidemic, slaughter in war, the calamity of extermination of families resulting from political struggle, the adversity occurred along the road of relocating all make it more difficult for people to survive in such a precarious time, hence the emergence and prevalence of far-fetched and suspicious legends-for people would rather believe in these legends than to sacrifice their own lives. Under such atmosphere, whether it's a powerful sorcerer or the illiterate common people, most people still keep alert to the uncommon things around and observe the hints of death. Stories in this theme are the legends of the "Omen of Death".

Except for people who commit suicide, most people are not aware of how and when they die, which makes the concept of "death" creepier and more fearful. Especially in the age of unrest, many of the above-mentioned unexpected disasters and uncommon adversity not only concern the people involved but also arouse the attention and the opinions of the public, connecting the former events as the omen of death and latter events as evidence of the omen. Furthermore, along with the basis of the concept of the five elements, there are more and more stories spreading with the news of people's death. The mostly-seen omens include many uncommon phenomena, such as dogs walking and talking like humans, worms coming out from the rice pot, a great deal of blood emerging from the ground, or some grim objects protruding out from nowhere, like a red-eye monster from the toilet, a dead man's head with moving eyes, or digging from the ground a large amount of money. Documents concerning predestination like "The Book of Life and Death" or "The Heaven-SentCommand"are also recognized as the notifications of death.

As soon as there are unusual phenomena appearing as an omen of death, the ones involved usually panic and would not resign themselves to the omens. Instead, they would make efforts to retrieve the life that will be eliminated soon.

However, being an omen of death, once it appears, no one can avoid it. The helplessness is sad yet it is where the fun of the stories plot lies.

一、兒子的命被買走了 東晉·陶潛：《搜神後記》卷五

王導子悅為中書郎，導夢人以百萬錢買悅，導潛為祈禱者備矣。尋掘地，得錢百萬，意甚惡之，一一皆藏閉。

及悅疾篤，導憂念特至，積日不食。忽見一人，形狀甚偉，被甲持刀。問是何人，曰：「僕，蔣侯也。公兒不佳，欲為請命，故來爾。公勿復憂。」導因與之食，遂至數升。

食畢，勃然謂導曰：「中書命盡，非可救也！」言訖不見。悅亦殞絕。

Death Ransom

Dong Jin Dynasty (317-420CE) Tao Qian (365-427CE) "Sou Shen Hou Ji"

Wang Dao's（王導）（272-339CE）son, Yue（悅）, served as the magistrate official. One night Dao（導）dreamed of someone paying a million dollars for Yue's life. Thus, Dao secretly held a ceremony to dispel the misfortune. Before long, his family members found one million dollars while digging in the ground. Dao was very concerned about this, and carefully hid all the money.

When Yue was seriously ill, Dao was so worried that he could not even eat for many days. Suddenly he saw a sturdy man in a suit of armor, holding a broadsword in his hand. When asked by Dao about his identity, he replied, "I am Duke Jiang（蔣侯）❶ . Your son is not in a good condition. I intend to negotiate for his life, that's why I come here. Please do not worry." Dao then served him food, and Duke Jiang ended up eating a large amount of food. After he was done, his countenance suddenly changed. He said to Dao, "The life of your son has ended. There is nothing that can be done to save him." He then disappeared after saying this. Yue then passed away afterwards.

---

❶ 蔣侯 Duke Jiang：The general Jiang Zi Wen（蔣子文）lived in the Han Dynasty（漢朝）and died on the battlefield. Afterwards, his spirit haunted the Jiang Nan（江南）region for a long time. To put an end to the haunting, the King of Wu（吳）knighted him as Duke Jiang. In addition, people set up temples to worship him to keep distresses away.

二、偷看生死簿　　東晉・干寶：《搜神記》卷五

　　漢下邳周式，嘗至東海，道逢一吏，持一卷書，求寄載。行十餘里❷，謂式曰：「吾暫有所過，留書寄君船中，慎勿發之！」去後，式盜發視書，皆諸死人錄。下條有式名。

　　須臾，吏還，式猶視書。吏怒曰：「故以相告，而忽視之！」式叩頭流血。良久，吏曰：「感卿遠相載，此書不可除卿名。今日已去，還家，三年勿出門，可得度也。勿道見吾書！」

---

❷　里 li：The character li is a traditional Chinese measuring unit of distance. Its length is close to half a kilometer.

<u>式</u>還，不出已二年餘，家皆怪之。鄰人卒亡，父怒，使往弔之。<u>式</u>不得已，適出門，便見此吏。吏曰：「吾令汝三年勿出，而今出門，知復奈何！吾求不見，連累為鞭杖。今已見汝，無可奈何。後三日日中，當相取也。」

<u>式</u>還，涕泣具道如此。父故不信，母晝夜與相守。至三日日中時，果見來取，便死。

A Glance at the Book of Orbituary

Dong Jin Dynasty (317-420CE) Gan Bao (？-336CE) "Sou Shen Ji"

During the Han Dynasty（漢朝）（202BCE-220CE），a man named Zhou Shi（周式）from Xia Pei（下邳）once went to Dong Hai County（東海郡）. On his way he met an official holding a scroll, asking for a ride. After walking for more than five kilometers, the official told Shi（式），"I will go to temporarily to visit someone. I have to leave this book in your boat. Under any circumstances, please do not open it." When the official left, Shi secretly opened the book and found a list of the dead, with Shi's name was listed inside.

Shortly after, the official returned while Shi was still reading the book. The official said in anger, "I specifically told you not to read that book, yet you neglected my words!" Shi kept kowtowing ❸ even after his head started bleeding. After a long period of time, the official said, "I am grateful that you gave me a ride despite the long distance of the journey. However, I am not able to delete your name off the list. Leave now and return home, and do not go out of your house for three years, then maybe you can survive. Don't ever tell anyone that you had read my book."

Shi then returned to his home, without leaving his house for two years. His family thought this was strange. One day their neighbor came to a violent death. Shi's father was angry with him because he did not want to leave the house to pay condolence. Without any choice, Shi then left the house. Just then he saw the official, who said, "I ordered you not to go out of your house for three years, yet now you have left your house. You knew what you should have done, but you couldn't! The person I was supposed to seek was never sought, from this I was punished by whips and canes. Now that I have seen you, I have no other choice. Three days later at noon, I will come and take away your life."

---

❸　叩頭 Kowtow : The highest form of respect in Chinese etiquette used to show one's obedience or used to apologize or plea for forgiveness from a severe mistake. It is the act of kneeling down and placing one's hands and forehead on the ground. When used an apology, one must knock his/her forehead on the ground.

When Shi got back, in tears he told his family of his situation. His father still did not believe him, but his mother watched over him all day long. At noon of the third day, they saw the official come and take Shi away, and Shi died.

三、踏上不歸路　東晉‧干寶：《搜神記》卷九

吳諸葛恪征淮南歸，將朝會之夜，精爽擾動，通夕不寐。嚴畢趨出，犬銜引其衣。恪曰：「犬不欲我行耶？」出仍入坐。少頃復

起，犬又銜衣，<u>恪</u>令從者逐之。及入，果被殺。

其妻在室，語使婢曰：「爾何故血臭？」婢曰：「不也。」有頃，愈劇。又問婢曰：「汝眼目瞻視，何以不常？」婢蹶然起躍，頭至於棟，攘臂切齒而言曰：「<u>諸葛</u>公乃為<u>孫峻</u>所殺！」於是大小知<u>恪</u>死矣。而吏兵尋至。

On the Road of No Return

Dong Jin Dynasty (317-420CE) Gan Bao (？-336CE) "Sou Shen Ji"

Zhu-Ge Que(諸葛恪)of Wu Kingdom(吳國)(222-280CE) returned from a failed expedition in Huai Nan County(淮南郡). The night before he had to go to the royal court meeting, he grew anxious and could not sleep at all. He dressed formally and just about ready to leave when his dog gripped his clothes. Que（恪）said, "My dog does not want me to go?" Then he went back indoors and sat down. After a short period of time he got up again and the dog came and gripped his clothes once more. Que ordered his entourage to take the dog away. In the end he went to the royal court, and was ambushed for assassination.

At that time his wife was at home and asked her maid, "How come you smell like blood?" The maid replied, "No, I don't!" Before long, the blood smell became sharper and sharper. She asked the maid again, "Your eyes are rolling back into your head, why do they look so strange?" Suddenly the maid jumped into the air and hit her head on the beam of the house, throwing her arms all over the place and grinding her teeth saying, "Mr. Zhu-Ge has been murdered by General Sun Jun（孫峻）（219-256CE）." From this, all the family knew that Que was dead. Shortly afterwards, the military came to arrest the family.

四、箱子裡的索命天書

南朝 宋·劉義慶：《幽明錄》卷四

衡陽太守王矩為廣州。矩至長沙，見一人長丈餘，著白布單衣，將奏，在岸上呼矩奴子：「過我！」矩省奏，為杜靈之。入船共語，稱敘希闊。

矩問：「君京兆人，何時發來？」答矩「朝發。」矩怪，問之，杜曰：「天上京兆。身是鬼，見使來詣君耳。」矩大懼！因求紙筆，曰：「君必不解天上書。」乃更作，折卷之，從矩求一小箱盛之，封付矩，曰：「君今無開，比到廣州可視耳。」

矩到數月，悁悒，乃開視。書云：「令召王矩為左司命主簿。」矩意大惡，因疾卒。

Heaven's Decree

Nan Chao Song Dynasty (420-479CE) Liu Yi-Qing (403-444CE) "You Ming Lu"

Wang Ju（王矩）(?-306CE), the chief magistrate of Heng Yang（衡陽）, had been transferred to serve as the chief magistrate of Guang Zhou（廣州）. When he arrived at Chang Sha（長沙）he saw a man about ten feet tall, in a formal white gown, holding a royal document calling for Ju's（矩）servants, "Carry me on to the boat." Ju looked over the document. He then knew that the name of the man dressed in white was Du Ling Zhi（杜靈之）. Du came inside the cabin and chatted with Ju.

Ju asked, "You are from the capital city, what time did you depart from the city?" Du answered, "I set out this morning." Due to the long distance of travel, Ju thought it was strange to arrive so quickly, so he continued asking questions. Du said, "The capital city I am referring to is the capital city in heaven. I am a ghost and was sent to visit you." Hearing this, Ju became extremely frightened. Du asked for a brush pen and paper, then wrote down something and said, "You definitely cannot read the words of heaven." Then he wrote once more and rolled the paper up. He asked Ju for a box and put the scroll inside, sealed the box, and handed it over to Ju , ordering him not to open it until he got to Guang Zhou.

Upon arriving at Guang Zhou, for several months Ju felt depressed, so he opened the scroll inside the box. It wrote, "Wang Ju is recruited to serve as the Defied Judge of Life's （司命）chief of staff." Ju was quite disheartened after he saw it, and died of an illness afterwards.

五、預見滿地腥血　東晉·干寶：《搜神記》卷二

宣城邊洪為廣陽領校。母喪歸家，韓友往投之。時日已暮，出告從者：「速裝束！吾當夜去。」從者曰：「今日已暝，數十里草行，何急復去？」友曰：「此間血覆地，寧可復住？」苦留之，不得。

其夜，洪欻發狂，絞殺兩子，并殺婦，又斫父婢二人，皆被創。因走亡。數日，乃於宅前林中得之，已自經死。

Foreseeing the Upcoming Bloodshed

Dong Jin Dynasty (317-420CE) Gan Bao (？-336CE) "Sou Shen Ji"

Bian Hong（邊洪）of Xuan Cheng（宣城）was the military officer of Guang Yang（廣陽）. He returned home to fulfill the

mourning after his mother's death ❸, and his friend Han You
（韓友）intended to stay overnight at his place. When it was
dark, Han（韓）walked out and told his entourage, "Let's pack
up quickly. We are going to leave here tonight." The members
of his entourage said, "It is dark now and we have traveled
more than ten kilometers in the grassland, why are we
rushing to leave?" You said, "There is blood everywhere. How
could we stay here any longer?" Although the entourage
requested to stay, Han still insisted on leaving.

That night, Hong suddenly went mad, strangling his two
sons and killing his wife. Then he slashed two of his father's
maids until they were seriously injured. Hong then fled from
home. After several days, he was found dead, hanging from a
tree in the woods in front of his home.

---

❸ 母喪歸家: In Chinese traditional culture, after one's parents pass away,
for three years they cannot work or get married and must stay in a small
hut near the tomb and maintain a sad state of mind in condolence for their
parents.